SPECIAL FORCES:
THE OPERATOR

Cindy Dees

NEW YORK TIMES BESTSELLING AUTHOR

HARLEQUIN®

ROMANTIC suspense

Heart-racing romance, breathless suspense

AVAILABLE THIS MONTH

From passionate, suspenseful
and dramatic love stories to
inspirational or historical,
Harlequin offers different lines to
satisfy every romance reader.

New books available
every month.

HRSATMIFC0719

Dear Reader,

Welcome to the third installment in the ongoing adventures of the Medusas!

I cannot tell you how much fun it has been to revisit my first-ever women Special Forces operators and see what they're up to these days. Thank you so much for the opportunity and for all your emails and letters asking for more Medusa stories. I hope you're enjoying the team's new adventures even half as much as I am.

Many moons ago, I wrote about the Medusas operating at the Winter Olympics, and it seemed only fitting that this time around the team should be sent to work at the Summer Olympics. Thus, this story was born.

Throw in a fun setting, the whole Medusa team and a supersexy hero. Stir until well blended. Serve hot, of course. Voilà, the perfect recipe for exciting suspense and a truly yummy romance.

As always, I encourage you to pour yourself your favorite reading drink, sit back, settle in and enjoy the wild ride that Medusa Rebel McQueen and her perfect hero, Avi Bronson, take us on as they race to save the day and find love.

Let the games begin...

Warmly,

Cindy

They waited in silence as the first course of their meal was served: hors d'oeuvres of wild mushrooms stuffed with crab, escargot and truffle pâté.

He silently took pleasure in watching the orgasmic expressions crossing Rebel's face with each new flavor she encountered. She was a great deal more expressive than she likely thought she was. But then, a man like him was adept at catching every nuance of facial and body language, too.

Eventually, he leaned forward. "I did get one interesting piece of intel from my people this afternoon."

She looked up expectantly from her potato-leek soup, abruptly all business, food forgotten. He sent a silent mental apology to the chef.

"I'll share it with you, but on one condition," he murmured.

"What's that?"

He stood up, went around the table and held out his hand to her. "Dance with me."

* * *

Mission Medusa: A fierce team of warriors who run into the danger zone...

* * *

SPECIAL FORCES: THE OPERATOR

Cindy Dees

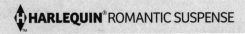
HARLEQUIN® ROMANTIC SUSPENSE

Recycling programs
for this product may
not exist in your area.

ISBN-13: 978-1-335-66207-1

Special Forces: The Operator

Printed in U.S.A.

New York Times and *USA TODAY* bestselling author **Cindy Dees** is the author of more than fifty novels. She draws upon her experience as a US Air Force pilot to write romantic suspense. She's a two-time winner of the prestigious RITA® Award for romance fiction, a two-time winner of the RT Reviewers' Choice Best Book Award for Romantic Suspense and an *RT Book Reviews* Career Achievement Best Author Award nominee. She loves to hear from readers at www.cindydees.com.

Books by Cindy Dees

Harlequin Romantic Suspense

Mission Medusa

Special Forces: The Recruit
Special Forces: The Spy
Special Forces: The Operator

The Coltons of Roaring Springs

Colton Under Fire

Code: Warrior SEALs

Undercover with a SEAL
Her Secret Spy
Her Mission with a SEAL
Navy SEAL Cop

Soldier's Last Stand
The Spy's Secret Family
Captain's Call of Duty
Soldier's Rescue Mission
Her Hero After Dark
Breathless Encounter

Visit Cindy's Author Profile page at Harlequin.com for more titles.

Chapter 1

It started as a hot tub party.

It quickly devolved into a hot tub orgy.

Rebel McQueen was supposed to provide security for a dozen members of the US women's softball delegation in the midst of it, but she'd last seen her charges disappearing into a mass of gorgeous naked bodies that was the Norwegian men's water polo team.

Acute regret speared into her.

Where did she go wrong with her life that she was a lousy security guard while these other young women of her approximate age and physical ability were partying with possibly the hottest guys on the planet?

The "hot tub" was actually a giant swimming pool in the Olympic Village that had been heated to spa temperatures for the duration of the games. Easily two hundred athletes were in the pool now, engaging in every manner and combination of sexual play.

She got it. They were young, athletic, far from home, and had precompetition adrenaline galore before the games opened tomorrow night. But she was responsible for those softball players, and she couldn't spot a single one of them right now. All she could make out in the churning water were writhing limbs and the occasional flash of a pale face. The rest of it could just as easily have been a feeding frenzy of sharks.

The Medusas—the highly classified, all-female, Special Forces team she was part of—were an ultra-under-the-radar part of the American security contingent at these games.

Tonight, the American security staff was undermanned, and she'd volunteered to help out. But she'd had no idea she was in for this! The Medusas had been briefed that the Olympic Village would be a wild party scene, but nothing in her Special Forces training had prepared her for a frat party with twenty thousand wild children determined to play. Hard.

Play. Not a word that had meaning in her world. *Duty. Honor. Country.* Those words, immortalized by General Douglas MacArthur, were the ones she lived by.

Oh joy. Word of the orgy must be spreading, for more athletes started arriving at the pool in a steady stream, stripping naked and jumping in.

It was arguably the best-looking group of naked people Rebel had ever seen, at any rate. Idly, she played a game of "guess the sport based on body type."

There went a lean, no-fat marathon runner.

Disproportionately massive torso and skinny legs? A rower.

Big gut, wreathed in muscle—weight lifter.

A crowd began to form around the edges of the pool. Whether they were purely spectators to the debauchery or waiting for an inch of open water to join in, she couldn't tell. But they elbowed Rebel back from the pool with their muscular, jostling bodies.

Swearing under her breath, she let herself be propelled back. Her orders were to be inconspicuous. Instead of resisting, she occupied herself with watching the watchers. Which was why she happened to glimpse a familiar face in the crowd. A face that made her lurch. A face that emphatically should not be here.

The face of a terrorist.

Surely she'd made a mistake. She moved quickly around the pool, trying to keep an eye on the man, who looked shockingly like Mahmoud Akhtar. Mahmoud led a terror cell that kidnapped her teammate, Piper Ford, last year.

Piper's fiancé was an undercover CIA officer who'd helped her escape from Mahmoud, and who'd captured photographs of the entire cell of Iranian operatives. Rebel had looked at an eight-by-ten glossy photo of Mahmoud posted in the Medusas' ready room every day for the past eight months. She *knew* his face.

And she'd just seen it here in Sydney, Australia.

Next to Mahmoud, a second man stood up from where he'd been squatting by the edge of the pool. *Yousef Kamali.* Mahmoud's second-in-command and also a glossy photo on her team's personal Most Wanted wall.

She wove through the throng of people to the spot where Mahmoud and Yousef had been standing and turned in a slow three-sixty.

No sign of the two men.

She *had* to be wrong. No way could known terrorists gain access to the Olympic Village. Not unless the Iranian government had given them credentials that attached them to the Iranian Olympic team…

Nah. The Iranians wouldn't be so brazen.

She spied two males wearing black tracksuits with green-white-red stripes down the arms and legs. *Iran team uniforms.* She swore under her breath.

The pair was moving away from the pool area quickly. Purposefully.

Frowning, she debated whether to leave her post and follow them. It wasn't like the softball girls were leaving this party anytime soon. But she was responsible for their safety, which technically included apprehending terrorists.

The Iranians approached a streetlight with its pole-mounted surveillance camera and, as she looked on, both men simultaneously turned their faces to the right.

Away from the camera.

Sonofa— That was the deliberate act of someone who didn't want to be identified. The act of a trained operative. Or a terrorist.

She took off running, but the two men were well ahead of her, and more athletes were streaming toward the pool. She dodged and weaved, doing the whole fish swimming upstream thing, desperately trying to keep the Iranians in sight. But she was only five foot four, and it was darned near impossible to see over the glamorous amazons that were most Olympic athletes.

Finally, she broke out of the worst of the crush and glimpsed her quarry passing through one of the checkpoints to leave the Olympic Village. She put on a burst of speed as they scanned their credentials and stepped onto a city street.

She flew through the checkpoint without bothering to scan herself out. She couldn't lose the Iranians! Once they hit the giant street party outside the village, following them was going to get immeasurably harder. She had to close as much of the gap as she could before they lost themselves in the crowds. Sydney was in full celebration mode, and this part of the city had been completely shut down to allow foot traffic to fill the streets.

Rebel raced through crowds of revelers, but the Iranians picked up speed in front of her, and she stretched out into a full sprint. The men turned a corner and disappeared.

When she approached the intersection, she slowed, turning the corner fast and low. It turned out to be a relatively quiet, dark street lined with closed office buildings. And it was empty. She raced down it, searching side to side for the Iranians. Nothing. She burst out into another crowded thoroughfare.

Where did they go?

There. To her left. She gathered herself to take off running again just as the men disappeared into a building ahead.

Without warning, big, hard hands grabbed her by both arms, dragging her back into the dark street she'd just emerged from. She stumbled backward, fetching up hard against a building. Immediately, she was flattened against it by a living wall of muscle.

Chagrin roared through her. She'd gotten so focused on chasing her quarry in front of her that she'd forgotten to watch her own tail. *Stupid, stupid, stupid.* She knew better.

"Let go of me," she ground out. The terrorists were getting away!

"Who are you?" a male voice rasped from over her head.

"The person who's going to hurt you if you don't let me go. *Right. Now.*"

"Little thing like you?" Humor laced her battering ram's voice.

No help for it. She was about to be conspicuous.

Avi Bronson yelped as the fleeing suspect, a tiny, shockingly quick female, stomped painfully on the top of his left foot. He swore when she grabbed his thumb off her shoulder and gave it a vicious wrench.

"Damn, woman! You've practically dislocated my thumb."

A normal man would step back from the tiny virago now throwing painful elbows at him, kneeing him dangerously close to his groin and scratching at his face. But he was a trained Special Forces soldier, and the last thing he dared do was let this woman get an arm's length between them where she could really wind up with a fist or foot and actually damage him.

He leaned in against her, using his superior size and weight to mash her even flatter against the wall at her back, silently thanking his wool suit coat for absorbing the worst of her attack.

She went still abruptly.

"Are you done?" he asked cautiously.

"Yes." Her tone was surly. Not even close to subdued.

"If I step back from you, will you stop attacking me?" he tried.

Too long a pause. Then, "Yes."

Liar.

He jumped back all at once, throwing up his fists to defend himself. And just in the nick of time. She flew at him like an angry bird.

But then she surprised him by spinning away and taking off at a dead run down the street. Genuinely irritated now, he gave chase.

Crap, she was fast.

Of course, she had the advantage over him in weaving through the heavy crowd, being as small as she was. He struggled to keep sight of her as she dodged among the civilians ahead of him.

Then she did a weird thing,

She came to a dead stop in front of a giant discotheque, staring at it in what could only be utter disgust.

Avi screeched to a stop beside her. "Ma'am, I'm going to have to ask you to come with me—"

"Oh, save it," she muttered, yanking out a set of Olympic credentials from inside her jacket. The holographic ID card hanging from a lanyard around her neck and declaring her to be from the American delegation, certainly looked authentic.

"Nonetheless. I need you to come with me," he repeated.

She finally turned her full attention on him, and he was taken aback by her giant blue eyes, glaring at him as indignantly as if he'd kicked her puppy. "Who are you?" she demanded.

"Olympic security," he said shortly.

"I showed you my credentials. Let's see yours," she challenged.

"Not here," he muttered. A lifetime of being reviled and targeted for being Israeli had taught him to be deeply reticent about announcing his nationality in crowded, public settings. Not to mention, he was not about to air Olympic security business on a street full of half-drunk spectators.

"Why won't you show me your credentials?" the woman demanded.

"Just come with me, will you?"

"I can't. I need to get surveillance video from inside this club."

"I can get you the footage faster than anyone in there can if you'll *come with me*." He said the last few words through gritted teeth. This woman was really starting to get under his skin. She was blithely ignoring him as if she didn't give a flip for being stopped by Olympic security.

"Fine," she declared. "There are at least four exits from this place to three different streets, and thanks to you, I have no way of knowing which direction the men I was following went. I've lost them."

"Lost who?"

She blinked, as if abruptly becoming aware of being closely surrounded by dozens of Olympic guests. "Uhh, nobody I care to talk about out here in the open."

"Hence my *request* that you come with me." He emphasized the word *request* to make it perfectly clear that this was, in fact, not a request at all.

The woman took several quick strides away from him, back toward the Olympic Village and then had the gall to stop and look over her shoulder at him. "Are you coming or not, He-Man?"

He lurched into movement, not sure whether to be amused or fantasize about strangling her. He fell in beside her, matching his long stride to her shorter one. "Are you always this touchy?" he murmured.

"You haven't seen anything, yet. We're in public and I have to behave myself."

"Good Lord."

"Oh, praying won't save you from me."

He glanced down at her in something approaching shock and she continued, smiling sweetly all the while, "When we get back to the village, I'm going to give you a piece of my mind…and chew off a chunk of your hide while I'm at it."

Amused. He was definitely amused. A grin crept across his features. She reminded him of a little angry sparrow—her feathers all puffed up and flapping her wings furiously at the big bad hawk. She looked ready at any second to fly at his head and peck at him.

"You're cute when you're mad," he murmured as he took her by the elbow to guide her through a particularly thick cluster of drunks spilling out of a bar into the street.

Her biceps flexed under his fingers and he noted that her arm was rock hard within his grasp. She definitely worked out. But then, the Olympics drew the fittest people on Earth into one place.

Leaning in close to her and using his big body as a shield, he protected her from jostles and errant hands as they passed through a group of loudly singing young men wearing Irish national soccer team paraphernalia. One of them, carrying a brimming full pitcher of beer in each hand stumbled, and Avi spun in front of the woman, taking a hefty slosh of beer down his back for his trouble.

While the drunk mumbled a slurred apology, Avi merely rolled his eyes and ushered the woman onward. Cold, sticky wetness made his shirt cling to his back as the beer soaked through his suit.

"Thanks," she muttered reluctantly.

"You're welcome."

There was a bit of a delay getting her scanned into the village since she hadn't scanned out properly when she left, but the guard sorted it out quickly enough when Avi flashed his own senior security credentials.

"I have to make a phone call," she announced, stopping just inside the fenced enclosure surrounding the large campus of dormitories, dining halls, workout facilities and delegation headquarters. Sighing in frustration at yet another delay, he nonetheless stopped and waited while she pulled out her cell phone.

He listened with interest as she said, "Tessa, it's me. I need one of you to head over to the north village pool and take over babysitting the women's softball team. I've got another situation to sort out right now." A pause, then, "I'll tell you about it when I get back to Ops. Speaking of which, could you call Major T. and have him meet me at the ops center ASAP?"

Avi heard an exclamation that sounded like surprise from the person on the other end of the call.

The woman snorted. Then, "He's never off duty. He eats, sleeps and breathes the job. And I seriously have to speak with him. We have a potential situation."

Spoken like a true security operator. Avi frowned. Who *was* this woman?

She was speaking again. "…join us after you fish the women's softball team out of the pool and tuck them back in their rooms." She added, "Oh, and their clothing is in a pile at the northwest corner of the pool. Yes. *All* of their clothing. It's an orgy over there. Thanks. Bye."

She pocketed her phone and glared up at him. "Let's make this fast. I have someplace to be."

He crossed his arms and smirked down at her. "All right. Let's try this again. Who are you?"

"This is still far too public an environment for me to answer that. And I'm certainly not telling you anything without you showing me proper identification."

"Fair enough. Come with me." He turned and headed toward the Israeli security operations center. Returning the favor from earlier, he glanced back over his shoulder and asked wryly, "Are you coming, She-Woman?"

The woman lurched into motion, scowling. Smiling

a little to himself, he led her to his delegation's headquarters.

The atmosphere was all business inside the Israeli security operations center. Ever since Munich almost fifty years ago, the Israelis operated on the assumption that their athletes were active terror targets. And it was up to the men and women in this room to protect those athletes—the finest flowers of Israel's youth.

He didn't stop in the main area crammed with desks, video monitors, computers and mostly big, capable men. Spying an empty office, he stepped inside, turned on the light and waited for his prisoner to join him. Not that he would call her that to her face. His ribs and foot still ached from her initial assault. She might be tiny, but she had sharp elbows and knew how to use them.

In the bright light of the office, he got a good look at her face. She had smooth, soft-looking skin, regular features that grew more pretty the longer he looked at them, and those big, blue eyes of hers. They were her best feature, for sure. Her hair was a soft chocolate brown shot through with strands of gold, like she spent a fair bit of time outside. He already knew she was stronger than her small stature suggested.

She pulled out her credentials again and this time he did the same. Silently, they exchanged badges.

"Rebel McQueen," he read aloud. "That's an unusual name. Did your mother dislike you?"

"No. She was a fanatical Steve McQueen fan. He was an actor—"

"I know who he was. *The Great Escape* is one of my favorite movies."

She mused, "Allied prisoners break out of Nazi prison camp. I could see why that movie would be popular in

Israel." The woman continued, "Anyway, McQueen's nickname was 'the American Rebel.'"

He commented sympathetically, "You must have to explain that a lot."

"You have no idea." She rolled her eyes, and they traded brief smiles of commiseration.

She glanced down at his identification. "Avi Bronson. Israeli Defense Forces? Mossad?"

"Sayerat Matkal," he replied. Not that she would have any idea what that was. Which was the point. His team didn't advertise their existence, let alone their presence at a venue as public as the Summer Olympics.

"Unit 269?" she blurted.

"You know who we are?" he blurted back, shocked that she'd heard of his special operations unit. It wasn't the sort of thing most civilians knew about.

"Yes," she replied impatiently. "You guys are the primary hostage rescue unit for the Israeli Defense Forces. I'd have thought most of you security types here would be *Mista'arvim*—counterterrorism units."

He shrugged. "I did a stint with them a few years back. I also rolled with *Shayetet* 13 early in my career."

"The Navy SEAL equivalent, huh? Well, aren't you the overachiever?"

He frowned down at her "Okay, so you know more about Israeli Special Forces units than the average bear. How is that?"

"It's my job?"

"Don't be cute with me. What do you do as a member of the American delegation, Miss McQueen?"

"Lieutenant McQueen. US Navy. Roving security for the American delegation. Sometimes it's handy to have female security guards. We can go places men can't."

He frowned. "Regular US military personnel aren't assigned to Olympic security details."

She shrugged, offering no further explanation of why she, a military member, was here on a distinctly civilian assignment.

His mental antennae wiggled wildly. She wasn't telling him the truth. Or at least not the full truth.

"Why did you flee the village without scanning out properly?" he tried.

"I told you. I was following someone. I didn't have time to mess with scanning my ID."

"And who were you following?" he asked gently when she didn't continue.

She huffed. "I thought I saw a guy named Mahmoud Akhtar."

"Akhtar? Here?" Mahmoud Akhtar was the kind of guy who made men like Avi lose sleep at night. Akhtar was highly trained, highly intelligent and highly radicalized. He was a known agent of the Iranian government and believed to be a wet operator—meaning his skills and missions covered everything up to and including terror and assassination. It could not possibly be good news for the Israeli delegation if Akhtar was here in Sydney. "Are you sure?" Avi asked the woman curtly.

"No. I'm not sure." She sounded exasperated. "I was trying to get close enough to make a positive identification when you decided to go all Neanderthal and tackle me."

"I didn't tackle you. I merely stopped you for questioning." She opened her mouth, obviously to argue, and he took an aggressive step forward to loom over her. He had nearly twenty-five centimeters—ten inches—on her in height. "If I had tackled you, you would have been smashed flat on the ground. And I would have handcuffed you." He added, "As it was, I probably should have tackled you. But I was exceptionally restrained."

She snorted. "You should have been even more restrained. Mahmoud and his buddy, Yousef Kamali, got away, thanks to you."

He frowned, reluctant to believe her claim that an international terrorist had been strolling around the grounds of the Olympic Village. But caution dictated that he take her seriously, of course.

She didn't *seem* delusional.

And the fact that she even knew who Mahmoud Akhtar and his sidekick, Yousef Kamali, were, meant she had some sort of access to classified material—also indicative of a not delusional female.

Still. Akhtar here? It would be a huge risk for a terrorist of his notoriety.

She interrupted his skeptical train of thought, demanding, "You said you could get me video from that nightclub. I want to see it right away. I might be able to make a positive ID from that."

"Come with me." He led her into the main room and gestured for her to sit at his desk. Reaching past her shoulder, he typed into his keyboard quickly, calling up the Israeli link to the entire Sydney CCTV—closed-circuit television—system.

Clicking on the map of downtown Sydney that popped up, he selected the nightclub. It took a moment, but then his screen flashed up black-and-white imagery of the exterior of the disco where Rebel had finally stopped running.

"Do you have interior video feed?" she murmured up at him.

He glanced down at her and was close enough to see that her eyelashes were long and silky, a soft brown that matched her hair. And she smelled good. A gentle, sweet scent like vanilla, warm and inviting. A study in contrasts, she was turning out to be. Sharp words, sweet mouth. Hard elbows, soft skin. Tough attitude, gentle eyes.

"Interior video?" she repeated.

Oh. Right. He shook himself out of staring at her and typed again. Planting both hands on the desk, he leaned forward beside Rebel to study the crowd gyrating on-screen. He hit the pause button and froze the image. Face by face, he scanned all the people in the frame. He didn't see anyone resembling the Iranian terrorist.

Rebel leaned back. "This is hopeless. The crowd is too thick to spot my guys without a full forensic analysis of this video. What if we run the video in real time and see if we can spot Mahmoud and Yousef entering the club?"

He estimated it had been fifteen minutes since he'd detained her, and he backed up the video twenty minutes to be safe. He hit Play.

He pulled up a rolling chair from the next desk over and sat down beside Rebel. Their shoulders rubbed together as they both leaned forward, staring intently at the moving images in front of them.

Both of them jolted at the same moment as two men wearing black tracksuits entered the frame. They bumped into each other, and Avi mumbled an apology at the same time Rebel did. Their gazes met, startled, and she looked away immediately, a blush staining her cheeks. Was she shy, or did she find him attractive, or both? *Hmm. Interesting.*

She stabbed at the video monitor. "Those are my guys."

"Unfortunately, that's only the back of their heads," he commented. "Let me see if there's another angle." He advanced the video frame by frame in search of a good facial shot of the men.

Nothing.

He pulled up the second camera in the club, and damned if the men weren't moving through the space with their heads turned to the side, avoiding being seen clearly on that camera, too.

Rebel leaned back in disgust. "They did that same trick when they were leaving the village. They turned their faces away from the surveillance cameras as if they knew exactly where they were."

He pushed away from the desk and leaned back in his chair, linking his hands behind his head as he stared at her. "Let's say you're correct, and that's Mahmoud Akhtar. How did he get into the Olympic Village?"

"Obviously, the Iranians gave him credentials."

"Their entire delegation undergoes thorough background checks by the International Olympic Committee. And my people run our own background checks above and beyond the IOC's. We would have spotted him."

She threw him a "duh" look. "Obviously, the Iranians substituted him after the fact in place of someone who passed the background check."

"Or he could have stolen the credentials. But either way, the next question is why?" he asked reasonably.

"Because the Iranians have something planned to disrupt the games."

"Like what?" he asked, interested to see how she answered. The Israelis had spent the past four years running possible scenarios of their own and preparing to stop each one.

She shrugged. "He won't be operating alone. Last time we had contact with him, he was the leader of a six-man cell. The man I saw with him tonight, Yousef Kamali, was one of those men. My guess is Mahmoud has reconstituted his team."

Avi jumped all over her slip of the tongue. "We? We who? What group are you really a part of?"

She threw him a withering glare. "A group you don't need to know about."

He arched a skeptical eyebrow at her. "Did you not hear who I work for?"

She shrugged. "I stand by my statement."

Huh. So she worked for some superclassified security team the Americans had put together—that included women. His Mossad buddies would find that interesting.

"You never answered my question," he pressed. "What do you think Mahmoud and this hypothetical team of his are up to?"

"I have no idea. But I know a guy who might be able to make an educated guess."

"I know several guys who've spent the past few years making educated guesses," he snapped. "Give me more than that."

"I don't *have* more. But I can tell you one thing. If Mahmoud Akhtar is here, he's up to no good."

"On that, we are agreed." He met her gaze grimly, and this time her big blue eyes were brimming over with worry. An urge to rock his chair forward onto all four legs, gather her into his arms and comfort her shocked him into stillness. This woman was the last person he would expect to accept comfort from him. Such a prickly little thing, she was.

"Would you like to come with me to my security team's meeting?" she said all of a sudden, surprising him mightily.

"Do I have the proper clearance to attend it?" he asked, his voice as dry as the desert.

She rolled her eyes. "I can't guarantee my boss will let you stay, but you Israelis are an obvious possible target. It makes sense to loop you into at least some of what we know about Mahmoud."

"Gee. Thanks."

"In the spirit of Olympic cooperation, I'm offering you an olive branch," she said with a huff. "Take it and be grateful, already."

"Fair enough. Thank you." He quoted quietly, "Behold, how good and how pleasant it is for brethren to dwell together in unity!"

"Should I recognize that?" she asked.

"It's your Bible. Psalms 133."

She frowned. "I don't get much time for religion in my work."

"Hmm. My work is all about religion. Or freedom of religion, at any rate."

"Right now, a threat to your peoples' freedom is walking around out there, no doubt planning something dastardly. Although I'd put it at about equal odds between your country and mine as to which one is the primary target," she replied.

He asked, "When was the last time your people had contact with Akhtar? What were his targets at that time?"

"Last fall. And his target was a schoolteacher. He planned to kidnap her and blackmail her husband into filing a false report on a nuclear facility in Iran. Instead, Mahmoud accidentally kidnapped one of my teammates. She escaped with the help of an undercover man on the team. We got to the teacher's husband—a nuclear facilities inspector in Tehran—before Mahmoud did, and the husband filed a report showing that Iran was trying to import nuclear triggers from Russia by way of Turkey."

"I heard about that!" Avi exclaimed. "Wasn't there

some sort of shoot-out in Tehran? Several major arms dealers killed and the deal scuttled? Our…sources…report the Iranians were livid."

She shrugged looking entirely unrepentant.

"You were involved with all of that?" he asked incredulously.

"You don't have to sound so surprised." She was back to being defensive. And her hackles were standing up again. Maybe she was more like a baby badger than a hedgehog.

"C'mon, then," she said briskly. "Bring your Olympic credentials and your fancy security clearance with you. You'll need them both to hear what my team has to say."

Chapter 2

Rebel jumped as Avi's big, warm palm landed lightly in the small of her back. The power and gentleness of it sent crazy zinging sensations ricocheting in all directions through her body. She inhaled light and fast, her adrenaline levels ready for combat—or sex.

Oh, c'mon, Self. You've been around plenty of hot special operators in the past year. This one is no different.

Except the tingling didn't go away. And her breathing didn't settle down.

"This way," he murmured, guiding her through the maze of Israeli security personnel at their desks. "There's a rear exit where we won't be seen."

Now he was getting the idea. She liked—she needed—to operate under the radar and away from the prying eyes of the public as much as possible. They slipped out into the warm night and, by unspoken mutual agreement, wove around the edges of the Olympic Village, mostly avoiding the surveillance cameras whose feeds were shared with all of the security delegations.

She swiped a key card she pulled out of a zipped pocket inside her jacket and stood before a retinal scanner to gain entrance for herself and her big Israeli guest into the back entrance of the American operations center. It had its own building containing both offices and housing for the large contingent of security specialists in Sydney to protect American athletes.

Vividly aware of the big man following her and the curious glances being thrown his way, she led Bronson across a room much like the one at Israeli operations, crowded with desks and video monitors. This room, too, was half-filled with big, capable-looking men and a few serious, focused women. Ignoring them, Rebel led her guest to the conference room and ushered him inside.

Her boss, Army Major Gunnar Torsten, looked over her shoulder at the Israeli. He did a double take. "Avi?"

"Gun? Long time no see," the Israeli exclaimed.

Rebel looked on in disgust as the two men shook hands warmly and clapped each other on the back. Of course, they knew each other. Torsten was fond of saying how small the Special Forces community really was.

The men were a study in physical contrast. Where blond Torsten's hair was straight and buzzed short, the Israeli's dark hair was wavy and thick enough to run her fingers through it. Torsten was fair and blue-eyed, where Avi Bronson was bronzed and brown-eyed. But that was where the contrast ended. Both men were tall, fit, and moved with confident grace. Also, they both had that particular cool look in their eyes announcing they were lethal, and furthermore, that they knew it.

"What brings you to the Land of Oz, Avi?" Torsten asked.

"Olympic security detail. You?"

"Same."

Torsten glanced at Rebel. "You summoned me, Lieutenant McQueen?"

She winced at his dry tone, not sure whether to interpret the use of her title as formality for the guest's benefit or a signal that she was in trouble for her presumption. Her boss was a very hard man to read.

She responded grimly, "I spotted two men tonight who looked shockingly like Mahmoud Akhtar and Yousef Kamali."

Torsten sucked in a sharp breath. "You're sure it was them?"

"I only saw them from a distance, but I *know* Mahmoud's face. I'm pretty sure it was him."

Torsten stared at her for a long moment as his expression passed through shock and chagrin, ending up wreathed in speculation.

She watched her boss cautiously as he placed a phone call on the speakerphone sitting on the table in front of him. He said without preamble, "Piper, how quickly can Zane join us?"

Rebel's teammate answered briskly over the speaker, "He can be here in twenty-four hours from when I call him, sir."

That wasn't bad, given that the flight itself took on the order of twenty-two hours.

"Make the call," Torsten said quietly. He disconnected the call to Piper.

Avi piped up. "Who is this Zane person?"

Torsten answered, "CIA officer. Embedded with Mahmoud and his cell in the US for several months last year. Best expert we've got on the bastard."

"And who are these ladies you're working with?" Avi asked, gesturing at the phone and then at Rebel.

The room fell silent. Rebel stared at Torsten, who stared at the Israeli.

Torsten asked obliquely, "You're still operational, my friend? You've still got all your clearances?"

"Yes to both." Avi was frowning and looking back and forth between her and Torsten, now.

Rebel watched apprehensively as Torsten stood up, closed the conference room door and came back to the table to sit. He wasn't going to brief in the Israeli, was he? Her safety, and that of her teammates depended in no small part upon the secrecy around them.

Torsten said, "I command a team of women called the Medusas. They're a fully operational Special Forces team. I have four more operatives out working in the village, right now."

Piper and Tessa, original team members along with Rebel, were probably still working on fishing the women's softball team out of the pool party and herding them back to their quarters.

Gia Rykhof and Lynx Everly, the two newest additions to the team, were working a media event for the US Women's Gymnastic team, tonight. These Olympic Games were Gia and Lynx's first operational assignment. They had more training to do before they would be fully up to speed, but both women could still handle themselves in most any situation.

"An entire team made up of women?" Avi repeated blankly.

"Correct," Torsten answered briskly.

Avi Bronson was not the first man to react that way to hearing about the Medusas, and he would not be the last. But it still bugged Rebel that he acted so surprised and didn't automatically take her and her teammates seriously.

Chauvinist.

Torsten leaned forward, asking Avi, "What have your people got on Mahmoud and Yousef?"

"Nothing recent that I'm aware of. Not until I caught up with your...operative...earlier after she raced out of the village without scanning out properly. She's the one who brought Mahmoud Akhtar to my attention and claims to have seen him."

"Claims to have seen him?" Rebel echoed in annoyance. "I know what I saw!"

Torsten intervened smoothly. "Avi believes you. And so do I. Where did Mahmoud and Yousef go?"

She answered more calmly, "I followed them out of the Olympic Village to a discotheque. They entered from one street, crossed the club and must have exited onto another street. I lost them when your buddy, here, tried to detain me and prevented me from following them."

"I was just doing my job," Avi protested.

Rebel glared at him. Damned if his dark eyes and darker soul didn't light up with amusement in response. He seemed to think she was hilarious. As long as he didn't think she was a joke—and he stayed out of her way next time—she could live with him laughing at her.

"Did they act like they were fleeing you or moving toward a specific destination?" her boss asked.

"Unknown." She shot another disgusted look in Avi's direction.

Torsten followed up tersely with, "Where in the village did you first spot Mahmoud and Yousef?"

At least her boss was taking her seriously. She answered, "They were standing beside the north pool. I don't know if they saw me and I spooked them or if they just turned and left. But either way, they left the pool and headed for the nearest exit. Interestingly enough, they turned their faces away from every surveillance camera they passed."

"Which suggests they know the security layout of the village," Torsten replied. "Have they been added to the Iranian delegation?"

Avi jumped in. "I cannot believe the Iranians would try to slip terrorists into the games on official credentials. The scandal if they got caught would be humiliating."

Rebel shrugged. "In my experience, the Iranians will suffer a humiliation or two if it means they can destroy an enemy."

Avi met her gaze head-on. "Truth."

"Possible targets?" Torsten threw out.

Rebel ticked off, "American athletes, Israeli athletes, a large public venue containing lots of athletes, a large venue containing lots of spectators—"

Avi interrupted, "In other words, everyone and everything at the Olympic Games."

Torsten drummed his fingers on the tabletop, a rare sign of tension from her excessively self-disciplined boss. "When Zane gets here, we'll see if his people have any chatter on what Mahmoud might be up to."

Zane's people being the CIA.

A spear of jealousy for Piper stabbed Rebel. Zane and Piper were wildly in love, and he was about to come join her for possibly several weeks in a beautiful, romantic locale. *Lucky dogs.*

Rebel's last boyfriend had dumped her when he found out she'd agreed to join some kind of special team that was going to involve her traveling all over the world for several years to come. As long as she'd been stationed at a desk and never deployed, he'd been all over her naval career. But as soon as it had interfered with his convenience and comfort, she was history.

Jerk, she thought tiredly. Not that she could blame him entirely. She'd volunteered for the Medusas knowing full well it might break them up. Maybe she'd taken the job partially *because* she thought it might break them up. Which made her a coward, at least in the romance department.

But how often did a woman get a chance to be on one of the most classified—and cool—teams on the planet? To serve her country in a direct, meaningful way? And to fulfill a lifelong dream of doing something awesome?

That had been her main reason for joining the Medusas. Dumping the loser had been a side benefit.

Avi was talking, and she yanked her attention back to the discussion at hand. "...will touch base with my Mossad contacts and see if they've heard anything about Mahmoud Akhtar. How should I let you know what I find out?"

Torsten answered, "Why don't you liaise with Rebel, since you two already know each other? I'm up to my elbows in alligators chasing down other rumors and threats, but I want to give this possible sighting of Akhtar highest priority. I'll pull Lieutenant McQueen off her other security rotations for now so she can follow this up specifically."

Avi nodded, the ghost of a grin flitting across his face. Was he pleased that she would be working with him? Or was that indulgence for the little girl playing commando with him? God, he was as hard to read as Torsten.

The Israeli glanced at his watch. "It'll take me an hour or so to find out what the Mossad knows and to take a shower and change clothes." He glanced at Torsten. "On the way here, I took a beer down my back defending the honor of your girl. Had I known she was an operator, I'd have let her take the beer in the face."

The men traded grins, and she bit her tongue. She was standing right here, while they talked over her head and called her a girl. Of course, she knew Torsten actually thought highly of her, or else he wouldn't have invited her to be a Medusa in the first place, nor would he have passed her through the rigorous training program. He'd washed out plenty of other women without any compunction.

But it bothered her that when he was around a male counterpart he reverted to Neanderthal talk about her and her sisters-in-arms. Of course, it was entirely possible he was speaking in sexist terms intentionally to relax Avi about the whole idea of working with a female special operator. Torsten was fully that calculating a guy.

Avi stood, and she was vividly aware yet again of how big a man he was. He had to be pushing six foot three. And every inch of him was solid, functional muscle. He wasn't thick, but he wasn't exactly a beanpole, either.

His face was a wee bit on the long side for Hollywood, but his nose was proportional to his face, his cheeks and jaw were just the right amount of craggy, and his smile was wide and beautiful when he shook hands with Torsten.

All in all, he was a ruggedly handsome man in an understated way. Like most special operators in her experience. They didn't draw attention to themselves, and a person's eye tended to slide past them without stopping to really notice them. But then, she supposed she could be accused of the same thing. She never wore makeup and left her hair its natural mousy brown color. She wore boring clothes that hid her figure, and in general, she worked hard not to be noticeable.

Avi glanced at his watch and then speared her with a penetrating look that made her feel positively naked. "What say we reconvene at ten o'clock for a late supper? Have you eaten tonight?"

Supper? Him and her alone? Her stomach leaped against her ribs until she silently admonished it to behave. She managed what she hoped was a nonchalant shrug. "Okay. That'll give our guy in Washington some time to track down any intel from our end—"

Torsten's and Avi's cell phones rang at the exact same moment, exploding in stereo in the small room. As they reached for their phones, she saw red lights illuminate all over the ops center through the glass window—including the emergency phone from the International Olympic Committee's operations headquarters.

And then her own phone vibrated in her pants pocket.

Uh-oh. She didn't even need the hackles rising on the back of her neck to know it was something bad.

She jammed the phone to her ear and immediately heard screams and shouting from the other end. Over the din, Piper yelled, "There's been an incident at the pool. Bring everyone you can. And bring bottled water and first aid kits!"

Torsten and Avi were already moving, sprinting for the door. She darted out right on their heels without stopping to ask why water was necessary. She trusted her teammate and expected the need for water would become clear when they got to the scene of whatever had happened.

She and the two men each grabbed a case of bottled water from the stack in a storeroom and raced outside to a golf cart, leaped in and drove at the electric vehicle's top speed—close to twenty-five miles per hour—to the pool.

The scene was utter chaos when they arrived. Naked athletes laid all over the lawn around the pool in various degrees of distress. Many of them appeared to have suffered some sort of burns on their skin and had angry red patches, and even raw wounds, on their bodies. Most were coughing and rubbing their eyes, and some were vomiting.

A few people, obviously trying to render first aid, were moving among them, but the victims vastly outnumbered the medics. Thankfully, though, help was starting to arrive as golf carts and running coaches and trainers got wind of the problem.

She leaned forward and shouted in Torsten's ear that the American athletes would probably be congregated by the northwest corner of the pool where they'd left their clothes.

He headed that way, but had to stop well short of the pool because of the sprawl of humanity on the ground.

She tumbled out of the golf cart dozens of yards short of the pool, grabbed a case of water and picked her way through the mess as quickly as she could. The athletes moaning and crying at her feet acted like people who'd just escaped a burning building full of smoke as they coughed thickly and nursed what looked like burns.

The medics on scene appeared to be trying to attend to the most severely affected, but coaches and team officials were shouting for their own athletes to be seen first. The result was a disorganized mess with no semblance or proper triage and sorting of patients into those who could wait and those who could not.

Rebel looked around for the fire and saw no smoke, no flames, no building with people pouring out of it.

"There! Tessa and Piper!" Torsten shouted at her, pointing off to their right.

She followed him toward her teammates, weaving between victims as fast as she could. Avi veered away as someone shouted at him—probably an Israeli athlete or coach. Ignoring him, she ran to her own teammates.

"What the hell happened?" Torsten demanded.

Piper looked up from the legs of one of the women softball players where she was pouring bottled water over several angry, palm-sized burns.

"Athletes were partying away in the pool, and all of a sudden, people started coughing. Shortly thereafter, they started thrashing around and screaming. Other athletes started pulling them out, and then people started screaming about acid in the water."

"How can we help?" Rebel asked quickly. All of the Medusas had emergency medical training, but most of Rebel's to date had been classroom theory and not practical field experience.

"Grab bottles of water and flush the wounds. There's definitely something caustic in the water that has to be washed off the skin of anyone who was in the pool. A few of our girls need eyewashes, but I don't have the right solution or equipment to irrigate their eyes."

Rebel spent the next few minutes rinsing off the American women's skin and reminding them not to rub their eyes. The girls were coughing up a lot of mucus, and their eyes were watering copiously. But fortunately, none of them seemed badly injured. The softball players claimed to have been on the far side of the pool from the worst of whatever had happened.

The Medusas handed off the American athletes to another American security type who escorted the women to an ambulance where an eye washing station had been set up, and the Medusas grabbed their remaining bottled water and headed for the most seriously injured athletes.

It was a frantic race to provide breathing support for those who were struggling to get air, to keep the people puking their guts out from choking, and to get as many skin wounds rinsed and dressed as possible. Over the next half hour, though, the plentiful medics and team coaches nearby arrived and gradually got ahead of the crisis.

More ambulances pulled up, and the most seriously burned athletes were carted away to area hospitals. The less seriously injured limped away to their rooms to take more complete showers, and gradually, the lawn around the pool calmed.

It was nearly midnight before the scene was fully cleared of victims, leaving behind only police and security types for the most part. Rebel pushed loose strands of hair back from her face and made her way over to where Torsten and Avi Bronson had their heads together.

They glanced at her as she joined them and kept talking in grim undertones.

Avi was saying, "…Aussies are saying they think someone accidentally shocked the pool. It should have been closed, but they got their wires crossed."

"What did they shock it with?" Torsten responded.

"Concentrated chlorine."

Rebel frowned. "Wouldn't whoever have poured it into the pool seen it filled to the brim with people and refrained from putting caustic chemicals in the water?"

"This pool has an automated cleaning system that releases chlorine into the pool from several dozen injection points along the bottom of the pool for more rapid and even distribution of the chemicals."

"Snazzy," she commented wryly.

"Did someone forget to turn the system off?" Torsten asked.

Avi nodded. "That's what Olympic officials are saying."

Rebel frowned. "If the chemical was supposed to be distributed evenly, then why weren't the American women athletes affected much? Why were athletes on one side of the pool hit worse than the rest?"

"Could be your athletes were in a part of the pool where the water wasn't being churned up as actively," Avi offered.

She didn't argue, but the explanation didn't sit right with her.

"I don't know about you," Avi commented, "but I'm hungry. I haven't eaten since noon, and it's been an active evening for me." He threw her a significant look.

She got the message. Chasing her had been part of that activity. Rolling her eyes at him, she remarked, "Gee. My teammates and I have been trained, in a crisis, to ignore simple bodily urges like hunger. I would have thought a big, macho guy like you would know how to do that, too."

Torsten grinned and slapped Avi on the shoulder. "Score one for the lady."

"Yes, but the crisis is over," Avi retorted. "Now is the time to attend to my body's needs."

Well, hell. There went her stomach jumping around like an excited puppy again. She was *not* interested in his body's needs—hunger or otherwise.

"How about that supper you and I were going to have?" Avi asked her.

Panic flitted through her belly. "Are you hungry, sir?" she asked Torsten. "Do you want to join us?"

"Nah. I'll have a pile of incident reports to fill out after this mess. I'm going to head back to the office and get started on that. You two go eat."

Her and the hot Israeli alone? Together? She didn't know whether to be delighted or terrified… Definitely terrified. She'd never dated anyone in remotely the same realm of hotness—not a date, dammit. It would be a working supper. No more.

He glanced at Avi. "Can I give you two a ride some-where?"

"Sure. Drop us off at the north gate."

He wanted to leave the village, did he? She'd assumed they would just go to the huge, inflatable tent that was the village dining hall. The white tent would easily hold two football fields and was ringed with food stations offering literally any kind of food a person could imagine, from every corner of the world. Chefs and food were shipped in to meet the wants and needs of each delegation present.

They arrived at the gated checkpoint, and Torsten stopped the cart. Avi hopped off and held out a hand to help her out of the backseat. More hesitantly than she wanted to let on, she laid her hand in his palm. His hand was big and warm and gentle, encompassing hers lightly as his fingers wrapped around her hand.

She had no doubt that hand could crush her windpipe. Casually. Hence the gentleness of Avi's grip was striking.

Drat. There went her stomach again.

He released her hand, but her stomach didn't go back to normal.

Sheesh. He was just being polite. And she appreciated the gentlemanly gesture. It was always a bit of a balanc-ing act being around men—she didn't mind being treated like a lady as long as they understood that she was per-fectly capable of taking care of herself, too.

Although truth be told, she doubted Avi actually took her the least bit seriously. The good news: it wasn't her job to convince him of anything. She was merely here to trade information on Mahmoud Akhtar and then get on with her regularly scheduled life.

Avi, however, seemed inclined to go for a stroll and enjoy the sights. To that end, he led her away from the gate and wound into the blocked-off streets still impressively jammed with partying pedestrians. With the games starting tomorrow, everybody who planned to attend the Olympics was pretty much in town by now.

"Have you gotten an opportunity to get out and see Sydney, yet?" he asked her, leaning in close to be heard without shouting.

Gosh dog it, she really did need to eat, if for no other reason than to weigh down her stomach and keep it from hopping around like a bunny in her belly.

"I haven't done any sightseeing," she confessed. "We hit the ground running when we got here and dived right into helping with our delegation's security requirements."

"You Americans. Always in such a hurry."

"We get more done that way," she retorted.

"What's the point, though, if you miss the beauty of life along the way?"

"Philosopher, are you?"

He shrugged. "I enjoy every moment as much as I can. And I try not to take anything for granted before I die. Life's short, after all."

"That's a pretty dark view of the world," she responded.

"I live in a country where every time you step out of your house you knowingly put your life at risk. And I don't exactly have a boring, routine job."

"Still. I try not to dwell on death. I would rather focus on being and staying alive."

"On that we are in complete accord," he murmured, ushering her across a blocked-off street crowded with pedestrians. They slipped into a dark little restaurant called The Adler, and the sudden silence was a relief from the noisy party outside.

The bay window of the restaurant held a large, carved wooden mountain with little wooden skiers mounted on its painted slopes, and a collection of cuckoo clocks hanging above it. She was going to go with this being a Swiss-themed joint.

They had no trouble getting a table and sat down in a booth in a back corner. A tea candle in a glass globe gave out most of the light, and the table had an odd well cut into the middle about a foot deep.

"What is this place?" she asked curiously.

"Fondue joint," Avi replied. "Best cheese fondue this side of Zermatt, Switzerland."

"Huh. I took you for a steak and potatoes kind of guy."

He leaned back and grinned. "Perhaps you're guilty of misjudging me as badly as I initially misjudged you."

"What did you initially take me for, then?"

"A groupie who managed to sneak into the village to pick up hot athletes," he answered frankly.

"Gee, thanks," she replied sarcastically.

He shrugged unapologetically. "You wouldn't be the first one."

He wasn't wrong of course. Just yesterday, the American delegation had chased out a half-dozen drunk Polish guys from the American athlete building. They'd claimed to be looking for an American high jumper who was also a high-fashion model and on the covers of all the fashion magazines these days.

"If you're not a steak and potatoes guy, then how would you describe yourself?" she challenged.

A waitress came and Avi ordered quickly in German: some sort of meal package for two, and then Rebel's limited German gave out as he and the waitress conversed in the tongue quickly and fluently, ending on a laugh. Rebel had to stop herself from glaring off the flirting waitress, which privately stunned her. She had never been the jealous type before, and it wasn't like she had any claim on Avi Bronson, thank you very much.

The waitress brought a fondue pot filled with a creamy cheese sauce, a platter of bread cubes and a handful of long dipping forks.

"It's hot," Avi warned her. "Don't burn your mouth."

She nodded and dipped a bread cube in the smooth sauce that smelled lightly of wine and Emmentaler cheese. She blew on the bite and popped it in her mouth. "Oh my God," she groaned. "That's fantastic."

"Told you."

"I will never question your culinary recommendations again."

He smiled a little as he dipped a cube of his own. "I take my food very seriously."

"What else do you take seriously? You never answered my question of how you'd describe yourself."

He shrugged as he swirled a bread cube in the pot. "I would like to think I'm on my way to becoming a Renaissance man. You know what I do for my work. In my free time, I enjoy art, music, reading and good food."

"What kind of art?" she asked.

"Modern interactive art is my passion, but I enjoy a good Rembrandt as much as the next person."

"Music?"

"Every kind. Except Nazi-metalhead."

"Books?"

"That's a bit tricky. I prefer history or dead poets, but I make myself read literature and pop fiction."

"Why?"

"To be well-rounded."

"That all sounds terribly intellectual and dry. What do you do for fun?"

He leaned forward, and a boyish smile hovered on his lips. "I kill people."

"Oh, puh-lease." She rolled her eyes at him. "You must

suck at your job if you have to whack people often. The idea is to get in and get out without being spotted and without ending up in a fight. Or didn't they teach you that part in Israel?"

He laughed outright at her pithy observation. "Well, damn. Most women are unbearably turned on by knowing I can kill."

"Sorry. It's just an unpleasant part of the job to me."

The waitress removed their cheese fondue, which they'd mostly polished off between them, and replaced it with a bubbling pot of hot oil and a platter of meats and vegetables.

"What makes you happy?" Avi asked when they'd demolished most of the main course.

"Happy?" she echoed. "I don't believe in happiness."

"Why ever not?" he exclaimed.

"Because it's a lie. People confuse pleasure with happiness, and most humans only want pleasure. Which is transient, fleeting and passes quickly. It's not worth ruining my life in pursuit of a few moments here and there that constitute mere pleasure."

"Wow. Cynical much?" he murmured.

She shrugged. "Don't get me wrong. I enjoy my work. I take deep satisfaction from it, in fact. But that's because I'm doing something important that will improve the quality of the world... I hope."

Avi shuddered. "What a dreadful way to go through life."

"What's dreadful about being committed to my career?"

"Nothing. I'm committed to mine, as well. Passionately."

"Why passionately?" she followed up.

"Because I live in a small country surrounded by

larger enemies. Israel's ongoing survival is always an open question. Unlike your country with oceans on either side of it and no enemies on Earth who can match your power, my country is tiny and imminently crushable. It takes many people of passion to keep her safe."

"Just because the United States is big and powerful doesn't mean we can stop working at staying safe. We have lots of enemies, and our size and power makes us a prime target. Hence, the need for people like me."

He nodded. "We have a point of agreement, then. Both of our countries need robust security forces to ensure their safety."

"Speaking of which, when do you expect to hear from your people about our friend? I'm dying to know what they have to say about him."

One corner of his mouth turned up sardonically. "Are you in such a big hurry to jump in bed with him, then?"

She frowned across the table at them. They might have to speak elliptically about Mahmoud Akhtar in public, but she wasn't loving the sleeping with Akhtar analogy.

Avi grinned unrepentantly. "Lighten up a little, Rebel. It was a joke."

"Again, you didn't answer my question."

He sighed. "You need to learn how to slow down. Relax a little. Like now. Enjoy the good food and exceptional company. There will be time later for business."

Great. He was clearly determined to torture her.

Except when the dessert course came—a rich, silky, dark chocolate fondue and a platter of succulent fresh fruit, berries and delicate ladyfinger cookies—she forgot her impatience and lost herself in savoring the delicious sweets.

"Be careful, Rebel. You're looking suspiciously close to happy over there."

"I didn't say I don't like pleasure. Just that I don't live for it."

"I fear, mademoiselle, that you are missing out on most of the best things in life with that grim philosophy of yours."

"I am who I am," she retorted. She refrained from reminding him she didn't owe him a blessed thing. After all, she was supposed to work with this guy and trade information. No sense in antagonizing him outright.

"That's a rather Socratic take on life," he commented. "How does the saying go—I know that I am intelligent, because I know that I know nothing."

She retorted, "I know I'm intelligent, because I know better than to read people like Socrates and let them put my mind all in a twist."

Avi laughed warmly. "Touché." He signaled for the bill and handed over a credit card before Rebel even had a chance to grab for the bill.

"Next meal's on me," she declared.

"If it makes you feel better, I'll let you buy me supper sometime," he said evenly as he signed the check and tucked the receipt in his pocket. "But it's not necessary. I won't think any less of you as an independent woman because you do or don't insist on paying your own way."

"It's a matter of principle for me," she admitted.

"How so? Don't you like being taken care of?"

"More like I don't like being smothered."

He paused in the act of standing up to study her intently. After a moment, he finished straightening to his full height and gestured for her to precede him from the restaurant.

Dammit. Too revealing a comment. She shouldn't have said that. She slid out of the booth and headed for the front door.

The Adler was a narrow space, and as they slipped past a group of loud drunks at the bar, Avi placed a protective hand in the middle of her back. The touch was light, impersonal even, but it also declared clearly to all the men they sidled past to leave her the hell alone.

Lord knew, she could break in half most any man who groped her. But for some reason, she took comfort in Avi removing the need for her to be defensive for a change. Sometimes it got damned fatiguing having to be on guard against drunks, lechers and general idiots.

They'd left the restaurant and were strolling back toward the village through still shockingly crowded streets before Avi murmured quietly, "Who smothered you, Rebel?"

She opened her mouth to declare it none of his business, but surprised herself by saying, "Basically all the men in my life."

"Even Gunnar Torsten?"

"You have to admit he's an intimidating man. Hard to know. Demanding. While I wouldn't say he smothers any of us, he is challenging to work with. But at least he believes women have a place in the…community." She omitted the words Special Forces, but Avi would know what she'd meant.

"It's an interesting idea, building an entire team of women operators. I'd love to talk with you about it sometime, hear more about what you do."

She shrugged. "Major T. obviously thinks you have the clearance to know about it, so I have no problem talking with you."

"Perfect. What are you doing for dinner tomorrow?"

Gulp.

Chapter 3

Avi showed up at the American security center exactly five minutes early for his date with the fascinating American woman, Rebel. He was beginning to think her name fit her better than her parents could have imagined when they gave it to her.

He'd worked with enough American Special Forces teams over the years to know that in the American military, if a person wasn't five minutes early, they were late.

Rebel was seated at a computer, frowning intensely at it when he stepped into the busy space. The Israeli command center had been hopping most of the night as well, tracking which of their athletes had been injured in the pool accident and rescheduling preliminary competitions for them. The IOC had been more understanding that he'd expected, actually. But then, the accident in the pool had been the host committee's fault.

"Hi, Rebel," he said quietly so as not to startle her.

She glanced up at him just long enough for color to bloom on her cheeks. *Interesting. An autonomic response to him, huh? Good to know.* Particularly since he was deeply intrigued by her, too.

"Whatcha working on?" he asked.

"Check this out." She handed him a crude diagram she'd drawn on a piece of paper. A rectangle took up most of the sheet of paper, and it was filled with tiny numbers—hundreds of them from zero to nine.

"What am I looking at?" he asked.

"I've spent the day asking every injured athlete I can get a hold of how bad their injuries are—I developed a scale from zero to nine to log the severity of their symptoms—and where they were in the pool when they first noticed them. Then I mapped all of that information in a rough diagram of the pool. Notice anything interesting?"

It leaped out at him right away. All of the nines were clustered tightly together about halfway down the east side of the pool. The eights and sevens clustered around that bunch of nines, and the numbers grew steadily smaller the farther away the victims had been from that spot of origin on the east side of the pool.

He looked up at Rebel. "What do you make of this?"

"I don't think the excessive chlorine in the pool was introduced through the automated chlorination system. I think it was put in the pool by an individual standing beside it, right about there." She jabbed at her drawing where all the nines were centered.

"The IOC has already closed the investigation," he commented.

"Of course they have," she replied scornfully. "They don't want any hint of sabotage or an attack of some kind to sully their games."

"They also don't want to panic anyone by having wild

rumors or unsubstantiated accusations floating around," he observed.

She looked up at him, her gaze frustrated. "I get that. But I think the evidence is clear. We are, in fact, dealing with an act of sabotage. Combine that with my spotting Mahmoud Akhtar and Yousef Kamali at the east side of the pool last night, and you do the math."

He sighed. "We don't have a positive ID on either man. We can't even confirm they're here."

"Is that what your Mossad contacts said?"

"They said they've heard nothing to indicate that Akhtar or Kamali is outside of Iran, let alone here and active."

"That doesn't mean they aren't here. It just means your people don't know they're here," she countered.

"What does the CIA have to say on the subject?"

She shrugged. "Zane is due to land in about an hour. I'll let you know what he says."

Tonight, Avi had chosen a more formal restaurant for them. He'd made a reservation for seven thirty, and it wasn't the kind of place that held a table for a party if it was late. "We need to go," he announced.

Rebel stood up, and he glanced at her dark, tailored business suit. It was expensive fabric and well made, but it did nothing to enhance the body beneath it.

They were outside the village and close to the restaurant before he asked, "Why do you wear suits like that? Do you want to make yourself look like a man?"

"I find that men are easily distractible creatures. Also, as a group, they're not generally taught to judge a woman by her intellect or skill at her profession, but rather to judge her by her looks. If I want them to think of me as a professional, I have to look like one. And that means not girl-ing up."

"You don't think it's possible for a woman to be attractive and do a job?"

"Of course I think it's possible. I just don't think it's possible for men to perceive an attractive woman as a professional."

"That's a pretty dim view of men, Ms. McQueen."

She shrugged. "I call it as I see it."

"You really have been surrounded by stupid chauvinist jackasses, haven't you?"

Her gaze jerked up to his.

"Why do you look surprised that I might have liberated views of women?" he asked. "Women have served side by side with men in the IDF since the founding of Israel in 1948."

"Apparently, I was born in the wrong country," she responded dryly.

"A mistake that can be rectified. I'm sure there's a place in my country for a woman with your special abilities."

She laughed. "Thanks, but I'm good with where I'm at. The Medusas are unique."

"Other countries are training women Special Forces operatives."

"True. But none of them are fielding entire teams made up of women who do the same sorts of missions as men. Most add a single woman to a team here and there. Also, not many countries are giving women full SF training. They're modifying the training for women and not making them meet the same standards as men."

"You had to meet men's standards?" he exclaimed, startled.

"What would be the point if we didn't?" she snapped.

He absorbed that in silence as they reached the restaurant. He held the door for her, and as she slid past him he muttered, "All the men's standards?"

"*All* of them."

"But…you're so tiny."

"Lower muscle to weight ratio for me to overcome. And I fit into small spaces my male counterparts don't. Makes for great sniper nests that hostiles don't spot."

"You're a—" He broke off, realizing belatedly that they were standing in a posh restaurant, and it probably wasn't the ideal place to blurt out that his dinner companion was an assassin.

"Not my specialty," she murmured. "I'm mainly a photo intelligence analyst. I look at live video images from drones and interpret them in real time."

"So you have an eye for detail?"

"You could say that." Her voice was as dry as the Negev Desert.

Their table was ready, and he followed Rebel and the maître d' into the private dining room Avi had reserved for them. The decor of the room was dark, with paneled walls and burgundy carpet. Crisp white linen covered their candlelit table, though, and the places were precisely set with Limoges china and Lalique crystal. The table looked like a glittering jewel nestled in a bed of dark velvet. It was impossibly romantic.

Which was exactly the point. He'd set a personal goal of teaching the overly serious American commando how to loosen her collar a little and enjoy the finer things in life.

The maître d' seated Rebel and then retreated, leaving the two of them alone. He sat down across from her and unfolded his crisply starched linen napkin, spreading it across his lap in anticipation of the culinary delights to come.

"Where have you brought me?" she asked in alarm. "I'm afraid to breathe hard, lest I break something."

"The food is outstanding, and we can speak in private, here. And my government is picking up the tab, so don't worry about the cost."

"Cost? I bet his place doesn't even put prices on the menu."

He smiled. "They don't. Shall I choose a wine for us?"

"You'd better. All I know about wine is it's bad if it's still bubbling."

He laughed, shocked. "Still bubbling? That's obscene."

"That's Boone's Farm in a box."

"Boone's Farm? That's not actually wine. It's—" he searched for a proper description "—corn syrup, food coloring and rubbing alcohol."

She laughed, and he stared, shocked at what happened to her face when her customary intensity gave way to actual joy. Her eyes sparkled, color came to her cheeks, and the fineness of her bones, the soft perfection of her skin came to life. It was as if her entire being smiled for a moment.

"You should laugh more often," he declared.

The laughter faded from her eyes, and determination to make her laugh again came over him. But first, their waiter arrived, and Avi ordered a ridiculously expensive bottle of wine to go with the chef's choice.

The waiter left and Rebel leaned forward, looking distressed. "What are we eating tonight?"

Avi shrugged. "Whatever the chef serves to us. I've eaten here several times and he has never disappointed me."

"But what if it's something weird?"

"I thought you Americans do a half-decent survival school. After eating bugs and worms, are you really that worried over what a Michelin three-star chef is going to make for you?"

She leaned back, looking disgruntled. In a heartbeat, she'd gone from stunningly beautiful to fluffy kitten cute.

"You're quite the chameleon, Rebel."

"How so?"

"I've identified at least four versions of you so far, and each one is entirely different."

"Do tell." She sipped the wine the waiter had poured for her, and abruptly, her attention riveted not on him but on her glass. "Holy crap," she muttered.

"Is it ruined?" he asked quickly. "Cork in the wine? Soured?"

"No. I had no idea wine could taste like this. I don't even like wine. But this is…amazing."

He leaned back, grinning. "Ahh. Welcome to the civilized world. Where pleasure is more than fleeting and people achieve actual happiness."

She scowled at him, back to being a hedgehog—prickly, but still adorable.

He sipped at his wine, savoring the complex bouquet. "So tell me this. Why would men like Mahmoud and Yousef bother dumping chlorine in a pool? It's a far too low-level attack—too amateur for men of their training and skill."

"Agreed. Unless it was some sort of test run. Maybe they were checking the emergency response. Or maybe they wanted to see if any sophisticated monitoring and detection equipment was brought out and used."

An interesting theory. He replied, "It's not as if poisoning a bunch of people with a chlorine attack is likely to succeed without being detected. It stinks to high heaven, and people have some time to run away from the fumes, and in this case skin burns, before they're seriously injured or killed."

"Obviously," she retorted. "But what if they're planning to use some other poison gas in a larger attack? Why go to all the trouble of setting up a lethal attack if you know the Olympic security team is prepared to detect it and stop it?"

"But we *are* prepared to identify the usual nerve gasses."

She shrugged. "I know that, and you know that. But do the Iranians know that? Or are they testing the edges of our defenses to measure what we can and can't respond to?"

"Or maybe a few drunk hooligans thought dumping a bunch of chlorine in the pool would be a funny joke."

She studied him long and hard enough that he began to wonder what she was thinking about him. Only perverse stubbornness stopped him from asking. The same stubbornness frustrated his parents to no end, but had also saved his life on countless occasions when he refused to give up in the face of impossible odds. Hell, he was beginning to think getting this woman to relax and enjoy herself a little was one of those damn near impossible tasks.

Clearly, she intended to keep the talk over dinner entirely business. *So be it. For now.*

"Fine," he conceded. "If it was, in fact, an attack, you're likely right. It probably wasn't random drunks. Have you considered the timing of the attack? Could it even have been your terrorists?"

She shrugged. "Mahmoud and Yousef left the pool about thirty minutes before everyone started reacting to the chlorine. They would have had to use some sort of dissolving packaging or pellets that melted slowly for the timing to work."

"Okay," he replied. "That's a plausible hypothesis. Do you have any proof of it?"

"There are no lights in that pool, hence no underwater video. I've checked the security cameras for last night, but the crowd is so dense around the pool I can't make out anyone who might have dumped anything in the water."

"So your theory will have to remain just that. A theory."

"A scary theory that you and my bosses would do well to take seriously," she retorted.

"I'm sorry. I didn't mean to make you angry," he murmured.

"I'm not angry. Just worried."

"Fair enough. If you're worried, I'm worried," he responded gallantly.

"Really?"

He met her gaze squarely. "Yes. Really. Even if I don't know you that well, yet, I do know Gunnar Torsten. And anyone he trains is someone to take seriously."

They waited in silence as the first course of their meal was served, hors d'oeuvres of wild mushrooms stuffed with crab, escargot and truffle paté.

He silently took pleasure in watching the orgasmic expressions crossing Rebel's face with each new flavor she encountered. She was a great deal more expressive than she likely thought she was. But then, a man like him was adept at catching every nuance of facial and body language, too.

Eventually, he leaned forward. "I did get one interesting piece of intel from my people this afternoon."

She looked up expectantly from her potato-leek soup,

abruptly all business, food forgotten. He sent a silent mental apology to the chef.

"I'll share it with you, but on one condition," he murmured.

"What's that?"

He stood up, went around the table and held out his hand to her. "Dance with me."

Chapter 4

Rebel gulped. If there was one thing in the whole world she was terrible at, it would be dancing. "But, there's no music," she protested, praying the excuse would divert Avi.

He walked over to an intercom panel on the wall and pressed a few buttons. Lilting violin music suddenly blared. He turned the volume down and then turned to her, holding out a hand.

She looked around in panic. The room was plenty large enough to accommodate dancing. There were no apparent cameras to make an embarrassing record of her clumsiness. She resorted to confessing, "I'm a terrible dancer."

"Well of course you are. Dancing is about expressing joy. And we've already established you need a lot of work in that department."

She frowned, not appreciating being called a failure at anything, even if it was true.

He captured her hand, which she realized in some shock was waving around nervously, and tugged her to her feet.

"You're going to regret this," she warned him as he drew her into his arms.

"Put your right hand on my waist and your left hand on my shoulder…assuming you can reach my shoulder."

She snorted. "Very funny. I'm not *that* short."

"In my world, you're practically a midget."

Her eyes narrowed in challenge. "You'd be surprised the things I can do that a giant lout like you can't even begin to do."

"Sounds like a fascinating conversation for another time. But right now, I'm giving you a lesson in waltzing. First, listen to the music. *One*-two-three. *One*-two-three. Do you hear the downbeat?"

"Yes."

"On each 'one,' I'm going to step forward with my right foot, and you're going to step backward with your left foot. Like this. I'll take it slow." He placed both of his hands on her waist and guided her through the step.

Thank goodness. He just did the back step several times, and she caught on quickly.

"Now, we're going to step to the side on the second and third beats. Like this. Step-together."

She nodded after a few repetitions.

"And now we put them together, and we find the rhythm of the music. Just relax, and let me lead, okay?"

"Since when is this a trust exercise?" she blurted.

He smiled down at her a little ruefully. "Leave your left hand on my shoulder and put your right hand in mine." She grasped his hand, as always stunned by the electric energy flowing from him.

"I have to say, Rebel, I didn't expect you to discover

my real motive so quickly. This is entirely about trust. That and loosening you up a little. You are a smart one, aren't you?"

She might have answered, but he whisked her backward and into a whirl around the room that took her breath away. His hands moved her with effortless power, but still, she had to concentrate on relaxing and releasing the habitual tension from her body.

Ahh, but when she did, they were suddenly dipping and swooping, turning in light, swift circles until she felt like a swallow in flight. It was actually a rather fantastic sensation. The music lifted them off their mortal feet, spinning them into a breathless world of candlelit magic.

Or maybe it was the big, graceful man staring down at her, his eyes as dark as midnight, the expression in them bemused. If there had been any humor in his expression when they started the waltz, by the time the song ended, it was long gone.

The music shifted into some other, more formal rhythm, and they came to a stop beside the table. His hand was warm and firm on her waist, and his fingers flexed, tightening momentarily against her side.

He released her abruptly, stepping back almost as if startled. She knew the feeling. She was shocked to her toes. That had been an almost-sexual experience. And it had been wonderful. Which begged the question of why he'd insisted on dancing with her. Had trust and getting her to chill out been his only motives, after all? Or had he been subtly demonstrating to her that he knew how to woo a woman?

For no doubt about it, he most definitely knew what he was doing in that department.

It almost made a girl wonder if maybe the problem

with sex in her life prior to this had been men of inadequate knowledge rather than the sex itself.

Hmm. Sex with Avi Bronson. A suddenly fascinating concept.

The door opened, and their waiter wheeled in a cart loaded with what turned out to be the most delectable food she'd ever tasted. Quail roasted to tender perfection with herbed skin that was crispy and savory, oyster stuffing that made her groan in delight and tender asparagus that was so fresh and light she wanted to ask for more—and she didn't even like asparagus, normally.

She refrained from licking her plate, but it was a struggle. She looked up at Avi in regret. "You do realize you've ruined me for ever enjoying an MRE again."

"You *like* dehydrated military food?" he exclaimed.

"I did. But now… I shudder to think what it will taste like in comparison to this."

He smiled indulgently. "My work is done, then."

Something disappointed landed with a thud in the bottom of her stomach. Drat. She'd really hoped he might be interested in showing her more of these sophisticated pleasures she'd heretofore had no idea existed.

"Why the sad face?" he asked quickly.

"I'm sorry this meal has to end."

"Never fear. We have several more courses to go."

"Where am I going to put more food? You do realize I'm going to have to work out like mad for a week to burn off all these calories."

He shrugged. "I'll go for a run with you tomorrow if you'd like. After all, it's my fault you indulged like this. I'm obligated to help with damage control."

Hmm. That would be interesting. She enjoyed running and was one of the fastest Medusas. "You're on."

She was done with dessert and sipping a cup of coffee

so good it nearly brought her to tears when she finally remembered to ask, "By the way, what was the piece of intelligence you said you'd gotten?"

He sighed. "And, the pleasant interlude ends. Back to business, eh?"

She smiled a little at the disappointment in his voice. "Sorry."

"When you apologize like you mean it, I'll know I've broken through that workaholic exterior of yours."

"Good luck with that." She set down her coffee cup. "The intel?"

"Right. A source in Tehran reports that Mahmoud has spent the past six months or so training with a team of approximately eight operatives on a military base. They were seen going in and out of mocked-up buildings repeatedly."

"Sounds like they were training for a specific attack," she commented.

"That's how I would interpret it, as well."

"Any information on what the buildings looked like?"

"No. Our source isn't that highly placed."

"Still. Are you going to take me seriously now when I say I saw Mahmoud and Yousef and that I'm convinced they dumped the chlorine in the pool?"

"I always took you seriously, Rebel."

"Yeah, but no one else is likely to."

"Do you want me to put forward your theory to the IOC security team because they would take me more seriously?"

She sighed. "I appreciate the offer, but I expect Major Torsten will tell them about it if he thinks I've adequately backed up my theory with evidence."

"He's a good man. He won't take credit for your work. You'll get the credit."

"Or the blame," she added.

Avi shrugged. "If you think you're right, stick by your guns. Who cares if you got this one wrong? We all make mistakes from time to time. Better to be overcautious and be wrong than say nothing and have a preventable attack happen."

"Yes, but this is the first time the new Medusas have worked the Olympic Games. If I'm making a wrong call and people get all worked up for no reason, the egg will be on all of my teammates' faces along with mine."

"You're a team, right? Wouldn't you suffer a little humiliation on behalf of one of your sisters?"

"Well, yes."

"And they would do the same for you. Don't second-guess yourself. Trust your gut."

He was right. She took a deep breath. "Thanks for the pep talk."

"Anytime."

The waiter brought back Avi's credit card, and he signed the check quickly.

"Do I want to know what that meal cost?" she asked.

"No. But it was worth every shekel to watch you enjoy yourself like that."

Alarmed, she let him hold her chair as she stood up. Had she made a spectacle of herself? The idea sent shivers of horror across her skin. If she'd learned nothing else in her father's repressive home, it was that women should never, ever, draw attention to themselves.

"What were you thinking about just then?" Avi asked, startling her out of dark memories.

"Nothing."

Avi responded evenly, "I'm not letting you get away with putting me off like that. Tell me what you were thinking about."

"Why do you care?"

"Because it put pain in your eyes. I want to know what or who hurt you."

He sounded half-prepared to go out and beat up bullies on her behalf. Which was sweet. And strange. She wasn't accustomed to any man looking out for her. In fact, she'd spent most of her adult life making sure no man needed to look out for her.

She glanced up. He was staring down at her expectantly. He looked ready to stand there all night, not moving an inch, until he got his answer.

Well, hell. She huffed and then admitted, "I was thinking about my father."

"Your father? Why would he put such pain in your eyes?"

"Because he wasn't—isn't—a very nice man. He believes that women should be seen and not heard. And that women should stay out of men's way."

Sarcasm lacing his voice, he responded, "He must love your job choice."

"We don't speak."

"Ahh." A pause. Then Avi said quietly, "I'm sorry. I shouldn't have pried, and I'm sorry your father is a jerk. But thank you for letting me know what I have to overcome."

"I beg your pardon?"

"Well, now I know that not only will you be sensitive to feeling smothered, but you'll also have issues with domineering men."

"I don't—" She broke off. "Okay, fine. I do."

He gifted her with a smile so beautiful she could hardly look at it or at him. Lord, he was a handsome man.

He said, "Thank you for your honesty. I value it more than just about any trait in my friends."

Only friends? And there went her stomach again, dropping into her shoes in disappointment. Since when did she want to be more than friends with this man?

Since he'd taught her how to waltz and introduced her to fine cuisine—and not only saw her as a soldier, but also saw her as a woman.

Which also made her feel naked. Vulnerable. Most people ignored her, and she tended to prefer it that way. Too bad he hadn't seen her as more. It would have been nice if this man had looked at her and seen a woman of interest, maybe even a potential romantic interest.

But no. He'd seen a friend.

It was better than nothing. But not by much.

If only she was more capable at the whole romance and seduction thing. But that was like wishing she could hold the moon in her hand. It was never going to happen.

Their walk back to the Olympic Village was quiet, and Avi was content to let Rebel stew in her thoughts. He was prepared to move slowly with her, take his time and let her work out whatever she needed to work out in her head before he pushed her to the next level. She wasn't the kind of woman a man could proposition for cheap sex after a date or two and expect an affirmative response.

Huh. Since when had he started to consider sleeping with her?

He thought back and pegged it at the moment when she'd shown him her map of the injured athletes in the pool. Her passion and intensity had been sexy as hell.

He glanced sidelong at her as they crossed a busy street crowded with drunks. She was a tiny little thing, but it was easy to miss that because of how big her intellect and confidence were. Oh, she hid both well. As any good special operator should. But they were there. And sexy, too.

When he'd finally gotten her to relax into the waltz, she'd been light as air in his arms. A good natural athlete, she was, to pick up the dance so quickly. In touch with her body. Which was promising for more intimate dances—

He should really stop imagining sex with her. They both had a job to do. And although this was far below the usual level of danger he operated in, both of them needed to give the security of their respective delegations their full attention.

Maybe after the games were over he could volunteer to do some training with the Medusas, possibly as an instructor, or in some sort of exchange program with his team to run scenarios using teams of women operators. He could sell it to his superiors as an observation trip to see if the Israelis should consider training a female Spec Ops team of their own.

The more he thought about it, the more he liked the idea.

"Does your team ever run exercises with foreign teams?" he asked abruptly.

"To date, we've mostly had individual foreign instructors come to our main training facility to work with us as we come up to speed. We haven't worked with full teams. You'd have to ask Major T. if he ever plans to put us in the field on exercises. Right now, he's keeping our existence under pretty close wraps."

As well he should. The Medusas were safer the fewer people knew they existed. And apparently, he'd also developed a sudden interest in the safety of the Medusas, along with Torsten.

"This is my stop," Rebel announced, jerking him out

of planning how to sell an exercise with the Medusas to his boss.

They were, indeed, standing in front of the American security team's building.

"Sweet dreams," he murmured, leaning down to kiss her on the cheek.

She froze, startled as most Americans were when they first encountered the European habit of kissing pretty much everyone. He smiled to himself as he turned away. He was enjoying throwing her off balance far more than he should. But it would be good for her to pop that boring bubble she tried to hide in.

As for him, he was headed for his room to change into dark clothing, and then he was going to stake out the small apartment building the Iranian delegation was staying in by itself at the request of the Iranian government. Not that he blamed them. The Israelis had insisted on having a facility to themselves, too.

Midnight had come and gone when Avi spied movement out the back door of the Iranian building. He zoomed in his binoculars. Four men and two women, dressed in the black tracksuits of the Iranian team slipped outside.

Apparently, the mice were planning to play while they were away from the cat. Although, the Iranian government usually kept a ridiculously tight leash on its athletes overseas, too. Which explained why he was surprised this bunch tonight had made it out of their quarters successfully. He waited for any possible tails to slip out of the building to follow the athletes, but none did.

He briefly debated staying to watch the building or giving in to his curiosity to see what the Iranian athletes did when off the leash. His curiosity won.

They were almost out of sight, now, heading toward

the south end of the village and the many athletic complexes clustered there. He had to hurry not to lose them. There were plenty of facilities open around the clock in the village—the dining hall, gyms, game rooms, media rooms, medical and physio offices. So why were the Iranians headed toward the sports complex at this hour? The venues would all be closed, locked up and locked down.

Were the Iranian athletes maybe hoping to check out competition venues before the event? Except the men and women would be competing in entirely different sports. Were the men escorting the women to their venue perhaps?

He trailed along behind the group as it approached the gymnastics venue and peered in the banks of locked doors. He doubted they could see much besides the concourse around the exterior of the facility and a few tunnels leading down into the bowl of the competition floor. They walked almost a full circle around the field house and then veered off toward the natatorium.

The group gave the same rather inexplicable treatment to the swimming venue, peering in briefly, but making no attempt to get inside, and then circling the building. He knew for a fact that Iran hadn't sent any athletes to the game in either gymnastics or swimming. So why the interest in these venues?

His confusion grew as the group disappeared around the side of the basketball venue next. The big stadium could easily seat twenty-five thousand people. As far as he could tell, the Iranians merely walked around the outside of the building and made no attempt to go inside.

Something else dawned on him as the guided tour of all the big venues continued. The six athletes in front of him didn't appear to be having any fun. They weren't talking and laughing. There appeared to be no joking around and only minimal conversation.

Were they casing the venues in preparation for future crimes?

The idea crashed across his brain, along with cold dread, wrecking his concentration on the surveillance. How could these people be doing anything else? This had to be a reconnaissance trip of some kind.

Which said nothing good about who the people in front of him were.

What were the odds the Iranians had sent some sort of terrorist strike team to the Olympics posing as athletes? There were plenty of sports where no minimum time or score was required to qualify to participate.

What if the group in front of him was not only athletes but also terrorists?

Funny, but his very next thought was worry for Rebel's safety. She would be squarely in the line of fire from these people, and he had no way of knowing if she was adequately prepared to take them on and survive, let alone win.

He moved stealthily now, slipping from shadow to shadow, closing in to a range where he could get high quality surveillance photos of all the athletes. It took a while, but when he was fairly certain he had solid face shots of each athlete, he backed off to a safer range.

The Iranians went to every single major indoor venue in the Olympic Park, roaming laps around outside the giant structures before finally turning back toward the Olympic Village. The group returned quickly to the village and slipped back inside the Iranian team building. He was close to certain they hadn't spotted him, which made their behavior all the more perplexing.

He estimated they'd spent no more than ten minutes

circling each venue, which was barely long enough to have a fast look around. It certainly wasn't long enough to do any kind of a decent reconnaissance or a walk-through of an attack. Which was good news at least.

But it did beg the question, what in the hell were they up to?

Avi assigned one of the junior members of the Israeli security contingent to keep an eye on the Iranian team building overnight, so he could get a little rest, himself.

He fell asleep still wondering what the Iranians were doing, and coming up with no answers. Which was frustrating in the extreme...

Until he dreamed of Rebel and his frustration became sexual in nature and climbed heretofore-unscaled heights.

He woke sweating and horny. Naked, he rolled out of bed, poured himself a glass of water and downed it in supreme irritation at himself. He was a professional, and so was she. He owed her more respect than to imagine her naked and moaning in his arms, lost in pleasure.

But it wasn't like he had control of his subconscious. Like it or not, he had a thing for his colleague. Under other circumstances, he might have gone with the flow. Seen where things went between them. But as it was, he had a gut feeling something bad was unfolding around them both, and it required his full attention. And hers. *Dammit.*

Chapter 5

Rebel's pulse leaped as Avi held the door to the briefing room for Gia and Lynx bright and early the next morning. Zane had made an initial report directly to Major Torsten when he'd arrived last night, and then he'd been allowed to get some sleep before briefing the whole team. Today the Medusas were meeting in a secure conference room that had no windows, was tucked in the middle of the American security headquarters and was lined with reflective metals that would repel any efforts to snoop on the meeting.

Rebel was a bit annoyed with her teammates for intentionally leaving the seat beside her empty. Sometimes it bugged her that all the women knew each other so well and could read the most subtle signals from one another. Obviously, her interest in the hot Israeli hadn't gone unnoticed by her girls. *Dammit*.

As long as Torsten hadn't picked up on her crush, she

would be okay. God help her if the boss figured it out, though.

And honestly, she liked the way her stomach fluttered when Avi sank into the chair beside her with a brief, warm smile for her. It was an intimate expression, a private thing between them, a definite acknowledgment that they were more than vaguely acquainted coworkers.

Well, okay, then.

Her tummy bubbling with fizzy happiness, she turned her attention to Piper's fiancé at the front of the room. Zane fiddled briefly with a projector, plugging a flash drive into its side and picking up the wireless clicker.

"Good morning, ladies and gentlemen. I apologize for the hasty nature of this briefing—I didn't have long to pull it together before I left Langley yesterday—day before yesterday…international date line, right?"

Rebel smiled sympathetically. Jet lag was a bitch when fifteen time zones were crossed.

Zane flashed through the most recent photos of Mahmoud Akhtar and Yousef Kamali, most of which the Medusas already had posted in their ready room. Zane then blasted through a quick sitrep on Iran in general, ending with an assessment declaring the probability high that Iran would try something during or soon after the Olympic Games.

If the Iranians didn't act for themselves, they might act as proxies for Russia, which was furious at continued sanctions against many of its athletes for illegal doping.

Zane continued, "We've been in contact with our source at a classified Iranian Special Forces training facility, and he reports seeing Mahmoud Akhtar about six months ago working with a team of approximately eight operatives. They appeared to be running some sort of kidnapping or hostage scenario. Mock apartments—or perhaps hotel rooms—were the target."

Rebel echoed the low groan around the table at that. Twenty-thousand athletes and nearly that many coaches, support staff and officials occupied the many dormitory-style buildings of the Olympic Village at this very minute.

Zane finished with, "Our report also indicates that a large contingent of senior officers and government officials observed the exercises and offered comments and suggestions to the team."

Avi leaned forward at that. "Your source is sure about that last bit?"

"I should say so," Zane answered dryly. "He was an eyewitness to the exercises."

Avi nodded thoughtfully but said nothing more.

Now why had he asked that? Rebel made a mental note to ask him about it later.

"As for how Mahmoud and Yousef slipped past the IOC background checks and Australia's border security, we believe they may have arrived by ship up to two months ago, perhaps landing in a port of entry nowhere near Sydney and making their way overland to this location."

Avi added, "Which is indicative of nefarious intent. Or perhaps they were smuggling something into the country."

"Exactly," Zane agreed.

"Weapons, maybe?" Major Torsten threw out.

"Maybe," Zane replied doubtfully. "We have to assume they have plentiful black market contacts and will have no trouble obtaining whatever weapons they need inside Australia. Given the amount of terrorist activity in Indonesia over the past year, we can confirm that pretty much anything short of nuclear weapons would be available in this region of the world to anyone with enough cash."

Rebel leaned forward. "What kind of gear were Mahmoud's guys wearing while they ran their training scenarios?"

Zane looked at her quizzically, and she elaborated. "Were they wearing civilian clothes, or were they tricked out in full Spec Ops gear? Body armor? Night optical gear? Urban assault weapons? Explosives? Their equipment might give us some hint as to what kind of assault they're planning."

"Good point," Zane responded. "I'll have to get back with you on that."

Which was to say, he would have to pass the question on to the CIA's contact.

Avi nodded slowly beside her. "They can use overwhelming force to blast through the village security, or they can use subterfuge. They don't really have any other choices, given the level of surveillance and security measures deployed here."

"What kind of subterfuge could they use?" Rebel asked quickly. She sensed Avi was thinking about something specific when he made that comment.

She listened in dismay as he relayed having followed a group of Iranian athletes late last night who'd acted like anything but athletes. Not only was that news alarming, but she was disappointed he hadn't invited her to go along on his little surveillance outing.

Not that he owed her or Gunnar Torsten anything of the like. But still. They were supposed to be working together.

Or maybe she was overreacting and letting her hots for the sexy Israeli cloud her thinking.

Beau Lambert, a former Navy SEAL and due to marry

Tessa Wilkes in a few months, commented from the far end of the room, where he lounged with a knee propped against the edge of the table, "No offense, Z, but why did you have to come all this way to give us this briefing in person? We all know what the tangos look like and what we have to do, which is spot the bastards and take them down."

Torsten jumped in to answer, "I asked him to come here."

Everyone, including Rebel, looked at her boss expectantly.

He continued grimly, "I have an idea, and I'm fairly sure Zane would've jumped on a plane the minute he heard about it, anyway."

"Which is?" Piper—engaged to Zane—asked ominously.

Torsten looked the willowy blonde square in the eye. "I want to use you as bait to draw our terrorists out, Piper."

"Hasn't she been through enough?" Zane blurted.

Rebel knew that he, more than most, understood how traumatic being kidnapped last fall by Mahmoud Akhtar and his men had been for Piper. The other women of the Medusas had spent the past six months listening to her nightmares and watching her struggle to sleep at night. They might not know the gory details, and Zane had— according to Piper—prevented anything really bad from happening to her. But Rebel and the other women knew it hadn't been a picnic for her to get over the experience.

Torsten ignored Zane's outburst and instead stared steadily at Rebel's friend and teammate. Piper stared back at him for a long time. It didn't take a rocket scientist to know that Torsten was silently asking Piper if she was up for the mission or not.

Finally, she nodded once. Tersely. "I'm down for being bait," she said shortly.

"Piper—" Zane started.

"Not now," she said with quiet conviction.

Yikes. Rebel smelled a knock-down-drag-out in Piper and Zane's immediate future. Avi, blissfully unaware of the personal relationship between the pair asked eagerly, "Will Mahmoud come out of hiding to go after your operative, Gun?"

"Oh yeah," Torsten said dryly. "Mahmoud's got a gonzo hard-on to kill both Piper and Zane."

"What kind of trap are you thinking?" Avi plowed on. "Public appearances with a loose net of our people surrounding them? Will Mahmoud or Yousef recognize anyone else in this room? I can probably add some warm bodies from my delegation to flesh out the detail if that would help."

"Yes, I'm thinking of using a bull's-eye configuration," Torsten responded. "Piper and Zane in the middle with a team deployed around them in concentric rings. Better chance of spotting the bastards inbound instead of having to rely on nabbing them outbound. And no, Mahmoud won't recognize anyone in this room besides Piper—well, and Zane. That's why, if Zane would like to be bait, too, I'm good with that—"

"Hell yes, I'm doing it, too. No way is she doing this alone!" Zane burst out.

Torsten nodded as if fully expecting that response, and then continued, "The warm bodies from your working group would be appreciated, Avi. As you know, everyone here has other security duties to attend to, as well. We won't be able to provide round-the-clock coverage by ourselves. Not to mention that from the moment we expose Piper and Zane, I want full drone overwatch plus boots on the ground around them at *all* times."

Zane seemed slightly less in danger of an imminent stroke after that pronouncement, but the guy still looked none too happy at this whole bait development. Rebel felt for him. Zane had been superprotective of Piper ever since he'd pulled her out of Mahmoud's clutches and the two of them had nearly died in the process.

Torsten was speaking again. "I'll build a watch schedule and distribute it later today. As soon as all the necessary assets are in place and a good opportunity presents itself, I'll pull the trigger."

"How about tonight?" Rebel asked. "If we can get Zane credentials today, he can come out on the infield with the rest of the American security detail after Team USA has walked in the opening ceremony. We ought to be able to parade Zane and Piper right past the Iranian delegation."

Avi chimed in, "If I'm right that some of the Iranian athletes are actually government agents, they should report back to Mahmoud."

Piper added, "Particularly if pictures of Zane and me are posted on their ready room walls, too."

Zane snorted. "I'm going to be damned offended if we're not on their Most Wanted list."

Everyone chuckled, a welcome break in the tension permeating the briefing.

"All right then," Torsten bit out. "We'll put you two in front of the Iranians tonight and then wait for them to make their move."

"One more thing," Avi asked, his voice dropping into a sober register. "Will you be green-lighting your team for a kill? My people will want to know."

Torsten sighed. "I sincerely doubt the United States

government will give us permission to kill foreign nationals on Aussie soil, especially during their Olympics. The diplomatic fallout would be effing ugly."

"Do you need me to get the go-ahead from my government, instead? If Israel were to take the lead in the operation, we'd be operating under my country's rules."

His implication being clear that Israel would not withhold permission to kill Mahmoud and his team if it came to a confrontation.

A slow grin spread across Torsten's face. "You make an excellent point, my friend."

Avi stood up. "Then I'm going to suggest we reconvene in the Israeli command center when your schedule is built, Gunnar, and we'll launch this little fishing expedition as an Israeli-led operation."

The meeting adjourned, everyone stood and side conversations broke out. Beneath the general chatter, Avi murmured to Rebel, "Are you still up for that run this morning?"

It took her a second to remember he'd offered to help her run off last night's sumptuous feast. "I'll have to change clothes, and then you're on."

He nodded slightly and then turned away from her as Zane approached to introduce himself and make nice with his foreign counterpart.

Rebel slipped out of the briefing room and headed for the elevator. Her room was on the fifth floor and she hurried down the hall to change, more eager than she ought to be at the prospect of having Avi to herself for a little while, even if she had a sinking feeling he was going to run her into the dust.

She had barely changed into the cutest running shorts and tank top she'd packed for this trip before a knock sounded on her door. She opened it to find Avi standing there dressed to run. "That was fast," she commented.

"I could say the same of you. I'm accustomed to women taking forever on the serious business of choosing what to wear."

Rebel shrugged. "It's easy when you have a grand total of one suitcase full of clothes to choose from. Come in while I put my shoes on," she said. Now why did she sound all breathless like that?

He stepped into her spartan room and a frown crinkled his brow. "Don't you find these white walls...and linoleum floor...and white bedding a bit institutional?"

"I find them very institutional. But I didn't come here for the decor. I came to do a job. This is merely where I sleep."

"What do you do in your off time?"

"What off time?" she retorted.

He shook he head. "I like my downtime. I never pass it up when I can get some."

She glanced around her room, her second shoe tied. "Doesn't your room look about like this, too? I assumed all the rooms in the village were identical."

"Ahh, but I'm not staying in the village."

"You're not? How did you arrange that?" She locked the door behind them and tucked the key in the pocket sewn inside her shorts.

He strode down the hallway, not answering until they reached the elevators. "I have pull within my government. I asked for an upgraded room in a hotel."

"Wow. Must be nice," she commented as the elevator door closed behind them. He turned to face her, bringing them chest to chest, fully as close as they'd been last night when waltzing.

"It's very nice," he murmured.

Was he talking about having pull or about…this? She blinked up at him, suddenly feeling like a baby owl hit by a blinding spotlight. She had no idea how to act around a man like him. No idea even how to feel. She was in way over her head with this guy.

Ahh, but what a nice way to drown.

Their run went about like she expected it would. He started out way slow, taking baby steps to match his longer stride to hers. She got impatient, sped up to her normal run speed, and he matched her with ease—and a little surprise.

As she tore along, loving the wind in her hair, he asked, not appreciably out of breath, "Why didn't you tell me you're this fast?"

"Would you have believed me if I had told you?"

"Possibly. I'm learning quickly not to underestimate you or your friends."

"Smart man."

"Thanks."

She glanced up at him and was startled to see him looking back at her rather more warmly than he should if they were just casual friends out for a jog together. Startled, she yanked her gaze back to the paved trail winding around the perimeter of the Olympic Village.

"What?" she muttered without looking back at him.

"I find you utterly fascinating."

"Why?"

"I've never met a woman remotely like you."

"Hah. You said yourself that women have been serving in the Israeli Defense Forces since the 1940s."

"I'm not talking about that," he replied evenly.

"What then?" she asked nervously.

"You're so tough and so vulnerable at the same time.

How can the two exist simultaneously in the same person?"

"I have no idea what you're talking about," she retorted.

"Liar," he replied mildly.

She opened her mouth. Closed it. He wasn't wrong. Furthermore, she suspected the more vehemently she denied it, the more stubbornly he would insist that he was right. Instead, she sped up, pushing herself to bring home the last mile at top speed.

Of course, Avi kept up with her like it was all a stroll in the park. Which, honestly, was fine with her. She'd learned long ago that it wasn't a competition between the Medusas and their male counterparts. They were all on the same team, pursuing the same goals—the safety of the civilian populace and order and stability in the world. As long as she was fast enough to do the job, she didn't have to be faster than Avi or any other man.

When they arrived at her door, Avi grinned. "Well, that was invigorating. We should do it again."

"I'm up for it if you are," she replied, secretly delighted that she hadn't been so slow that he'd found running with her to be tedious or boring.

"I would offer to feed you real food tonight, but I'm going to be tied up with opening games all evening."

"Same," she replied in real regret. "But you're spoiling me. I'm actually starting to question the quality of my food choices."

"Bit by bit, I'll corrupt you, my pretty."

She laughed up at him. "Is that a promise or a threat?"

"Which would you prefer?" he asked, suddenly serious.

"Depends on what you mean by corruption, I suppose."

"Hmm. I'll have to think about that and get back to

you on it. Until later, then." He dropped quick kisses on both of her cheeks, startling her again with the whole kissing thing.

He whirled and took off running toward the Israeli headquarters. He had a beautiful stride, long and strong, like the man himself.

Sheesh. How besotted did a girl have to be to enjoy watching a guy run?

She turned as well, jogging into the American security headquarters to grab a quick shower before she had to report to the Olympic Stadium to help with a massive, last-minute security sweep before the public was allowed to enter the venue. Immediately after that concluded, she was assigned to guard the American athletes as they waited to enter the stadium for the parade of athletes. Once the American team was inside the stadium, she was to shift over to watching Piper and Zane, who were slated to roam around the infield at the edges of the American team and try to get spotted by the Iranian delegation.

Torsten wasn't worried the Iranians would try to pull anything during or immediately after the opening ceremonies because everyone had to go through metal detectors and thorough personal security checks.

The real hunt would be on once the athletes were delivered back to the village after the ceremonies.

Avi didn't think the Iranians would try to take out Piper and Zane for a few days—he guessed it would take them that long at a minimum to get their act together and figure out how to respond to Piper's and Zane's presence. She hoped he was wrong. She hoped they never got their act together and tried anything violent against her friends.

Assuming the pair was actually here. And assuming the Iranians were up to no good.

The IOC had blown off her theory that the pair had been responsible for the chlorine in the swimming pool and was sticking with its explanation that the pool had accidentally been shocked.

Which was crap.

She knew what she'd seen—Mahmoud Akhtar and Yousef Kamali were here.

If she'd spotted them once, she could do so again. Then she would call in the Israeli commando team on standby and they would take out the bastards with help from the Medusas. Game over.

And then they would all believe her.

Chapter 6

Avi was assigned to escort the Israeli team in the infield of the Olympic Stadium during the opening ceremony, but he would rather have been with Rebel and her teammates as they formed a dragnet around Piper and Zane. Frankly, he would just rather be with Rebel.

Her combination of humor, spunk and confidence fascinated him. He'd been around plenty of women in law enforcement and even in the military, but he was still working to wrap his head around the idea of an entire team of women commandos. He had to give it to Gun, it wasn't a concept he would have thought up on his own.

The opening ceremony itself, as seen from the infield, was a riot of color, sound and fireworks, but the choreography meant for a television audience was mostly lost on the mob of athletes crowding the infield of the stadium. Still, it was a fun party.

Israel's team was separated from the sixty-five Iranian athletes only by Iraq, Iceland, and Ireland. Given his height, Avi was able to glance over at the Iranians from time to time as the Parade of Nations dragged on. He made a point, though, of being in front of the Israeli team as the Americans marched past.

Piper and Zane walked side by side, flanking the US team on the side that would pass right by where the Iranians stood. Fully a dozen of the Iranian athletes appeared to notice Piper and Zane specifically and watched the pair with laser intensity as they strolled past.

He changed radio frequencies from the Israeli security channel to the Medusas' private channel and muttered into the tiny microphone beside his mouth, "The lovebirds have been spotted."

Tessa Wilkes responded, "I concur. The target has been acquired."

Now, to wait for the Iranians to make their move. He would enjoy nabbing two of the biggest thorns in Israel's side over the past decade. Mahmoud Akhtar and Yousef Kamali had trained Palestinian terrorists, delivered arms to Syria, sabotaged infrastructure inside Israel, and were suspected of kidnapping and killing several Israeli businessmen in Europe.

Oh yes. He was going to enjoy taking those two down.

The lighting of the Olympic torch was moving, and then the athletes streamed out of the stadium in a mob as the party spilled outside. Coaches and security teams attempted and for the most part failed to corral their athletes to walk them back to the village together by country. The best the IOC was able to manage was keeping the athletes on the opposite side of a crowd barricade from the public, also streaming out of the stadium to continue its own parties elsewhere.

What a zoo. Total security nightmare.

Once the last Israeli athlete was finally checked back into the Olympic Village nearly two hours later, Avi was released from duty. He hurried over to the American security building where the Medusas had set up their surveillance on Piper and Zane. Hidden cameras were planted in the room the pair was sharing, as well as in the hallway and around the building.

The makeshift surveillance headquarters, where all the camera feeds were displayed on a bank of monitors, was two doors down from Piper and Zane's room.

Avi knocked on the door and when it opened, Rebel smiled warmly at him. *My, my.* The all-work queen of no play was thawing out nicely.

He slipped inside and was delighted to see she was alone in the room. She sat back down in front of the monitors and he leaned over her shoulder, bracing a hand on the desk beside her elbow.

Lord, she smelled good. Like a fresh spring day, all sunshine and flowers.

"How's it going?" he murmured.

"So far, so good. Piper and Zane are riding a bus with the US Men's Basketball team back to their hotel. I'm following it on the CCTV feed from the city of Sydney." She pointed at one of the screens as a charter bus pulled through an intersection.

"Anyone following them?" he asked.

"Yes. A crowd of paparazzi on motorcycles and mopeds."

"Ugh. Have you run facial comparison on the photographers against our database of terrorists?"

"I'm working on it," she murmured. He watched as she efficiently captured still images of photographers as they became available and compared their faces to the combined US-Israeli database of people of interest that

Zane had spent the day building in conjunction with his counterpart from the Mossad.

"You're pretty good at that," he commented.

"You don't have to sound so surprised that I'm competent at my job."

"And you don't have to be prickly about me giving you compliments. A simple thank-you will suffice," he responded mildly.

She pushed back from her computer and glanced up at him. "I'm sorry. Ingrained habit. Comes from years of working with men who were always looking for a chance to take a jab at me."

"I understand. Well, I understand as much as a man who's never faced discrimination based on my gender can understand."

The rigid set of her shoulders relaxed a little.

"I was merely expressing my appreciation of how exceptionally well you do your job. Male or female, you're really fast at spotting the images you need, isolating and enhancing them, and running them through the facial rec program."

Her shoulders relaxed a little more. "I have to be fast when I'm working in real-time imagery. Sometimes I only have a few seconds to relay vital intelligence to the guys on the ground before they run into whatever I spot."

"You look tense. Like you've been hunching over your screen for a while. Can I offer a purely professional neck rub?"

She looked startled, but even better, she didn't say no. He reached down and massaged her shoulder and neck muscles with practiced ease.

Rebel groaned under her breath and let her head fall forward. Her shoulders went the rest of the way down to their normal position. "Where did you get so good at this?" she asked.

"My mother had a brain tumor and used to get tremendous headaches. I learned to rub her shoulders and neck to give her a little relief. She used to get particularly tight right through here…" He rubbed his thumbs up the back of Rebel's neck into her hair until he reached the edge of her skull.

She gifted him with another groan that was so packed with pleasure it made his groin tighten in response.

Eventually, Rebel murmured, "Did your mother beat the tumor?"

"No. It was a glioblastoma—an aggressive form of cancer—and she only lasted a year."

"I'm so sorry." Rebel turned in her seat to stare up at him in naked sympathy.

"The military gave me a leave of absence, and I was able to be with her to the end. It was as nice as spending the end of a person's life with them can be. We made many wonderful memories, and she died peacefully with me and my brother at her side. She lived a good life."

He was startled to see tears welling up in Rebel's eyes and blurted, "What do you have to cry about?"

"You're so lucky you had that time with your mother. And I'm sad you lost her. You obviously were very close to her."

He shrugged, even more startled at the way the back of his throat had suddenly tightened up. "What about you?" he managed to choke out.

"What about me?" she echoed.

"Are you close to your mother?"

"My mother died shortly after I left home to go to college. And no, we were never close. I couldn't understand how she could let my father boss her around like he did, and she couldn't understand why I wasn't just willing to submit to the men in my life. We—" she searched for words "—didn't see eye to eye."

"How did she die?" he asked, sensing that Rebel wasn't telling him everything.

"She just...faded away. Her official cause of death was heart failure."

"But..." he prompted.

"But she quit going out of the house. And then she stopped getting out of bed. And then she quit eating. She went pretty fast after that."

"She starved herself?" Avi blurted in surprise.

"More like she fell into a depression so deep she couldn't pull herself out of the darkness. She didn't exactly kill herself, but she surely let herself die."

"Didn't your father try to get her help?"

Rebel threw him a withering look. "My father the narcissist, who can't see past the end of his own self-important nose? No. He let her go. Heck, for all I know, he was relieved to see her die."

"God. That's horrible." Avi reached down and took Rebel by the upper arms, drawing her to her feet and into his arms for a hug. He held her for a long time, unable to bring himself to turn her loose once she was nestled against his body, safe. And warm. And soft.

Which was a weird way of thinking about a trained commando. Even when she was relaxed and pliant, snuggled against him like this, he still felt the muscles wreathing her body. No doubt about it, she was one of the more fit women he'd ever held. And yet, the impression of softness was real. Maybe it was just her finally letting down her guard with him that made the impression. Either way, it was nice.

He wanted to keep her right here, plastered against his

chest and surrounded by his strong arms, where nothing and no one could hurt her. Weird. Of all the women he'd ever known, she was probably the one least likely to need his protection. Although his head knew that to be true, his instinct to take care of her wasn't listening for a second.

"A little air?" she finally mumbled.

He loosened his arms enough to let her turn her head, but that was all. At length, he managed to force himself to ask, "Are you okay?"

"Yes. I've been okay for a while. I made my peace long ago with my father being a bad person and with my mother not being strong enough to stand up to him."

Avi leaned back enough to stare down at her. "How did you become so strong? Where did you find the will to stand up to your father?"

"My mom used to say I inherited all of his stubbornness and none of her softness."

Personally, he had to disagree with the last part of that statement. But aloud, he merely said, "Thank God for your strength of will. It sounds like your stubbornness saved you from a terrible fate."

She shrugged, and her rib cage lifted and fell against his, her breasts rubbing against his chest in the most wonderful way. Dammit, they were colleagues and he had no business dwelling on her attractiveness. He yanked his thoughts back to the conversation at hand. A conversation that also had nothing to do with work.

He confessed, "If your stubbornness led you to join the military and become a Medusa, which brought you to me, then I'm doubly grateful for it."

Rebel stared up at him, blinking in slow motion as she took in the implications of what he'd just said. "You like me?" she breathed. "As in like-like?"

His mouth curved up ever so slightly. "Yes. As in like-like."

"Well, then. What are you waiting for?" she demanded.

"I beg your pardon?" He frowned down. What was he missing here?

"Kiss me already."

"Oh. My bad. I'm not usually so slow on the uptake—"

"Still not kissing me," she interrupted.

Such a feisty little thing. Laughing under his breath, he dipped his chin and captured her rosy lips with his mouth. Hers was soft—no surprise—and warm and eager and tasted as good as she smelled.

Aww, hell. He was in deeper here than he cared to think about. She surged against him, and he caught her up against him as she wrapped her arms around his neck.

Give the woman points for enthusiasm. She wasn't the least bit reserved in flinging herself into the kiss, and it was intensely sexy. He relished her full-speed-ahead approach to life—and to romance. Not many women could match the zest with which he threw himself into everything he did.

He tilted his head to fit their mouths more closely together and smiled against her mouth as her tongue slipped between his lips, seeking and exploring. Their tongues swirled and sparred as their mouths slanted across each other more hungrily, now.

He realized he was actually lifting Rebel off her feet, he was holding her so tightly in his arms. "I'm sorry," he mumbled against her mouth as he set her back down.

"Don't be. I love your strength and how gentle you are with me."

"I would never hurt you—"

"I know. I trust you," she mumbled back.

And then she was kissing him again, spearing her

fingers into his hair, and making him forget everything but the feel of her mouth against his, her body pressing against his, the smell of her, the taste of her—

He jumped as a female voice announced from a speaker on the desk, "We're pulling into the hotel, now. The driver will take us to the loading dock to avoid the fans and photographers in the lobby."

"Roger," Gunnar Torsten's voice replied, sounding tinny over the radios. "I'm right behind you. I'll deploy beyond the bus."

Groaning under her breath, Rebel tore away from him and sat down quickly at the desk, scanning the various video images before her hastily. "All clear on overwatch," she transmitted into the microphone on a stand in front of her.

Avi registered several impressions simultaneously. He was breathing hard. He was shockingly aroused, particularly given that this was an active work scene. And Rebel was blushing, her cheeks were stained practically cherry red. Thank God. It wasn't just him who'd had his socks blown off by that kiss.

She spoke to him without turning away from the monitors, "I should have asked when you first arrived. Did you want something?"

Besides that smoking hot kiss that he was still reeling from?

Yes. Another kiss.

His scattered thoughts struggled to form a coherent, work-related answer to her question. Why *had* he come here? Right. Chasing terrorists.

Man, she was giving him mental whiplash, swinging from work to that kiss and back to work like that. How did she do it?

Normally, he was great at compartmentalizing—at

separating work from play, at putting each aspect of his life in little drawers that he opened and closed as he needed or wanted to deal with the contents of each.

Not many woman had the capacity to knock him off balance like this, but clearly she was one of the few who could. And had. He stood back, bemused, and watched her comb through video images almost faster than he could register the content of the images. He was usually the guy out in the field on the other end of the radio from someone like this, and it was enlightening to see how much data she sifted through and how quickly.

"The rear of the hotel is clear," she reported. "No sign of Laurel or Hardy."

Laurel being the code name assigned to Mahmoud earlier, and Hardy being Yousef's code name.

The American basketball players filed out of the bus and ducked into the hotel's loading dock quickly—most of them were superstars in America and accustomed to these sorts of security measures. When the last man had disappeared inside, handed off to the private security team the basketball players had brought with them to keep away paparazzi during the Games, Piper and Zane strode across the parking lot and climbed into the armored, dark-windowed SUV Gunnar was driving. Avi and Rebel watched the CCTV feeds in silence as the vehicle headed back toward the Olympic Village.

Rebel leaned back, more relaxed now, watching the SUV make its way through the crowded streets. She glanced up at him, still standing behind her, watching over her shoulder.

"Did you actually come here for a reason, or just to kiss me?"

"Believe me, if I'd known we were going to kiss, I'd have been here sooner. I came to ask if you have all the video feeds you need from the city of Sydney and from the IOC security team."

"Yes. I've got full coverage of everywhere Piper and Zane should go over the next several days. I'll reassess our coverage needs as the Games progress."

"How much longer will you be in here watching the screens tonight?" he asked.

"Why? So we can take up where we left off?" she shot back.

"Would that be so bad?"

Her gaze slid away from his. *Hmm. Interesting.* "Why did you go so defensive with me, all of a sudden?" he asked quietly.

Her gaze riveted on the screens in front of her as if she didn't want to look up at him. He'd touched a nerve, had he? Interesting. He was dying to know exactly what nerve he'd hit.

He waited patiently for her to answer him. It was an interrogation technique he'd found over the years to be highly effective. Create a pregnant silence and then wait for the other person to break it.

Rebel sighed. "I'm sorry. I shouldn't have snapped at you."

"Apology accepted, of course. But I'm curious. What made you snap at me in the first place?"

"I thought we'd already established that I don't have a great track record with men."

He replied in disappointment, "I'd hoped we were well on our way to establishing that I'm not most men."

"I'm starting to get that. For one thing, most men wouldn't interrogate me on my motives."

He pulled up a chair and sat down beside her, stretching out his long legs under the desk. "I can't imagine why men wouldn't be curious about you. I find you utterly fascinating."

"Why?" she blurted.

"You're quite the study in contrasts. I can't say that I've ever met another woman quite like you."

"Surely, you've met plenty of female Mossad agents or women IDF soldiers."

"I have," he answered evenly. "But what I'm talking about goes deeper than the fact of you being both a woman and a warrior."

"Do tell." And her eyes were fixed unwaveringly on her monitors again. Which meant he was getting close to the heart of what made her defensive with men. Should he push or back off?

What the hell. They were only going to be together for a few weeks. "You're so confident in your work, and yet so unsure of yourself in personal interactions. Why is that?"

"You tell me, Sigmund."

He rolled his eyes. "Freud would have had a field day with you."

"Do tell."

"Answer me this. Why are you avoiding a direct answer to my question?"

He waited several heartbeats for her to provide an answer. Nope, she wasn't going to play ball. Awkward silences obviously didn't bother her. Although, with Gunnar having trained her, he probably should have expected she would be immune to such tactics.

Avi filled in the silence himself. "If I were to take a stab at answering the question of why you're unsure of yourself in relationships, I would say you've either had deeply negative interactions with most of the men you've dated…or perhaps you're wildly inexperienced with men in general and feel like you're in over your head with me. Which, I would take as a compliment, as an aside."

"Of course you'd take it as a compliment. Men are all about their egos."

"Ahh. A revealing comment, dear Rebel. It leads me to believe my first guess was the correct one. You've dated mostly flaming assholes who utterly failed to treat you the way a woman ought to be treated."

A burst of laughter escaped her.

Hah. Nailed it. Her exes were all jerks.

She asked more seriously, "How should a woman be treated, then?"

He smiled broadly. Now they were getting somewhere. "It would be my pleasure to show you."

She leaned back, staring openly at him. Her eyes were big and wide, as if she was surprised at a minimum or possibly even a bit afraid of his offer. He was tempted to dare her to take him up on it. After all, no Special Forces operator he'd ever known could turn down a dare. But if she had, in fact, been around mostly jerk males, he was probably better served by backing off and letting her make the next move. Not to mention she deserved the decency on his part.

Waiting out her response was harder than he'd expected it to be. Huh. He wanted her to take him up on the offer more than he'd realized.

"What would showing me entail?" she finally asked.

He shrugged. "It would entail whatever you're comfortable with. Decent men don't force women to do anything they don't want to do or are uncomfortable with."

"Hmm."

Suppressing a smile at her hedging, he said quietly, "They do, however, insist on yes or no answers to questions of whether they should proceed. Consent must always be clearly given."

He waited her out while the SUV carrying Piper and Zane shifted to another camera and pulled up at the gate to the Olympic Village. Rebel scanned the area around the guard shack and reported, "You're clear to open your window, Major T."

"Roger," came the clipped response from Gunnar.

"Why are you keeping the lovebirds under wraps in an armored vehicle?" Avi asked. "I thought the idea was to put them out as bait."

"It is. But we want to control when and where they're exposed. We don't particularly want to run a dozen-person dragnet around the clock, and neither our security contingent nor yours can afford to cut loose that many people. Major T. wants to orchestrate Piper and Zane's public appearances."

"Fair enough."

"Speaking of which, has the Israeli government green-lighted use of lethal force if necessary to stop Laurel and Hardy?"

"Not yet. It should come through shortly, though." Given the political sensitivity of using lethal force at an Olympic Games, the decision had been run up through the highest levels of the Israeli government, which took a little time even under the best of circumstances.

Gunnar delivered Piper and Zane to the back door of the American building, and Avi watched the pair ride an elevator to their floor, walk down the hall and enter their room.

"It must suck being together again and knowing they're on camera like this," he commented.

Rebel smiled at him. "Piper was complaining about that very thing earlier."

"You should shut off the camera in their room for a little while at least," he suggested.

"When the lights go out, I'll shift it over to a motion activated mode—and before you make a snarky comment about that, the motion sensor is pointed at the door."

"Nice. Do you have motion sensors in the hallway, too?"

"Yes, and one outside the window, mounted on the wall of the building. Major T. doesn't mess around when it comes to the Medusas' security. We have the best equipment there is."

"So, now that the lovebirds are tucked in to do what lovebirds do, does that mean you can relax a little?"

"Yes, but not how you mean."

"How do you mean it?"

She pointed at the hallway monitor. "Here comes Major Torsten now. He's going to spell me watching the cameras tonight. He's the lightest sleeper I've ever seen. He can doze in the bed and will wake up if any of the motion detectors sense anything and ping."

"Excellent," Avi purred.

Definite alarm blossomed in Rebel's oh-so-expressive eyes. *Good.* He liked making her a little nervous. She was the kind of woman who needed to be kept on her toes. If he didn't miss his guess, boredom would kill her interest in a man faster than just about anything else.

Avi moved his chair back to its position under the window. The hall door opened and he turned quickly. "Hey, Gun."

"Avi." A nod. "How's it going, Rebel?"

"All quiet on the western front."

"Great. You go get some sleep. The next few days you're going to get precious little of it while pulling double shifts working security for athletes and pulling shifts watching Piper and Zane."

"Yes, sir," she said crisply.

"I'll walk you out," Avi said casually. "Good hunting, Gun. I expect to have that green light from my government by tomorrow morning. I'll let you know as soon as it comes through."

"Perfect," Gunner murmured, already pulling up views of the Iranian team building on a couple of the monitors.

Avi followed Rebel into the hallway and closed the door behind her. They walked to the elevator in silence and didn't speak on the ride down. Rebel was obviously as vividly aware as he was of the cameras Gunnar would be using to watch them.

"Walk with me?" he breathed without moving his lips as they reached the lobby. Gunnar no doubt read lips, like most experienced operators could.

"Sure," Rebel uttered back, playing ventriloquist herself, and without so much as glancing in his direction.

It was a crisp, Australian winter night under bright stars. The temperature was cool and bracing, perfect for a brisk walk. He matched his stride to Rebel's, relieved that she was a quick walker and he didn't have to hold his stride back too much.

The Olympic Village was quiet tonight, in stark contrast to the wild parties of the past several evenings. Many athletes had preliminary competitions coming up now that the games had officially begun, and they were tucked in bed trying to sleep. Although Avi suspected they would mostly fail to get much rest. It had taken intense training and practice for him to learn to sleep in spite of pre-mission jitters, and it wasn't a skill many people successfully mastered.

"So what's your answer, Rebel? Shall I show you how real men treat women? Yes or no?"

Chapter 7

Rebel glanced up at Avi. His profile was so handsome it hurt to look at it. She murmured, "You do realize it's a bit arrogant of you to assume that you constitute a real man or a decent guy, right?"

His gaze glinted with amusement, spearing straight through her emotional defenses. *Fine.* They both knew *that* wasn't true.

Memory of that first kiss they'd shared swept through her, and desire to do it again nearly overwhelmed her self-control. Only the knowledge that Gunnar had access to camera views of this sidewalk prevented Rebel from jumping in front of Avi and demanding another kiss right now.

He said mildly, "I'm merely stating a fact, not trying to making a value judgment. I like women. I respect women. I do my damnedest to treat women well and make them feel good."

How good? What did he do that made them feel so

good? These and many other questions suddenly crowded forward in her mind.

"Yes," she declared in sudden decision.

"Is that your answer to my offer?" he asked cautiously.

"Yes."

He murmured low, "Outstanding."

He might not have said the word loudly, nor moved his lips when saying it, but he managed to pack the syllables with fervent relief. That, and a sure and certain promise of toe-curling passion.

"What comes first?" she asked a little hesitantly, now that she'd thrown her hat into the dating ring with him.

"Are you hungry?" he asked.

She laughed. "You're going to have to push me to the airport in a wheelbarrow if you keep feeding me all the time."

"My mother always said the way to a woman's heart is through her stomach."

"I thought that was what they say about men."

"Men and women aren't so different. While men may be in it purely for the food, women enjoy the intimacy of sharing a meal together. Admit it. You liked our supper last night. Wine, candles, a little waltzing…it created a mood, did it not?"

"Indeed it did. But it's a little late tonight for seven-course French cuisine."

"Ahh, my sweet, innocent Rebel. There are many more flavors of food romance than just that one."

Her stomach fluttered in anticipation. What did he have in store for her next? "You're going to have to work hard to top last night's supper."

"Challenge accepted," he declared, smiling. "Come with me."

He led her toward the giant dining tent in the middle of

the village. Long rows of tables stretched away seemingly forever, and Avi wound through the cavernous space to a food stand that advertised custom-made flash ice cream.

"What's your pleasure?" he asked her as she stared at a dizzyingly long list of possible flavors.

"I have no idea."

"What's usually your favorite flavor of ice cream?" he responded.

"My family always got vanilla."

"Bah. That's boring. We're here to live a little. May I order for you?"

She had to laugh at his enthusiasm. "Sure. Go for it."

He told the attendant, "We'll have chocolate, raspberry and coffee flavored…a scoop of each in two waffle cones, topped with dark chocolate drizzle, whipped cream and one of those meringue puffs for each."

"That's not an ice cream cone! That's an entire dessert!" she exclaimed.

"I'll take you running again, tomorrow," he said soothingly.

"I'm going to need to pull a 10K to work this off."

"Okay. I run 10K's for training every few weeks or so."

"Of course you do," she muttered.

"Don't you?" He sounded surprised.

"Well, yes," she allowed. "In our initial training, the Medusas ran one almost every day."

"There you have it."

She watched with interest as the ice cream attendant poured a liquid custard base into three metal stand mixers. The guy added pureed raspberries to the first, espresso coffee to the second, and a combination of chocolate syrup and chopped chocolate to the third. He turned the mixers on and then warned, "Ready?"

"Ready," Avi declared.

The attendant flipped handles beside each mixer and liquid nitrogen was blown into each mix through a tube. In a few seconds, the mixtures had frozen. The attendant let the mixers run just long enough to keep everything smooth and creamy, and then he turned the machines off, scooped up the flash-made ice cream into cones and put the toppings on them.

Avi passed one cone to Rebel and took the other for himself. They sat down at the end of an empty table facing each other.

"Bon appetit," he murmured.

Rebel took a cautious lick of the ice cream. The tartness of the berries, the bitterness of the coffee and the lush, creamy sweetness of the chocolate were a lethal combination. She groaned aloud. "Ohmigosh. That's amazing. You've got to stop introducing me to all this fantastic food! I'm ruined for plain vanilla ice cream ever again!"

"Excellent. My work here is done." He took a long swipe of the ice cream with his tongue and her lower belly tightened. Whoa. Who knew that watching a man eat an ice cream cone could be so sexy? Was he enjoying watching her do the same with as much relish?

She dared to glance up at him, and sure enough, his eyes were blazing with what she hoped was desire. She took a long, slow swipe of her own around the edge of her cone, catching the little dribbles threatening to escape the crispy edge.

Avi groaned under his breath.

Ooh. This was fun. Next, she pursed her lips and placed them on one of the scoops of ice cream, slurping at the sweet. She finished with a delicate lick using the tip of her tongue to smooth away the dent in the ice cream from her sucking.

Of course, Avi wasn't above a little payback. He licked and sucked at his ice cream sensuously, the expression in his eyes devilish as he savored the dessert, never taking his gaze off her.

Oh, two could play at that. She opened her mouth wide and stroked her mouth over all three scoops of ice cream, ending with a satisfied smack of her lips. The mix of all three flavors at once was incredible, and she repeated the maneuver.

Avi's eyelids grew a bit heavy, and his stare went hooded and dark, black fire blazing in them. In fact, his entire presence had abruptly gone very mysterious and inscrutable. But she wasn't fooled. She'd gotten under his skin with that R-rated display of ice-cream eating.

And she wasn't done with her cone, yet.

More dripping threatened, and she licked around the cone's crown again. She was forced to suck the tip of the cone as it started to leak creamy fluid, and then she went back to long, sexy swipes around the scoops of ice cream.

Of course, Avi gave the same treatment to his cone, and her breathing was shockingly affected by the sight of him making love to the sweet. Her chest felt a little tight, and she was suddenly unable to draw a deep, full breath without conscious effort.

Hubba hubba.

It was a race to finish the ice cream before it dripped and leaked everywhere, but she managed to keep up with Avi, and they both averted a potential mess. Although, a fantasy of letting ice cream drip all over his body and having to lick it up flashed through her brain. Based on the incendiary glint in his eyes, she gathered something similar had passed through her mind, as well.

Avi stood, and she stood as well, reluctant to leave the fantasy behind. "Shall we walk a bit?" he suggested.

"Please. That sugar's going to keep me awake for a while."

They went back outside and strolled along one of the many beautifully landscaped paths winding through the village.

"Tell me what you like, Rebel."

She frowned, not sure how to answer that. "I like my work. A lot."

"Why?"

"It's important, and I feel like I'm making a difference."

"What else do you like?"

"What do you mean?" she responded.

He chuckled under his breath. "You're really not very good at enjoying life, are you?"

"I'm sorry—"

He cut her off. "Don't apologize. Never apologize for being exactly who you are. Actually, I find your...inexperience...endearing. Please allow me to clarify my earlier question. What's your favorite food?"

"At the moment, I would have to go with ice cream."

He grinned at that. "Favorite activity besides exercising for work—which I already know you enjoy?"

"I love to ski."

'Have you ever surfed?"

"No, but it's on my bucket list."

Avi nodded firmly. "Done. Next time you and I get a day off, I'm taking you to the ocean."

The notion of wearing a skimpy bathing suit with him, sun and waves and sand—*oh my*. Her heartbeat just accelerated noticeably. "Don't hold your breath on that day off," she warned him. "It's likely to be after the games end before I get a down day."

"Same."

Same? He intended to see her even after the games

were over? Well, that certainly was a new wrinkle in whatever this was developing between them.

"What else do you like?" he asked.

"I like to sit by a fire and read a book on a snowy night."

"Ahh, there's my introvert coming through."

"Is that bad?" she asked quickly.

"Not at all. I'm an introvert, too."

"You? No way. You're Mister Sociable."

"And I get tired of being social eventually, then I want my alone time to recharge."

She nodded. "I totally understand that. I love being with my teammates, but sometimes I just need to get away and be by myself for a while."

"Anytime you want to be alone, let me know. I promise I won't take offense."

Wow. That was certainly considerate of him—

Ahh. That was what he meant by treating her well.

Huh. She couldn't remember dating a guy before who actually got her need to be alone sometimes.

"What am I going to do if you're perfect?" she mumbled more to herself than to him.

"I beg your pardon?"

Oh God. She'd said that aloud? "Never mind," she said quickly.

"I'm far from perfect," he mused. "I want to win every argument and tend not to give up even if I'm wrong. I'm told I'm stubborn to a fault. I don't like being told what to do. I prefer to be my own boss and not have to give orders much, either. However, when I do have to give orders, I don't like it when they're questioned, especially when bullets are flying overhead."

"In other words, you're an excellent special operator," she replied.

He smiled a little. "I'm still alive after fifteen years as one, so I guess I don't suck. But I'm told that makes me rotten long-term relationship material."

So this whole seduction thing was a purely short-term deal, after all? *Well, hell.*

She stared at the sidewalk while shock rolled through her. She was already thinking about something long-term with this guy? What was wrong with her? She'd barely established that she liked him, let alone going and doing something dumb like falling in love with him.

She knew her life had no space in it for long-term anything except her work with the Medusas. What was Avi doing to her head? How had he gotten under her skin so fast? Sure, he was a great kisser, but no kiss was worth throwing away everything she'd worked so hard for—

"What are you thinking about so intently?" He interrupted her raging thoughts.

"Nothing."

Avi laughed under his breath. "I learned a long time ago that women are never thinking about *nothing.*"

"Okay, then. Nothing I care to talk about right now," she amended.

He nodded a little. "Fair enough. We can just walk."

She blinked, startled yet again. Since when did the man she was with not push her to explain herself? She had to give Avi credit. The man most certainly knew how to seduce a woman.

But that was all it was to him. A seduction. An entertaining diversion while he was stuck here in Australia babysitting athletes and being bored out of his mind. She would do well to remember that while he was plying her with sexy food and long walks.

"I probably need to get back to my room and get some sleep," she announced. It was the last thing on her mind, but she surely didn't want to come across as desperate and thirsty.

He frowned, obviously sensing her abrupt change in mood, but he didn't comment on it. He veered back toward the American headquarters, and disappointment made her gut feel heavy all of a sudden.

Sheesh. Was she really that pathetic?

Maybe she should just go for the two-week fling and call it good. After all, he was the hottest thing this side of the international date line. And he was clearly completely at ease with the whole short-term thing.

Decisions, decisions.

Aww, what the heck. Why not go for it?

They reached the American security building and stopped out front. "Would you like to come up?" she asked as casually as she could muster.

"Not tonight, but thank you for asking," he answered calmly.

What? He'd turned her down? Didn't he find her attractive enough to sleep with?

He leaned in close to kiss her cheek and paused with his mouth on her temple, murmuring against her skin, "When we make love, it will be because you absolutely demand it and not because you think I expect it. I'm in no rush, Rebel. Sweet dreams."

He stepped back, gathering himself to turn away from her.

"Avi. Wait."

He went still, waiting and watching. He reminded her of a panther, as dark as the night itself, crouched in the shadows and ready to attack.

"May I ask for a kiss?"

His body hesitated, but his eyes blazed all of a sudden. His body won out and he didn't move.

Well, hell. She grabbed the front of his shirt, fisting her hand in the starched cotton. He wanted her to demand it from him? *Fine.* Using her considerable strength, she pulled him toward her.

All at once, he stepped forward of his own volition, grabbed her elbows and pushed her back against the wall of the apartment building. It took her a second to realize he'd maneuvered the two of them directly underneath a security camera, which meant they were in a blind spot, not visible to anyone inside.

His arms went around her and he swept her up against him like he had the first time, enveloping her body, mind and soul…

Then he kissed her again.

And what a kiss. His mouth was demanding. His tongue was demanding. The low sound in the back of his throat was demanding. She responded from a place deep down that she didn't even know existed before now. She kissed him back with abandon, holding nothing back. Her mouth opened for his, she sucked at his tongue, and she reveled in the way this big, powerful man let her inhale him, and how he inhaled her in return.

The cool thing was she didn't feel overwhelmed or overpowered, and surely he could have done both if he chose to. She felt like she met him on even ground, and he let her take the lead in their kiss if and when she wanted to. And the freedom to take charge was sexier than she could believe. She tugged his head down to hers so she could kiss him more deeply, more hungrily.

Huh. She was making noises deep in the back of her throat, too. Raw, hungry noises she'd never made before, but which came entirely naturally. She surged against him, loving how she didn't budge him and how he absorbed her strength into him easily, comfortably.

Thank goodness. She wasn't too much for him. The last time she'd been with the ex, he'd griped about how she'd gotten stronger than he was. Which had been true, of course. While she'd been working out ten hours a day training for the Medusas, he'd sat at home playing video games and drinking beer. *Loser.*

But Avi was fully as fit as she was, if not more so. He might be a man's man, but he was also a warrior woman's man.

Avi tore his mouth away from hers, and she was gratified to feel him breathing hard against her temple, his chest heaving. She'd done that to him? *Cool!*

"I promised I would wait to make love to you until you demanded it, but if we don't stop now, I'm going to demand it from you," he said gruffly.

"What if I'm okay with that?"

He smiled down at her, using his index finger to trace her forehead and cheek, scooping back a strand of hair that had escaped her serviceable bun. "I'm not okay with it. You have issues with men dominating you and pushing you around, and that's not how we're going to start our relationship. I'm sorry. That's not open to negotiation."

A relationship? As in more than a two-week Olympic fling? Really?

Lord, she felt like a yo-yo on a string bouncing up and down. Two-week fling. More than a fling. Just a fling. Full-blown relationship. Simple seduction. She had no idea *what* to think. Was that the point? Was he trying to throw her off balance? Or was she just hopelessly naive when it came to men?

Hope leaped in her stomach. It almost, but not quite, overtook the doubts raging in her mind.

As if on cue, Avi turned away from her then and strode

away into the night, leaving her staring after him, utterly flummoxed.

What the hell had just happened?

What man kissed a woman into a sexual frenzy and then walked away from her? Particularly after she made it crystal clear she'd like to make love with him? Surely, she hadn't read his signals wrong. He'd practically made love to her with his eyes while he was eating that ice-cream cone. She could have sworn he was totally down for sex with her tonight—if she demanded it.

Which she basically had, if not in so many words.

So. He was going to make her say it, was he? Maybe this wasn't about her at all. Maybe he just liked to make his women beg.

She wasn't sure whether to be outraged or amused as she made her way to her lonely bed. Either way, it left her wondering what on earth she was going to have to do to get that man to make love to her.

No surprise, she slept for crap. And it was all Avi's fault.

Chapter 8

That woman was going to be the death of him.

Avi's gaze strayed toward Rebel again from behind his mirrored sunglasses, and again dragged his attention back to the athlete he was here to protect. *Man.* He couldn't concentrate at all today. Not after that kiss she laid on him last night. Nor after the sleepless, uncomfortable night he'd spent afterward, trying and failing to cool his jets. He had it *bad* for her. Worse than he could remember having the hots for a woman in a long time.

Even worse, or maybe even better, depending on a person's perspective, it wasn't just about the sex. She was a fascinating and complicated person—smart, funny and just unpredictable enough to keep him on his toes.

Who'd have guessed she would turn eating an ice-cream cone into a sexy seduction? Or that she would grab him by the shirt and drag him into a kiss that nearly removed his tonsils? Or that he would barely have the will to turn away from her and go back to his own bed alone?

It had been a very close call. He had almost decided to make love to her right there against that wall last night. It had taken every ounce of his self-discipline to break off that kiss, step back and walk away from her.

And that kiss was *still* messing with his concentration today. It had been just a kiss. Nothing more.

And yet, here he was, distracted by even the slightest movement out of Rebel, some fifty feet away from him. He was hyperaware of her, tensing every time she even twitched, looking wherever she looked every time she turned her head.

Get your head together, man!

Today was the first round of the women's archery preliminaries. One of Israel's most promising medal hopefuls, a young woman named Hadassah Jacobi, was shooting her qualifying round at the Olympic archery venue, built in a city park and flanked by temporary bleachers. Flimsy fences at each end of the archery range were supposed to keep random spectators out.

He wasn't fond of the security here—the venue was far too open for his taste, far too easy for someone to slip in under the bleachers or around the end of the fences at either end of the range. But it wasn't like he had any choice about where the event happened.

Still. He wished the IOC and the Aussies would take the potential security threats to the games more seriously. He'd tried in this morning's daily briefing to bring up the subject of the pool incident again, but he'd been summarily shut down. The matter had been declared an accident, the case was closed and nobody on the IOC wanted to hear anything more about it.

Idiots.

But then, of all people, the Israelis understood more than most never to let down their guards. Never take

safety for granted. He'd responded to enough bus bomb-
ings, mortar attacks and outright assassinations over the
years to know that better than most.

It wasn't that the Olympic Committee didn't take security seriously. They just didn't take it as seriously as
he and his people did.

Avi glanced down the firing line, and near the far end
he spotted the American shooter. Rebel was parked close
behind her, hovering like a mama bear over her cub.

Each archer would shoot six sets, or ends, of twelve
arrows each at a target seventy meters away, with each
arrow scored for how close it came to the bull's-eye. The
scores out of this round would set the placement for the
single elimination rounds, where archers would com-
pete head-to-head against each other, tournament style.

Hadassah had just finished her fourth end and was in
the top ten shooters, looking solid to advance to the singles rounds, where she particularly excelled. The Israeli
coaches were relaxed, confident in their athlete.

Avi glanced to the other end of the firing line where,
just beyond the American archer, an Iranian woman was
struggling with her fifth round of arrows. She was on the
cusp of making the singles round and needed to bring it
home strong to advance.

It was probably no mistake that the Israeli and Iranian
athletes were at opposite ends of the shooting venue. The
Olympic Games might be about unity and peace, but
there was no reason to tempt fate and throw antagonists
together unnecessarily.

Although, Avi suspected the athletes wouldn't care
who stood beside them. It was the coaches and security
teams who would snarl and snap at one another.

Rebel backed away from the American delegation
slowly, easing off to her left, away from her shooter

and toward the Iranians. Instantly, Avi went on high alert. What had she seen? Had she spotted Mahmoud or Yousef?

"Yakob, take over watching Hadassah for me," he radioed tersely to his partner today.

"What's up?" the other security man asked alertly.

"Just checking out some movement down the firing line." The whole Israeli security contingent had been briefed that Mahmoud Akhtar and Yousef Kamali might be in Sydney, but they had not been briefed about the existence of the Medusas.

"Radio if you need backup," Yakob responded.

"Will do." He eased backward casually, blending into the crowd of coaches and equipment technicians milling behind the firing line, until he popped out the back of the press of bodies.

Stretching out his long legs, he walked swiftly toward where he'd last seen Rebel. The archery venue was in Centennial Parklands, a complex of several linked green spaces in downtown Sydney, dotted with massive fig trees and live oaks. The crowds were heavy in the park this morning, and Avi didn't want to call undue attention to himself, so he was forced to weave through the throngs at no more than a fast walk.

He used his height to search over the crowd for Rebel, but she was hard to find. Not only was she short, but she was also adept at making herself invisible. She'd been heading in exactly this direction when he'd last seen her slipping out of the archery venue, though.

A creeping sense of dread began to overtake him. Something was wrong. What had she gotten herself into? Urgency to find her sooner rather than later lengthened his stride even more as he searched for her. He bumped into a man and apologized absently, his gaze still roving all around. Where *was* she?

If she was out in the open, he would have already spotted her—and she wouldn't be in trouble.

But his gut was positively shouting at him that she was definitely in trouble.

He broke into a jog, thinking fast. Where would he go if he were a bad guy and was being followed by an Olympic security type? He would either head for the big crowds, or he'd go the complete opposite route and head for the most isolated area he could find.

Isolated. Isolated. Avi looked around frantically for any place in the park not mobbed at the moment.

Over there. A forested area with the spreading branches of jacarandas up high and brushy plants below. More to the point, it didn't appear that the crowds were walking through the bushes. Lamenting his suit and street shoes, which would provide no protection against a snakebite, he prayed not to encounter any of Australia's many deadly vipers as he eased into the dimness of the miniforest.

He slipped from shady spot to shady spot, pausing behind the trunks of towering jacarandas to peer about for any sign of movement. The grove was larger than he'd anticipated, though, and it was several minutes before he spotted what he thought might be a man, moving in much the same furtive fashion as he was.

Avi eased off to his left, circling around the other man to approach the guy from behind. *Oh yeah.* The man in front of him was definitely stalking someone. As Avi closed in, he made out more details. The man was wearing a dark suit, much like Avi's. It even had the same slight bulge under the left armpit, indicative of a weapon.

The guy crept forward patiently, taking one step at a

time and then waiting to see if he'd disturbed anyone or anything around him. *Oh yeah. Definite operator.*

The man had dark brown hair. A mustache. Dark tan—or maybe a naturally bronze complexion. Of course, being swarthy in coloring didn't automatically mean the guy was Middle Eastern, but Avi's gut vibrated with certainty. The man in front of him had to be from the Iranian delegation—

Avi tensed as the man suddenly sprinted forward, looking exactly like a tiger leaping to attack prey.

A shadow abruptly separated itself from a tree in front of Avi—a small form. Medium brown hair. *Rebel.* Damn. She'd been out here all along and he hadn't spotted her once?

The Iranian closed in on her from behind—too fast for Avi to shout a warning—and at the last second before the guy reached her, she whirled to grapple with her attacker in silent, violent struggle.

Avi burst out of hiding and sprinted forward, closing in on the pair at top speed. Nobody was attacking Rebel on his watch!

The Iranian stumbled back, obviously taken completely by surprise by Rebel's ability to fight back. But then the man closed in again. Avi was close enough to see the rage on the man's face, the intent to seriously harm or kill Rebel, now.

If possible, Avi ran even faster, putting every ounce of strength he had into reaching her before something terrible happened to her. He crashed into the man and Rebel, peeling the guy's hands off her throat by the sheer force of the tackle he laid on the guy.

The Iranian shouted incoherently, a sound of frustrated fury, as Avi's body weight bore him down to the ground. They smashed into the earth, and the Iranian—

maybe five foot nine and lean in build—got the worst of it by far as Avi landed on top of him heavily.

Avi both felt and heard the whoosh of air leaving the Iranian's lungs as he knocked the wind out of the assailant. Avi rolled off the guy and came up onto his feet. He dropped to one knee, planting his other knee solidly on the guy's throat. The Iranian stopped struggling completely, throwing his arms wide in what could only be interpreted as surrender.

"What are you doing out here?" Rebel demanded from behind him.

In his best Australian accent, Avi answered, "Savin' you, obviously. Are ya all roight, mum?"

He desperately hoped she caught on and pretended not to know him. Avi also prayed the Iranian would peg him, not as Israeli or Olympic security, but as just some random dude in the woods diving in to help a woman being assaulted.

"I had it under control. I didn't need saving," she declared.

"Looked to me loike he was ready to kill ya, mum."

"I let him get his hands around my throat so I could slip inside his guard and gouge out his eyes. I was about a second from taking him out, myself."

"Well, then Oi saved ya the trouble," Avi declared, never taking his stare off the man beneath his knee. To the Iranian, he said, "Who are ya, mate?"

"I'm with an Olympic delegation, you sonofabitch. Get off me." The man tacked a few choice curses onto the end of his statement. Obviously, the guy had his breath back if he could spit curses at Avi like that.

"Have ya got them fancy credentials, then?" Avi challenged.

"Inside pocket of my suit."

"Use your left hand and reach into your jacket," Avi instructed. "Pull out your credentials very slowly, mate. Failure to follow my instructions will result in my leaning on my knee and rendering ya unconscious…or dead if I happen to lean a bit too hard."

More cursing. But the guy did as Avi ordered and reached slowly into his suit to pull out his identification card.

"Take it if ya will, mum," Avi murmured.

Rebel skirted wide around the Iranian's feet and approached from the other side. She plucked the ID card out of the guy's hand and examined it carefully. "His name is Farhad Jamshidi. Athletic trainer for the Iranian delegation."

Athletic trainer, huh? So. The Iranians were sneaking in government types in coaching and support roles too, in addition to the athletes themselves. This guy had moved just like a Special Forces type as he'd sneaked up on Rebel. He was no civilian physical therapist.

"What are ya doing out here in the woods, mate? We've got snakes, ya know. Big, poisonous bastards that'll kill ya," Avi said to the guy.

"This crazy chick was following me, and she freaked me out. I was trying to lose her."

"And that's why ya attacked her?"

"I thought she was trying to hurt me."

Avi snorted. "Have ya looked at her, mate? She's half your size. Are ya trying to tell me a big strong guy loike you can't defend himself from a tiny little sheila?"

The Iranian scowled beneath Avi's knee, not appreciating the aspersions being cast on his manhood. But the dude was trapped in his cover story. Either he was afraid of Rebel and had been defending himself, or he'd been out here flat out trying to assault her.

Avi pushed to his feet, not being particularly careful as he did it. The Iranian sat up, coughing and choking. Avi stared down at the guy, his gaze flat and unreadable, he hoped. "Take my advice, mate. Don't attack civilians, particularly sheilas. We Aussies don't take kindly to our guests being jumped in the woods."

The Iranian threw one last spate of epithets at Avi before whirling and jogging away—limping as if he'd turned an ankle when Avi tackled him—back in the direction of the archery venue.

Avi dropped the Aussie charade, asking tersely, "Are you all right, Rebel? Did that jerk hurt you?"

"I already told you. I'm fine. I had things under control."

"I'm just glad I got here when I did," he responded fervently.

"You're not listening to me. I had him—"

"I heard you the first time. Look, I need to get back to my post. Do you need to get back to the archery venue, too?"

She huffed in something akin to exasperation. "Yes. I do."

He led the way, picking a path around and through the brush, keeping an eagle eye on the ground, searching for snakes that might strike at Rebel's ankles. She, too, was wearing street shoes that provided no protection against a snakebite.

They broke out of the grove, and Rebel moved up to his right side to walk beside him. He murmured, "Why did you follow Jamshidi away from the archery venue?"

"He fled from me. I saw him in the bleachers using a sniper's spotter scope to look at the American archer. Then he swung his scope down the line to look at your girl. I started to move toward him and he jumped out of

the stands and took off. That seemed like suspicious behavior, so I followed. I wanted to see if maybe he would
hook up with Laurel and Hardy."

She fell silent, so he finished for her, "Instead, he
lured you into an isolated area and turned the tables by
jumping you."

Rebel muttered, "I think we should add him to our
suspect list. He acted like the kind of guy I would expect
Mahmoud to have in his cell."

"Agreed."

"You should have questioned Jamshidi when you had
him down. Asked him what Mahmoud is up to."

Avi glanced down at her. "He wouldn't have told us
anything, and it would have tipped off Mahmoud that
we're onto him."

Rebel snorted. "When that guy reports back to Mahmoud that a woman was following him in the woods,
Mahmoud will know without a shadow of a doubt that
the Medusas are here and that we're onto him."

Avi grinned. "Jamshidi may not tell his boss that a
woman and some random guy in the woods made a fool
of him."

Rebel rolled her eyes at him as they approached the
archery venue once more. "Thanks for the completely
unnecessary bailout," she muttered.

"Anytime," he responded sincerely.

She veered away to go stand behind the American
archer once more, and he fell in behind Hadassah, who
was just finishing up her last end. The scoreboard showed
her in sixth place overall. A few of the top contenders
were yet to shoot in the afternoon's preliminary session,
but the Israeli woman was assured of making the single
elimination round. The Israeli coaches were enthusias-
tic, and the entire Israeli contingent was noisy and happy

as they boarded an athlete bus for the ride back to the Olympic Village.

But Avi's thoughts were dark. What was Mahmoud up to, with a full Special Forces team embedded in the Iranian delegation? Would the guy make some grand gesture to attack a huge venue, maybe in retaliation for economic sanctions against Iran, tightened again recently by the international community? Or would Iran go after one of its regional neighbors—Iraq or Israel being the obvious targets? Or would it go after America? From the pulpits of mosques, Iran's populace was frequently incited against the US.

Either way, his gut warned him that something bad was coming. And soon.

Chapter 9

Rebel went off Piper-and-Zane-watch at midnight, handing off the video monitors to Gia Rykhof, who showed a lot of promise for becoming another excellent live photo intel analyst for the Medusas. She had a gifted eye for detail and her information processing speed was improving rapidly. Rebel gave her three more months before she would be up to full speed with the best analysts in the US military.

About five minutes after twelve, Rebel's phone vibrated with an incoming text. The name associated with the phone number was TDAH. Frowning, she opened the message.

This is Avi. Are you off work? Would like to talk.

She replied, Yes. Just went off duty. In person or by phone? And TDAH?

Tall, Dark, and Handsome.

Rebel rolled her eyes. He was, indeed, tall, dark and handsome. But ego, much? Another text came through.

Meet where we last kissed in ten minutes. Come dressed for work.

Dressed for work as in geared up for special operations? Surely, he couldn't mean anything else. She jogged to her room and put on black jeans, a black turtleneck, and pulled her hair back into a ponytail. She strapped on the fanny pack that was actually a disguised utility belt. It held a razor-sharp field knife, zip ties, a small first aid kit, flashlight, flares, lock picks and various other bits of equipment that might come in useful. The Medusas hadn't been given permission to carry pistols when they deployed here, and she felt half-naked without a firearm. But she did know how to fight with that knife.

And she was proficient in unarmed combat, of course. Not that Avi had given her any chance to prove it, earlier. She was still annoyed at how he'd busted into the middle of her fight, tackling her opponent as if she wasn't capable of taking care of the guy herself. Sure, it had been chivalrous of Avi to help out, but she got the feeling he still didn't take her seriously as a soldier. And that rankled.

She slipped out the rear exit of the American security headquarters, hugging the building out of camera range, and slid around the corner to the spot where she'd kissed him last night. Strong, familiar arms wrapped around her, drawing her up against that warm, hard wall of muscle that made her feel so safe.

"Miss me?" Avi murmured against her mouth.

"No. I've been too busy doing my job to think about you," she mumbled back.

"I'm devastated. I thought about you all day."

She pulled back a little to glare up at him. "I didn't say I wasn't thinking about you. I just didn't have time to miss you."

"I love it when you're all prickly and indignant." He kissed his way across her cheek and nuzzled her neck just below her ear, sending crazy bolts of something shooting all through her body. The tingling ended in her fingertips and toes, leaving everything in between warm and wanting.

"Why do you like me prickly? That makes no sense."

He laughed quietly against her collarbone. Good grief, the things his mouth was doing to her skin! "You're cute when you puff up and act all tough."

"Cute? Am I going to have to drop you to get you to quit calling me that?"

He lifted his head to grin down at her. "You can try. Anytime."

Her gaze narrowed. Sometime soon, when he least expected it, she was going to put all six foot three of him on the ground. She'd trained against men every bit as big and strong as him, and she knew exactly how to leverage her lower center of gravity to win against a much-bigger opponent.

"Kiss me, Rebel. For I did miss you, today. I thought about this moment all day long."

His mouth closed on hers, and everything he'd made her feel last night came rushing back. The strange sensation of being wanted and seen as attractive flowed over her once more. All the sizzling desire low in her belly, all the breathless pull of him drawing him into their kiss, deeper and deeper, was all right there.

Heat burned across her skin. She must be bright red from blushing so hard. It was the curse of her fair skin. She could never hide embarrassment—or apparently, desire. *Oh joy.* Because she loved being a completely open book to Avi, compliments of her involuntary autonomic reactions to him. *Argh.*

They kissed until they were both breathing a little too hard, their hands roaming a little too much, their bodies straining toward each other a little too eagerly. They were totally going to end up in bed together sooner rather than later at this rate.

Gasping for air, Rebel broke off yet another smoking hot kiss crammed full of passion and unabashed lust from both of them. They absolutely had to stop unless she wanted to have sex with Avi right here, right now.

"Why did you tell me to dress for work?" she managed to pant.

He stared down at her, not comprehending. It took a moment for the raging desire blazing in his eyes to retreat just enough to be replaced by understanding. He closed his eyes as regret wreathed his face. "Right. Work. I can always count on you to bring us back to that."

"I beg your pardon?" she snapped. "I'm not the one who texted me to meet you in work gear. What else was I supposed to think except that you have something security-based planned tonight?"

Avi dropped his forehead to rest against hers lightly. "You're right, of course. I'm the one who suggested work. And I do have a scouting mission planned. Just give me a second to collect myself, here. You do…bad things… to my concentration."

As in she destroyed his focus on work? That would actually be pretty darned wonderful and give her all kinds of warm fuzzies if there weren't terrorists circling around the Olympics at this very minute, planning who knew what.

She felt his chest expand in a slow, deep breath. He held it for several seconds and then exhaled slowly. She recognized the four-count breathing technique she'd been taught to calm fear and focus the mind.

The next time he inhaled, she breathed with him, willing her body to chill out, ordering her lust to take a hike. The breathing exercise helped a little—but not a lot. Her body still buzzed with desire, her nerves jangling more than she cared to admit.

"Follow me," he finally muttered low.

"Where are we going?"

"Iranian headquarters. Thought we'd have a look around."

They slid into the shadows at the back of the Iranian building during a tiny gap when both rotating security cameras were pointing away from their path of approach. When Avi pulled out a fistful of lock picks, she realized with a start he wasn't just talking about looking in the windows. *Holy cow.* This was an aggressive move. Far too aggressive for Gunnar Torsten. They were at the Olympics, for crying out loud. If the two of them got caught breaking into the building of another delegation, they would be thrown out of the Olympics so fast their heads would spin.

"Are you nuts?" she muttered.

"No. I'm curious."

"Yeah, but…this isn't a good idea."

"Have you got a better one for finding out what these bastards are up to?"

She huffed. He had a point. Still. This was wildly dangerous. "What about their security system?" she breathed.

"Gonna pick the lock on the control box and disable it," he muttered back.

Ahh. "Need help?" She was excellent with locks. Her fingers were sensitive and Major T. said she had a real knack for breaking and entering.

"Nah. I got it."

She watched over Avi's shoulder as he did a reasonably credible job of picking the lock on a gray metal utility box. These buildings were originally designed and built to be part of a college campus and hadn't been wired for high security. Otherwise, this box would be safely tucked inside the building. But she was happy to exploit the weakness on behalf of her country, tonight.

Avi opened the gray door protecting the circuit breakers for the building, and together, they quickly traced the circuits. Working simultaneously, they threw the four circuit breakers for the security cameras and the door alarms. Then, moving quickly, they padlocked the box shut once more and hurried to the back door of the building. Avi pushed the door handle's thumb latch down and cracked the door open. No sound, and no lights.

Of course, the lack of a blaring claxon didn't guarantee that a silent alarm hadn't tripped somewhere else in the building. But as far as she could tell, they were in the clear. She nodded at Avi and followed him inside. If the layout of this building was anything like the American or Israeli buildings, the communications center would be in the front of the building, beside the lobby. Back here would be the commercial kitchen, laundry, janitorial closet and storerooms.

Avi opened the first door on the right and they slipped into the laundry. It was a large space with several industrial washers and dryers, but nothing special jumped out at Rebel. Avi led the way into the kitchen next, and again, nothing unusual caught her attention.

They crossed the hallway and eased into a storeroom next.

Now, that was interesting. A large gun safe sat awkwardly in the middle of the space, clearly brought in here by the Iranian security contingent in the past few weeks. A second locker, obviously hardened to contain ammunition, stood beside the gun safe. They were different models than the standard ones provided by the IOC for each security delegation. These looked significantly stouter than the IOC models.

Now, why would the Iranians need more substantial safes than everyone else?

Man. She would love to know exactly what kind of weaponry the Iranians had locked inside those things. What had Mahmoud brought into the country for his guys to play with? His team's gear would tell her and Avi a great deal about what the jerk had planned. If there were explosives in one of these safes, even just grenades, that would prove to the IOC that the Iranians were up to no good.

Avi picked up a chair and set it down beneath the ceiling-mounted light fixture just inside the door. He climbed up quickly and reached around the flat glass fixture to unscrew the lightbulbs inside. She put the chair back while he moved over to the safes to have a look. Quickly, he took pictures of all sides of both safes.

"You're not planning to try to break into those, are you?" she asked under her breath.

"Maybe. I have a little safecracking training. You look around the rest of the room while I work on these."

She moved deeper into the space, beyond the hulking safes. It was fully dark inside the windowless storage area, and she pulled out her flashlight, dimming it to its lowest beam before turning it on.

This space held a hodgepodge of sports equipment and assorted other stuff. There were massage tables, an empty ice bathtub, spare Iranian tracksuits, random sports gear and a huge pile of empty suitcases.

She pulled out small squares of cloth and randomly swabbed a dozen of the heftiest suitcases, then stowed the bits of cloth in a plastic zippered bag. She would test the cloth for explosive residue when she got back to the American compound.

As she was putting the baggie back in her pack, she glanced to one side and spied something that caught her attention. A dozen metal cylinders, like diver's oxygen tanks stood on the floor in one corner of the storeroom.

What did a bunch of world-class athletes need oxygen for? Sydney was right at sea level, and it wasn't like Olympic athletes tended to suffer from respiratory disorders. Some sort of oxygen loading therapy for pre- or post-performance for the athletes?

She snapped a quick picture of the tanks and moved on. A thorough search of the rest of the storeroom yielded no weapons, no tactical gear, no smoking guns to indicate that Mahmoud and company had anything nefarious planned.

"I'm done," she whispered as her search brought her back to Avi's side.

He murmured, "It would take me a couple of hours to get into these safes. Each one has upgraded locking mechanisms, which is informative in and of itself."

"I'm ready to move on," she responded.

He nodded and was just pocketing his picks when, without warning, the storeroom door rattled. Avi had locked it from the inside when they entered.

The sound of a man cursing under his breath in Farsi was audible inside. And a jingle of keys.

No, no, no! They were going to get caught—

Her adrenaline spiked at about the same instant her training kicked in. She knew what to do next. Hide in the shadows. Let her dark clothing do its camouflage work and don't move. The human eye perceived movement much more readily than it picked out stationary shapes.

She backed away from the door quickly, heading for the safes where Avi had already slipped around behind the big one. The hallway door opened and a slash of blindingly bright light spilled inside.

She froze, caught out in the open. *Oh God.* Was he armed? Was he was going to shoot her? No way could she claim to be pulling an innocent prank. This was a break-in, plain and simple, and her clothing and gear in her belt would give her away.

The silhouette of a man loomed in front of her, and she forced herself to stop, consciously suppressing the urge to turn and bolt. The Iranian was coming out of a brightly lit hallway into total darkness. He wouldn't be able to see squat.

Still. She felt naked standing out in the open right in front of the man like this. Slowly, she eased her right foot backward. Shifted her weight. Slid her left foot back.

The man half turned to fumble at the light switch and she took several quick steps while he was distracted. *Thank God.* The bulk of the gun safe was now between her and the Iranian.

Any second now, the guy would pull out a flashlight, and by then, she and Avi had to be hidden—or in position to jump this guy and knock him out. But the fallout of someone having been inside the Iranian building and taking out one of their people would be gigantic. Not getting caught at all was the only decent alternative.

The Iranian swore under his breath and continued to fumble around with the light switch.

Taking advantage of his focus on the wall and his turned back, Rebel gave a quick tug on Avi's sleeve and then faded backward quickly, keeping the gun safes between her and the Iranian as she glided deeper into the shadows. The best hiding place in the room was behind that giant stack of luggage, and she made for it now. Hopefully, Avi would get the message and follow her.

Thankfully, he did. She slipped behind the pile of suitcases and slowly sank into a crouch while Avi did the same beside her. They couldn't see whoever else might come into the storeroom nor could they track the guy already inside, but at least that meant the Iranian guy couldn't see them, either.

Someone swore in Farsi, and she heard the light switch being flipped back and forth quickly, clicking ineffectively. Eventually, the Iranian retreated, and the hallway door shut, throwing the storeroom into blackness once more.

"Let's go," Avi bit out low.

He paused beneath the light fixture, and lunged, his thigh parallel to the round. He patted his leg and pointed at her.

Got it. He wanted her to use him as a ladder and screw in those lightbulbs again. She ran to him and climbed up on his leg quickly. She reached up, but her hand barely reached the underside of the glass plate covering the bulbs.

A strong arm went around her waist and Avi lifted her off his leg. He stood up to his full height, and abruptly, her fingers banged the ceiling. Working fast, she reached behind the glass fixture and screwed in the bulbs.

"Done," she breathed.

Avi let her slide down his body, which would have been unbearably sexy were they not in imminent danger of being discovered. As it was though, her breath still hitched in the back of her throat momentarily.

He eased the storeroom door open and peeked out into the hall for a moment. He slipped outside and darted to his right. She followed suit, running lightly on the balls of her feet, racing for the rear exit right on Avi's heels. He opened the door carefully, slipped outside, and she followed suit. Just as she silently eased the exterior door latched behind herself, she heard two men's voices talking inside. Sounded like they were headed this way.

Avi had already moved around the corner of the building, and she bolted from the back steps, joining him quickly. *Whew. Outside.* If they got caught now, they'd be told to stay away, but they wouldn't have created an international incident—or been caught committing an actual crime.

She released the breath she realized she'd been holding. A wave of adrenaline slammed into her, crashing over her and making her whole body shake. Good grief, that had been a close call.

Avi turned to face the wall, reaching for the electrical panel once more. Crud. He was right. If they left all of the security-related circuit breakers thrown off, when the Iranians found them, they would be suspicious as hell. She and Avi needed to turn them all back on.

He went to work picking the lock again. Frowning, she pushed his hands aside, taking over the job. Thankfully, he didn't fight her. Using the picks she lifted out of his fingers, she popped open the padlock in a fraction of the time it would have taken him. Avi quickly threw open the metal door and they flipped on all of the circuit breakers they'd disabled before.

It took just a second to close up the panel, and then they turned to eye the security cameras. It was an agonizing ninety seconds or so until the cameras finally lined up, both pivoting away from them at the exact same moment.

"Now," Avi muttered.

She took off running for all she was worth beside him, sprinting for the cover of the nearest tree. He dived behind its trunk and she glanced over her shoulder. The two cameras were slowly turning back, coming to bear on the lawn they'd just crossed.

Safe. They'd made it.

Another surge of adrenaline startled her. Whether it was the letdown from the first adrenaline surge of fear or an actual sense of thrill pulsing through her, she couldn't tell. But her body tingled all the way to her fingertips, and she felt light and fast and more alive than she ever had.

Man, that had been fun.

Well, fun, now that they were safe and hadn't gotten caught.

Still. An urge to jump and shout and run nearly overcame her.

They stuck to the shadows as they moved farther away from the Iranian building, not ceasing their stealth tactics until they reached a main sidewalk well out of sight of the Iranian facility. Rebel stepped out of the shadows and began to walk normally beside Avi, who did the same.

"Good times," she commented.

He grinned down at her. "See anything interesting?"

"I swabbed a bunch of empty suitcases with explosive detection patches. And there was a stack of oxygen bottles that surprised me. What do athletes need with supplemental oxygen?"

"No idea. Maybe the team's planning on doing some scuba diving?"

"Tanks weren't the right kind for that. They looked like medical containers."

"Huh. Weird. Let's run those swabs right now."

It ended up being her running the swabs through the box-shaped detection machine while Avi looked up the make and model of safe the Iranians were using to store their weapons.

"The swabs are negative," she announced.

"I'm not surprised," Avi replied. "It would be nigh impossible to fly in anything nasty and get it past airport security in the international airports the Iranians had to transit to get here."

"If they're planning something, they would have to get some sort of supplies into the country, though," she said thoughtfully.

"Not necessarily," Avi responded.

"What do you mean?"

"They could've bought what they need on the black market here in Australia."

"Maybe. But it's not like illegal arms dealers hang out shingles and advertise Guns "R" Us."

Avi chuckled. "Agreed. Typically, it would take an established contact to make a fast arms sale. Which means either the Iranians planned whatever they've got up their sleeve well in advance, or else they used an Iranian government contact to make the arms buy."

She frowned at Avi. "In either case, you're suggesting that the Iranian government is involved in whatever Mahmoud has planned."

"Yes. I am."

"Wouldn't the Aussies pick up some sort of chatter about an arms sale to a bunch like the Iranians? The way I hear it, the Australian people take it as a point of pride that nothing bad will happen on their Olympic watch. Even criminals might inform on the Iranians if they tried to buy black market weapons and gear to hit the Olympics."

"Good point." He shrugged. "Maybe the Iranians brought in their gear by ship."

"You're assuming that the Iranians are, in fact, planning a terrorist attack in the next two weeks."

"That's because they are planning one. I can feel it in my gut."

She nodded, her gut also ringing with the rightness of his assumption. "Can we get manifests on all ships that have come into Australia for the past few months?"

"That would be a gigantic list. This is an island nation, after all. Do you have any idea how many ports of entry there are into this country?"

She shrugged. Major T. often lectured about the value of doing the hard legwork that normal people blew off as being too tedious. "We could search for ships that passed through the Middle East, maybe ones carrying Iranian cargo. That might narrow down the search. If nothing else, the Iranians won't expect us to go to all the trouble of sifting through hundreds or thousands of ship manifests to find their inbound gear."

"Maybe," he said doubtfully.

"It's worth a try. It's not like we have anything else to go on."

"Other than watching Mahmoud and Yousef directly," Avi replied.

"That would involve knowing where both men are, so we can set up surveillance on them."

Avi replied, "We'll find them, eventually. My guys are running facial recognition software on all the Olympic feeds, and will have it running on all the Sydney CCTV feeds by tomorrow."

"Facial recognition isn't flawless. What if our targets are wearing disguises?" she asked.

"You're giving them a lot of credit for being smart."

"Since when do Israelis underestimate their foes?" she shot back.

His stare was sharp as he looked up at her quickly, and she stared back unwaveringly. He'd gone full Special Forces on her, but she was no stranger to men exactly like him. Gunnar Torsten was every bit as hard a man.

"Point taken," he bit out. "I'll have my people pull up all the ship's manifests they can get their hands on, tonight. We should have a nice big stack of paper to wade through in no time."

"Thank you."

His gaze softened. The soldier had retreated behind the man once more. "You're welcome."

She smiled to take the edge off her criticism. They were both strong-willed people, and bound to disagree from time to time. It came with the territory of working with other special operators. The trick was to resolve the disagreement and then move on. No grudges, no after-the-fact snark. Just let it go. Apparently, Avi understood that lesson as well, for he said pleasantly, "Hungry?"

"It's nearly 2:00 a.m.!"

"The dining hall is open all night. And we can have ice-cream cones for dessert again."

She laughed ruefully. "I don't know if I could take another ice-cream eating session with you."

His eyes sparkled with humor. "No problem. Wait till

I introduce you to the banana-chocolate-hazelnut crepes the French cooks in the athlete's dining tent are making."

"Oh no. I'm doomed."

"Consider it a warm-up for better treats to come," Avi murmured under his breath as he ushered her out of the American building.

Gulp. And now she was definitely going to think about sex with him over every bite of whatever luscious treat he decided to serve her tonight. Who knew food could be full-on foreplay?

Chapter 10

Rebel took a break to stretch her neck and gazed around Avi's hotel room. Stacks of printed ship customs documents were everywhere. The two of them had eaten and blatantly flirted their way through the luscious dessert crepes while they attacked the foot-high pile the Israeli security office had printed for them.

They sorted the documents first by which port of entry they'd come from. Now she and Avi were working their way through each pile individually, searching for any ship that had transited the Middle East in the past few months and which was carrying any cargo originating in Iran.

It was four in the morning, and they'd identified eight ships so far that were possible candidates for Mahmoud and company to have used for smuggling illegal military equipment into Australia.

The next order of business would be to track down more detailed ship's manifests from each of the eight vessels and compare the listed contents against the weight and balance documents for the ship, and then to look more closely at the ship's crew.

Not that she expected Mahmoud or his team to show up on any ship's manifest. Mahmoud was too canny to make an amateur mistake like that. But he would have needed a way to get any smuggled equipment on and off the ship—which meant at least one crewmember was in on the hypothetical smuggling.

"I'm beat," Avi announced. "How about you?"

"I'm getting there. My eyes are burning and starting to water."

"Let's call it a night. We can pick this up in the morning."

She helped him lift the stacks of papers off his bed and set them on the floor around the edges of the room. All of a sudden, the bed loomed between the two of them while she stared at Avi and he stared back. Sexual tension was abruptly thick in the air, and potent attraction rolled off him.

Dang, he was a handsome man. He was an adult in every sense of the word, self-possessed, confident, and very sure of his ability to pleasure her. His words were right there between them, a challenge and a barrier. She would demand sex from him, huh? Temptation to do that very thing hovered on the tip of her tongue.

"What time do you go on duty tomorrow?" Avi asked.

"Noon."

"Perfect."

"I beg your pardon?" she asked quickly.

Avi threw back the covers and said casually, "Crawl in. It's too late for you to be walking back to your room alone, and it's too late for me to walk you there and back. I've already cost you too much sleep. Let's catch a few hours' rest and then we'll dig through the rest of this paper."

"Where will you sleep?" she asked cautiously.

"The floor will be fine for me."

"No way. I'm not kicking you out of your bed."

He paused in the act of reaching for the hem of his turtleneck. "Are you asking me to join you, Lieutenant McQueen?"

"I'm asking you to sleep in your own bed, Commander Bronson. I'll take the floor."

"Not a chance. Who do you take me for? A heathen?"

"You do know I've slept on the ground a lot. As in bugs and dirt and wet leaves, right?"

"I'm fully aware of that. But you're still not sleeping on my floor."

"We're at an impasse, then," she declared.

"No we're not. It's a king-size bed and we're both adults. We'll share it. I've already promised not to make love to you until you demand it, so you have nothing to fear from me."

She couldn't help but smile. "I have nothing to fear from you, anyway. I am capable of defending myself, thank you."

He might have successfully squished her against a wall the first time they ever met, but she also hadn't fought him full out. She'd had no desire to actually break his fingers or gouge his eyes out that night. And thank goodness she hadn't tried to permanently wreck his man parts. She might have need of those one day, as it turned out!

A skeptical look entered his gaze at her assertion that she could defend herself from him. It was there for just a second before it disappeared, but it bothered her, nonetheless. What was she going to have to do to get him to take her seriously as a special operator?

Avi stripped off his black turtleneck, revealing a torso that made Rebel gulp. His skin was tanned, his chest liberally sprinkled with dark hair and his abs—well. Suffice it to say the man had a serious six-pack.

He kicked off his shoes and took off his belt, but left his pants on as he sat down on the edge of the bed and then swung his feet under the comforter. He leaned back on a pile of pillows and linked his hands behind his head. He smiled up at her, a devilish glint in his dark eyes.

"Go ahead, Rebel. Crawl in."

He didn't add the phrase, "I dare you," aloud, but he might as well have.

Oh, she didn't like being dared to do anything. She had never been able to walk away from a challenge. Her current career being an excellent case in point.

Glaring a little in his general direction, she kicked off her shoes and reached behind herself to unstrap her bra under her turtleneck. Working under her shirt, she pulled her left bra strap down her left sleeve and slipped her hand out of it. Reaching up her right sleeve, she did the same. She finished with a flourish, pulling her bra out from under her shirt.

"How in the hell did you just do that?" Avi asked.

She grinned at him. "Put on a bra and I'll show you how."

He just shook his head. But the glint in his eyes was even more pronounced, now. She noticed that his gaze had a tendency to stray downward toward the formfitting spandex clinging to her now-unfettered breasts. She wasn't huge as women went, but she'd always privately thought she had a nice chest.

Avi seemed to think so, too.

She stretched out beside him, pulled the sheet up over her shoulder and rolled onto her side, facing away from him. Behind her, Avi turned off the light, and the room plunged into darkness.

"Good night, Rebel."

How could one person's voice sound both soothing and sexy at the same time like that? Good grief, it was intimate being here with him like this. His quiet voice caressed her skin as if it had been a physical touch, and his body heat warmed the space between the blankets, surrounding her in an embrace that might as well be his arms for real. It was comforting.

Except Avi was not a comfortable man. He was a challenging man. A restlessly energetic man. A frankly sensual man who dared her to let go of her inhibitions and experience more. Feel more.

Which was hard for her. She'd been taught her whole life to suppress emotions and feelings. To operate solely from a place of logic, and to be… Less.

The idea exploded across her mind with the force of a revelation. That was why she'd been such an angry child, a rebellious teen. Because she refused to be less than she was. If anything, her father's repressive attitude toward women had driven her to reach for higher goals, to push her own limits, to be… *More.*

In a way, she had her father to thank for where she was today. She doubted she would have gone to college, joined the military or, especially, tried for the Medusas without his disapproval prodding her in the gut for all these years.

"You've gone unusually quiet over there," Avi murmured.

"I was thinking about my father."

A burst of laughter escaped him. "You never fail to surprise me."

"What do you mean?"

"Here you are lying in bed with a reasonably attractive man who has stated his intent to make love with you, and you're thinking about your *father*? I must admit, that's a bit demoralizing."

"Oh. Umm. Sorry. I was thinking about how all his efforts to repress me only made me try harder and reach bigger in life. If I'm lying here beside you today, it's because of how much I hated him and resented his belief that I was good for nothing but cooking, cleaning and making babies. Thank goodness you're nothing like him."

"A complex and somewhat sideways compliment, but I'll take it. As for your father—" He expressed a curse crude enough to make her laugh out loud.

Still grinning, she said into the dark, "Fair enough. How is it you always know exactly the right thing to say to me?"

She could feel his smile, even though she couldn't see it. "Lots and lots of practice with women. You women are not really that hard to understand if a man takes the time to pay attention to you."

"There went my sense of being a special unicorn," she replied ruefully. "I'm as transparent as the next woman to you."

"Hardly. You've proven to be quite a challenge to analyze."

"Is that good or bad?" she asked doubtfully.

"Absolutely good. There's nothing I get bored with faster than a predictable woman."

"So, the key to keeping your attention is to keep you off balance? Thanks for that insight."

"Oh no," he groaned, laughing. "I've created a monster."

She rolled onto her back to stare at him. "Hah. Wait

until I start demanding sex from you. You're never going to get a moment's rest."

And just like that, he was looming over her, propped up on one elbow staring down at her. His eyes glowed like the last embers of a fire, banked but still hot enough to burn. His voice was low and dark, charged with promise. "Never fear, Rebel. I'm entirely up to the challenge. I look forward to it."

It was her turn to laugh at him, part in humor and part in nervous anticipation. "We'll see about that."

His voice was bare whisper of sound as he leaned in close. "Yes, we will, won't we?"

And then he kissed her, long and deep and passionately, until her toes curled with excitement and her belly fluttered with desire. He laid his hand along the side of her face, cupping her head as he kissed her, his fingers trailing across her ear and down her cheek to her jaw. They trailed away from her chin as he ended the kiss, and left her feeling strangely bereft as he flopped onto his back beside her.

"Aww, c'mon. That's not fair," she muttered.

A chuckle floated out of the darkness. "Whoever said I play fair?"

Chapter 11

Avi lay in the dark, listening to Rebel's light, even breathing. He was reminded sharply of getting caught in a rip current that whisked him away from the shore, no matter how hard he fought it, and deposited him far out at sea. Rebel had swept him off his feet without warning and dragged him completely away from the safety of his usual friendly but distant relationships with the women he slept with.

While he always offered to go slow with women— they liked having the freedom to choose—they rarely took him up on it. And furthermore, he was rarely in one place long enough for those who didn't act fast to get a shot with him, anyway.

But Rebel seemed to vacillate between being in an all-fired hurry to bed him and being in no hurry at all to take him up on his offer. More strangely, he was okay with her uncertainty. He found it charming. Innocent. Honest.

Sure, he had a little clock ticking in the back of his head whispering that they only had two more weeks here. But the larger voice in his head reminded him that he would likely have other opportunities to be with her, given that they were both in the incredibly tiny Special Forces community. And, since their countries were allies, they could be assured of running into each other now and then.

Except, lying here beside her tonight, that didn't sound like nearly often enough. He was comfortable lying beside her like this. Really comfortable. As if this was a place he would like to be more frequently than just now and then. The two of them fit.

She hadn't been scared of him when he went full Special Forces on her earlier at the Iranian headquarters, barking orders and being terse. And she made him laugh like few women could. She had the dry, sharp wit of an operator and used it with laser precision. She wasn't pushy, but she also wasn't timid. And the longer he was around her, the more he saw her quiet beauty.

He rolled on his side facing her and studied her profile, outlined by the faint city light creeping through the curtains. Her features were actually quite delicate. Soft, but with good bones. She was definitely not the type of women he would peg at first glance to be a special operator. Which was, of course, the point. Nobody would guess who or what she really was, and she would be able to infiltrate anywhere with impunity.

She stirred, and he went still, hoping she would settle back into sleep. But instead, she turned her head and opened her eyes to gaze at him. "Can't sleep?" she murmured.

"Something like that."

"Can I help?"

He smiled gently. "No. Go back to sleep. Sweet dreams." He rolled onto his back to stare at the ceiling and leave her to her rest.

But she shocked him by rolling over on her side a few moments later and snuggling up against his left arm. Her breasts, which were smallish and firm as it turned out, nestled intimately against his upper arm as Rebel's arm reached across his chest and settled there.

Every cell in his body went on high alert as her cheek came to rest against his shoulder, her left leg thrown over his. She was relaxed and breathing deeply. Definitely asleep.

By force of will, he slowly relaxed his muscles, one by one, until he was nearly as relaxed as her, at least physically, if not mentally. No way was he ever going to sleep, tonight…

He woke up sometime later, coming to full alertness all at once, the way he did when some threat approached.

"Aww, rats. I thought I could get out of bed without waking you up. But you're too light a sleeper."

Rebel. Talking in his ear. As in directly in his ear. The rest of it dawned on him all at once. He was in bed with her. They'd slept together. Platonically. And he'd liked it. Which meant he was either losing his mojo or this woman was doing bizarre things to his head.

He rolled on his side and gathered her against his bare chest, the soft fabric of her shirt not muting in any way the delicious press of her breasts against his chest. Their legs tangled, and their jeans did nothing to dampen his reaction to holding her like this, body to body, in a bed and alone together at last.

He glanced past her at the curtains. Sunlight streamed in at an angle that made him think it was midmorning.

And he felt refreshed, which placed the time at around 10:00 a.m. if he had to guess.

"Sleep well?" he murmured.

"Better than I have in ages."

"Aha. Sleeping with me is the key to happiness."

"We've already established that I don't believe in happiness."

"Right. Because we haven't made love, yet."

She laughed and her chest moved against his in the most fascinating way. "Tell me this, Rebel. If you're not feeling happy this morning, how *are* you feeling?"

"I feel…" She paused as if it was a struggle to even express a feeling. He waited her out, though. "I feel—" she tried again "—good."

"Good?" he echoed indignantly. "After all that thought, all you could come up with was *good*? Oh, my dear woman. We have serious work to do to correct your view of life."

"Oh yeah? You think you can fix me? What did you have in mind?" She had the audacity to be grinning up at him in open challenge.

"You did *not* just challenge me," he murmured.

"I'll bet you a kangaroo I just challenged you."

Grinning widely, he dipped his head and lifted her hair, kissing her neck just behind and below her ear.

"What are you doing?" she exclaimed as he sucked on the spot. Hard.

"Giving you a hickey so you have to wear your hair down today to hide it."

"Stop!"

"Too late." He pulled back to study in satisfaction the pink spot that was rapidly darkening.

"You are such a jerk!"

He laughed openly now, and pulled back the neck of her turtleneck to kiss his way further down her neck.

"Don't you dare give me another hickey!"

"I wouldn't dream of it. You have such soft, delicate skin. I would never harm it." He slipped his hands underneath the hem of her shirt and eased his palms up her ribs, reveling in how petite she actually was.

She had plenty of opportunity to protest or pull away from his hands, but she did neither. He had never been accused of being shy before, and he wasn't now, either. He slid his hands upward until they cupped her breasts, rubbing the pad of his thumb across the sweet little buds, delighting in how they beaded up instantly.

"Mmm. So responsive. You know what that means, right?"

"Huh. Whuh?" she mumbled incoherently.

"Yes. That. It means you'll achieve sharp sexual pleasure quickly and easily. Oh, sweet Rebel. Do you have any idea how many orgasms I'm going to be able to give you? Sex with you is going to be nothing short of amazing."

As he continued to tantalize her nipples, she made a faint sound that might have been protest, except at the same time her back was arching, thrusting her breasts more fully into his hands. Nope. Not a protest. Merely a sound of pleasure wrung from the back of her throat.

He'd had enough of her shirt blocking his view of her, and he impatiently pushed the fabric up around her neck. He stilled, captivated by the sight of her breasts. "Ahh, Rebel. So beautiful. Why do you hide yourself from everyone?"

"It's not like I'm going to run around topless," she muttered indignantly.

"You could if you wanted to. I know all the best top-less beaches in the Mediterranean."

"Of course you do."

He leaned forward to kiss the gentle valley between her breasts, breathing reverently against her skin as he murmured, "I'm not ashamed of enjoying women. I love to look at a beautiful body, and love even more making love to a beautiful woman."

Her back arched up sharply as he laved his tongue lightly across one of those oh, so sensitive nipples, and then he did the same to the other one. He pulled the eager little bud into his mouth, tugging at it with his lips and then lightly with his teeth.

She cried out, and her whole body moved restlessly against him this time. He ran his palms from her ribs along the length of her arms, and she realized what he was doing and helped, tugging her arms free of the sleeves and shucking the shirt over her head.

He gathered her in his arms again, relishing her warmth and satin softness against him. What the hell had he been thinking to declare that he wouldn't make love to her until she demanded it? He must be some sort of mad glutton for punishment. As it was, his groin was in enough pain at the moment to double him over in any other circumstances.

Her palms smoothed across his chest, measuring the width of his shoulders and looping hesitantly around his neck. He let her explore his body at her own speed, but it was torture holding himself perfectly still for her. She tilted her chin up and kissed him lightly, tentatively. And still he didn't move, other than to tilt his chin down to give her better access to his mouth.

Her tongue sipped at his lips, and then her mouth opened against his. He couldn't hold himself back any longer. He swept his tongue inside her mouth and kissed her voraciously, sucking at her tongue and inhaling her very essence into him.

Her entire body writhed against his, seeking more hungrily.

"What do you want, Rebel?" he asked against her lips. *Damn.* Was that his voice sounding so out of breath?

"I want you."

"I'm right here. You can have me."

"Can you take your pants off?"

"I can and I will." He rolled away from her and wrestled down the stubborn denim, which seemed determined to cling to his legs this morning. Finally, he kicked them free. And while he was at it, he got rid of his underwear, too. His erection sprang free, and he nearly groaned aloud in relief. He was still in pain, but now it was pain with the prospect of some relief in the foreseeable future.

He liked where this was heading. He rolled back to gather her close and was stunned to realize she'd gotten rid of her jeans and underwear, also. *Oh yes.* He definitely like where this was heading.

"What's your pleasure?" he murmured.

"I'm not sure I understand the question," she replied.

"What do you like to do in bed?"

"I'm, umm, not sure."

"Well, what have you liked in the past?"

"Not that much, actually."

He laughed under his breath. "Outstanding. Your previous lovers have set a low bar I'll be able to crawl over on my belly."

"Are you making fun of me?" she asked suspiciously.

"Good heavens, no. I'm pleased to have the honor of showing you how magnificent sex can be."

"Magnificent, huh? This I have to see."

"Are you asking me to make love to you?" He wanted there to be no misunderstandings between them, no room for recriminations or regrets.

She froze in his arms and stared up at him for a moment that stretched out agonizingly long for him while he held his breath. Finally, she murmured, "I guess I am."

"You're going to have to say it, love. I want utter clarity between us."

She exhaled hard. "Fine. I want you to make love to me—for us to make love together."

"You have no idea how glad I am to hear that. And when would you like this blessed event to occur?"

"Right now, of course."

"Again, my heart sings to hear that."

"Then why are you still talking?" she demanded, starting to sound a bit chippy.

"You didn't expect me to fall on you like some slobbering drunk, did you?" he asked, half laughing.

"Uhh, no. I guess not."

He swore under his breath. "Just how awful were your former lovers?"

"I don't know. I'll let you know when I've got someone to compare them to." She was sounding distinctly annoyed now.

"Are you telling me to get busy?"

"Yes. Yes, I am."

"Are you demanding sex with me, then?"

"Yes!"

Rebel wasn't sure if she was chagrined that he'd gotten his way and made her demand sex, or relieved to have finally given in to him and to her desire.

Avi surged up over her on one elbow, the humor fading rapidly from his eyes, leaving them dark and intense as he stared down at her. Truth be told, he was more than a little intimidating when he looked like this. He was no teenage boy or horny college kid. This was a man full grown. A warrior.

He lowered his mouth slowly, slowly toward hers, almost as if to ensure that she wanted this, too.

She briefly considered bolting, but then curiosity about what she'd been missing all these years overtook her trepidation. She waited in nervous anticipation of what came next.

He kissed her again, but this time, he wasn't messing around. He was done with laughter and joking, and he kissed her like he meant to sweep her off her feet and make her forget her own name.

His whole body was restless, moving against hers as his mouth slid across hers. His teeth captured her lower lip, and he bit her just shy of painfully. He pushed her gently onto her back and then he kissed his way across her jaw, down her neck and down to her chest.

Oh good. She'd liked what he did before a lot. Except he didn't stop at her chest. One of his palms was planted over her sternum as his mouth continued its downward path. He swirled his tongue in her belly button and she lurched at the not quite tickle that shot bolts of pleasure between her legs.

He kissed his way across her lower belly, and her abdominal muscles clenched so hard they almost hurt. She pressed her thighs together tightly against the burst of sensations exploding in her core.

But then Avi's hand was on the back of her knee, sweeping up the back of her thigh in a sensual glide that stole what little breath she had. His fingers plunged between the tops of her thighs from behind, and she opened her legs in surprise at the unfamiliar caress from that direction. And then his mouth continued its downward course, all wet heat and probing tongue and sucking pressure that made her lady parts engorge with lust.

"I've never…this is…oh my."

"Easy, Rebel. Just relax and enjoy. I want to know every corner of your body. You don't need to have any secrets from me. I find all of you beautiful."

Apprehension about where she jiggled and where she carried extra fat and where she wasn't proportioned like a fashion model fell away in the face of his gentle exploration.

He was thorough, kissing his way down the inside of her thigh and rolling her over on her stomach to kiss his way up the back of her leg. He massaged her rear end until she stopped clenching it in embarrassment, and then his fingers stroked between her thighs, coaxing them open once more.

The tip of his finger eased inside her tight passage and she gasped at the sensations that shot through her core. His finger eased a little deeper, and she was suddenly aware of how damp and pulsing and ready she was for him.

She turned on her side to face him. She gripped his erection in her fist, reveling in the velvet over steel hardness of him. He was a large man and well-endowed, and she frowned in sudden worry.

"What's wrong?" he asked immediately.

"I'm not sure…you're, umm, generous in size… I'm not…"

He laughed low, sounding a little amused and a lot delighted. "Never fear. It will all work out." He very gently eased her onto her back once more and his palm cupped her core.

His finger stroked slickly across the pearl of her desire, and then eased into her once more. He kissed her mouth in rhythm with the slow, easy glide of his finger, in and out, in and out.

"We're not trying anything until you're nice and relaxed and nothing will hurt. There's no rush. So just enjoy."

"I am. Believe me."

"Mmm. I can feel it. What will happen if I stroke a little faster? Like this."

What happened was she practically exploded. Her hips lurched and he laughed into her mouth. "Like that?"

"Uh-huh."

"How about this?" A second finger slid inside her while his thumb found the bud without and rubbed across it lazily with every stroke of his fingers.

She did explode then. A shower of shimmering pleasure broke over her and she cried out as it singed through her entire body. "What was that?" she blurted.

"An orgasm if I'm not mistaken." His voice was utterly deadpan, and she opened her eyes to glare at him. Unholy humor glinted in his eyes.

"Smart aleck. Are you always so smug?"

He laughed aloud, then. "I'll let you know when I achieve maximum smugness." And then he proceeded to give her no less than three more orgasms with his magic fingers.

She was panting and starting to feel a little wrung out when he finally murmured, "Now you're ready for me."

He shifted until he lay between her legs, the heaviness of his erection at her damp, pulsing entrance. And then the smooth, blunt heat of him was there, pressing slowly and inexorably into her.

He was right. Her body was ready for him and accommodated him, if not easily, certainly not painfully.

He was thick and huge and filled her so wonderfully that she nearly sobbed aloud. He withdrew a little bit and then eased home again, a bit more forcefully this time. She pushed back experimentally, meeting him halfway.

Oh my. That felt lovely. She did it again, matching his thrust with one of her own. They found a rhythm immediately, slow and languid as if they did, indeed, have all the time in the world.

It was incredible, staring up at him in the filtered morning light, seeing his smile, matching it with one of her own. Gazing deep into his eyes, she saw all the pleasure she'd put in them, and she knew her own eyes mirrored the same back to him.

The magic built slowly between them, and the intensity of their lovemaking gradually built until they both strained toward each other, their bodies crashing into each other, the orgasm building between them growing to epic proportions.

And yet it didn't come. Taller and taller the wave grew, racing toward shore like a tsunami entering a steep valley. It climbed the walls of her desire, building until she couldn't believe the size and power of it.

Avi gripped the headboard with his free hand, whether to use it for even more leverage or to stop himself from slamming into her so hard he hurt her, she wasn't sure. Either way, she gripped his broad chest with her arms and his thighs with her legs, and pulled him into her harder and faster.

He obliged, letting go of all restraint, and she did the same. The sex between them took on a life of its own, becoming a wild thing binding them together in a primal hunt. They raced toward their prey like lions, smashing into the orgasm they sought with complete abandon.

Rebel cried out, her entire body spasming and shuddering as one last, epic wave of pleasure ripped through her, tearing her apart from limb to limb.

Avi shouted with her, his voice hoarse as he emptied his body and soul into her in a massive, thrusting spasm that drove him all the way to her womb. She clung to him, her only lifeline in this moment of exquisite destruction.

Their mutual orgasm went on and on, but finally spent itself with one last shudder shared by both of them.

Avi collapsed, hanging between his elbows, which were planted on either side of her head. She stared up at him in wonder, shocked to the core of her being that sex could be that incredible.

He'd blown her into a million tiny pieces and then had put her back together again, whole and complete, but an entirely new woman.

She slipped one of her hands between them and reached up to brush a lock of his wavy dark hair back from his perspiration soaked brow. His eyes opened, and what looked like awe shone in their clear brown depths.

"Yeah. That," she murmured.

"Are you okay? I didn't hurt you?"

"Did I sound like you were hurting me?" she asked humorously. She had not been quiet in expressing her pleasure. She seriously hoped there was no one in the room next door.

He kissed her gently, reverently. "Thank you," he breathed against her lips.

"I'm the one who should be thanking you. You knew that existed. I did not."

His lips brushed across hers once, twice. "That was exceptional, even by my high standards."

"Whew. I'm glad to hear you say that. I was worried that there might be more I'm missing. I'm not sure I'd survive much more pleasure than that."

He rolled to his back and took her with him. She lay half across his body and relished the thud of his heart beneath her ear. It was still pounding hard, but slowing gradually.

He said reflectively, "I've never made love with a woman who was my physical equal before. I have to say, it makes quite a difference."

She knew the feeling. No guy she'd ever slept with before had come close to him in stamina or strength. And it was lovely being able to cut loose, knowing she couldn't possibly hurt him.

"I'm afraid, Rebel, that you may have spoiled me permanently for being with any woman other than an athlete of your caliber."

Hmm. It was just possible she was okay with that. She rather liked the idea of not sharing him with anyone else for a very long time to come.

Her brows slammed together. They couldn't possibly have a long-term relationship with each other. Not with their crazy schedules. And not to mention, his home was halfway around the world from hers.

And yet…

And yet. It wasn't possible. No matter how hard she wished for it.

Dammit.

Chapter 12

When Avi emerged from the bathroom after a shower, he still didn't feel like his feet were making full contact with the floor. Nope. He was definitely floating a few inches above the ground. It was hard to believe the effect that woman had on him.

Rebel was munching one of the bagels he'd ordered up from room service and studying a screen on his laptop computer intently when he stepped into the hotel room.

"Find anything interesting?" he asked.

She glanced up at him, and he couldn't resist leaning down to kiss her. She passed him a sheet of paper wordlessly.

"What's this I'm looking at?"

"It's the docking papers of a ship called the *IRAN Jahan*. Sails under a Panamanian flag."

"Yup. That's how the Iranians get around the sanctions against them. They sail under the flags of other nations. What's so special about the *Jahan*?"

"It docked in Adelaide nine days ago. I've pulled its manifest, and the cargo offload weight is about two tons light of the onload weight. Plus, part of the crew—the five Iranians on board—disembarked in Adelaide. There's no record from the dockmaster of them ever rejoining the crew."

"That's interesting. Do you have the names of the five crewmembers?"

"I do. I just finished running them through the American and Interpol databases, and they show nobody by any of those names and birth dates existing."

"Scoot over," he said briskly. "Let me run the names through the Israeli database."

It took a matter of seconds for the Mossad database to come back with an identification of two of the names—they were known aliases used by the Iranian MOIS, Ministry of Intelligence and Security.

"I think you may have found the needle in the haystack, Rebel."

"Great. What do we do next?"

"We run those names through the Australian credit card agencies and see if we can track their movements."

"We don't have access to those agencies' files—"

She broke off, catching his grin. "Speak for yourself, you law-abiding American, you."

He typed quickly, using a hack the Mossad had developed for moments just such as this, where vital information was needed and time was of the essence.

"Voilà," Avi announced. "Our boys rented a moving van in Adelaide and turned it in six days ago in Sydney. Now all we have to do is figure out where they drove the van to in Sydney. Since we've got full access to the CCTV system, that should be possible, if a pain in the butt."

"Maybe not so hard…" Rebel murmured, taking back his laptop. She typed quickly and then waited a few seconds for a video to load.

"Let's go back to, say, six days ago, and check the video for the Olympic Village. After dark, wouldn't you guess?" she muttered.

"For sure. If I had contraband to off-load, I would absolutely do it under cover of darkness."

She nodded, and he looked over her shoulder as she raced through four camera feeds simultaneously in blindingly quick fast-forward mode.

"How can you see all that?" he asked.

"Lots of practice." She reached for the keyboard and hit a flurry of keys all of a sudden. "There. Let me back up to it."

In a few seconds, the make and model of moving van the sailors had rented in Adelaide came into focus on the monitor.

She looked up at him grimly. "We have a positive link now to smuggled equipment and the Iranian Olympic delegation. Who do we tell about it?"

"The IOC security team, my people and your people," he answered grimly.

"Then what?"

"Then we hope the IOC takes the threat seriously," he answered even more grimly.

"Either way, I'm due at work in a half hour. I'll show the footage to Major T. and let him know you're going to the IOC with it."

"Why thank you, Miss Medusa Liaison. How very cooperative of you." He bent down to kiss her lightly.

She smiled against his lips. "I like liaising with you, Mr. Bronson."

"Ditto."

His crotch stirred with interest, and he sternly told his libido to cool it. He and Rebel both had work to do, and now they had proof positive of a credible threat at the Olympics.

What were the Iranians planning? What could possibly take two tons' worth of gear to pull off? Enough explosives to blow up the central stadium and automatic weapons for all of Mahmoud's men would weigh half that much.

He didn't like this.

Not one bit.

His mood went from bad to worse after his meeting with the IOC security team. They said in not so many words that they thought he was being paranoid and tilting at windmills to be tracking down shipments, which might or might not be from Iran, which might or night not have been off-loaded in Adelaide, which might or might not have been smuggled into the Iranian building by sailors who might or might not exist.

Just because his country had an axe to grind with Iranians didn't make him wrong.

Irritable as hell, he made his way to the American security office to report to Gunnar and his team on the IOC's reaction.

They all looked up with interest when he entered the conference room.

"The IOC didn't believe me."

"Of course they didn't," Gunnar said calmly. "I expected as much. But we'll continue investigating on our own." He added, "And this way, we're not beholden to anyone else. It's all good, brother."

Avi took a deep breath. Gunnar made a good point. Then he confessed, "Thing is, my internal alarms are going off. Something's going to happen soon. I can feel it."

Gunnar nodded. "I'm with you. Something's in the air."

Avi leaned forward. "Where do Piper and Zane make their next appearance?"

"We thought we'd dangle them at the Iranian men's soccer game this evening."

"Who does Iran play?"

"Germany."

Rebel spoke up. "We were just going over the layout of the stadium and picking a place to display the lovebirds."

"Could you guys quit calling us that?" Piper complained.

Avi leaned back and smiled, enjoying the round of ribbing and teasing that ensued. Thank goodness they didn't know about him and Rebel. He could only imagine the full broadside of harassment Gunnar would launch at him, let alone what Rebel's teammates would do to both of them.

Rebel asked, "What are the odds that we can distract Mahmoud from his primary objective if he spots Piper and Zane? Would he divert resources from the attack he has planned to come for the two of them?"

Avi nodded slowly. "An interesting hypothesis. It's worth a try."

Gunnar leaned forward over the schematic of the soccer stadium. "In the meantime, I doubt this venue is Mahmoud's target. It's too big, and there are too many exits. It would be easy for spectators to get away from whatever mayhem he could pull off there."

Zane leaned forward. "Which means Mahmoud probably won't have his whole team deployed in the soccer stadium, tonight. We might be able to isolate him from his men and grab him."

Avi winced. "We have permission from my government to kill him if he launches a terror attack. We don't have permission to snatch a delegation member from another nation."

Zane scowled. "So, we have to wait for him to hurt innocent civilians before we can move against him at all?"

Avi shrugged. "I don't like it any better than you do, but you know the drill. Operational teams have to play by the rules set down by their political superiors."

Everyone at the table groaned under their breath. It was the bane of Special Forces existence—being constrained by nonoperators—usually politicians—in how to do their jobs. More often than not, that interference caused the only snafus in otherwise smoothly planned and executed missions.

"All right. Is everybody clear on where to be and what to do?" Gunnar asked briskly.

Avi nodded along with the others, and they adjourned to go about their daily duties. This afternoon, he was providing security for an Israeli wrestler in the men's 97 kg class. Sadly, Rebel was assigned to the women's rhythmic gymnastics event, and it was going to be hours before he saw her again.

As he scanned the crowd at the wrestling venue, his thoughts kept returning to this morning's encounter with Rebel. It was strange not having to treat a woman in his bed like a fragile object that would shatter if he let go of too much restraint. He'd felt free with her. Like, for the first time, he could fully be himself and fully express himself sexually and emotionally. It had been exhilarating.

So much so that he was having a hell of a time concentrating this afternoon. Yet again, he had to remind himself to focus on the crowd. To look for body language, facial expressions, eye movement that might indicate someone was planning to do something bad, or even that they were thinking about something dangerous.

In a perfect world, security experts like him would spot a terrorist before they acted and nip attacks in the bud before they happened. In a perfect world, that was. In reality, security people usually were forced to react after the fact to contain and limit damage, rather than preventing it in the first place.

The Israeli wrestler made it to the round of eight before losing to the favorite, a Russian two-time gold medalist who looked like he'd be winning for a couple more Olympics to come. At least the Israeli athlete had the comfort of knowing he'd been trounced and that the match hadn't been close at all.

Avi escorted the guy back to the Israeli athlete's housing, where the wrestler cheerfully announced that he planned to spend the next two weeks drinking and getting laid.

Avi snorted. It must be nice to get to break training like that. In his world, he never had the luxury of letting down his guard for long periods of time. Even on vacation, he had to be aware of his surroundings and on guard for a bad guy to come after him.

Truth be told, the most relaxed he'd felt in months had been this morning in bed with Rebel after they'd made love.

And he was back to thinking about her, distracted, and not paying attention to his job. Man, that woman was bad for his concentration!

Rebel stood at the mouth of the concrete tunnel and looked down at the massive, screaming crowd. The game was just getting ready to start. The referee dropped the ball, and a renewed frenzy erupted in the stadium as the players ran down the field.

She looked around for people in the crowd who weren't enjoying themselves, weren't screaming, weren't fully engaged with the game. Those would be the people like her, here with completely different agendas than watching their favorite team win.

Most of the crowd was on its feet, and honestly, the spectators looked prepared to remain on their feet for most of the game. Which was a bit of a problem for her. She was short enough that it was hard to see over the heads of the people partying and throwing back beer.

Hence, her vantage point up here in the tunnel at the top of the first section of seats. Piper and Zane were due to stroll around the perimeter of the field any minute, and her job was to see if anyone left their seats to follow the pair.

A few latecomers were still making their way down to their seats, and Rebel moved left and right in the tunnel mouth to see past them.

There. She spotted Piper's blond hair and Zane's tall good looks off to her left. The pair was perhaps a hundred yards away, moving toward her. She scanned the crowd as best she could, looking for any reaction to the bait.

Piper and Zane walked slowly, talking and laughing with each other, pausing from time to time to watch the game beside them. They paused while a ball got kicked out of bounds a few yards ahead of them, and an Iraqi player scooped up the ball to throw it in bounds.

Rebel watched the pair resume their bait stroll around the field. They'd moved off to her right, and she was just about to key her radio to hand off overwatch to Avi, in the tunnel to her right, when Rebel spied a man in a dark jacket making his way out of a row of seats, pushing past other spectators.

More to the point, the man's attention seemed to be on Piper and Zane, rather than on the game beyond them.

"Possible catfish," she radioed. "One man. About twenty rows up, slightly behind the bait, paralleling their course."

A pause, then Avi's voice rumbled in her ear. "I have visual on him. Continue on course, lovebirds, for positive set of the hook."

Really? Did he have to carry the fishing analogy quite so far? Rebel rolled her eyes as she backed out of the tunnel and sprinted around the concourse toward Avi's position.

Gia's voice transmitted next. "I have the catfish in sight, as well. Lovebirds, time to make your exit."

Piper and Zane veered away from the field and commenced jogging up the long flight of steps toward the nearest exit. As soon as they turned, the man following them pushed to the steps nearest to him and commenced climbing toward an exit, paralleling Piper and Zane's course.

"Oh yeah," Avi commented. "He's taken the bait."

The plan was for Piper and Zane to get outside of the stadium if possible before their pursuer closed in on them. The fewer civilians nearby, the less chance there would be for collateral damage of bystanders.

Piper and Zane would be moving fast. They were both superfit, and several hundred stairs wouldn't slow them down much. Rebel and Avi needed to get ahead of the pair and clear the stadium exit for them. To that end, Rebel veered right and raced to the stadium exit, bursting out into a grassy area dotted with tents for vendors selling Olympic souvenirs and soccer team paraphernalia.

"I'm out," she transmitted.

A few seconds later, Avi replied, "I'm out, as well." He would have gone out the next exit over, the same one Piper and Zane would use.

"Here we come," Zane bit out.

"I'm in position at your eight o'clock," Gunnar responded.

"I'm on your four o'clock," Gia added.

The net was set around Piper and Zane. Rebel spotted them about four rows of tents over. They'd slowed to a walk upon exiting the stadium and were now walking quickly between the tents.

The plan was to set surveillance on whoever followed the lovebirds, interfere just enough with the person for Piper and Zane to escape, and then follow the follower back to wherever his home base was. The hope was that he would lead them to Mahmoud Akhtar. In a perfect world.

The man following Piper and Zane appeared to be around thirty years old, dark haired, and moving like an athlete. If she wasn't mistaken, Rebel spotted him muttering under his breath. The guy was wired for sound? *Interesting.*

"The catfish appears to be talking," she muttered into her own throat microphone, hidden beneath the collar of her oxford shirt.

"Look sharp for backups," Gunnar responded.

Rebel took her gaze off the catfish to scan all around for incoming hostiles. Any number of people were moving around out here, but none of them caught her attention especially.

Without warning, her radio erupted. Gia grunted, "I've been jumped."

Tessa responded sharply, "I'm headed your way—"

"Negative," Gunnar cut across her. "Stay on the love-birds."

No sooner had Rebel heard those words than an arm snaked around her throat and yanked her back against a hard body.

No air! She had no air!

Months of reflexive training kicked in and she bent forward hard and fast, flipping her attacker over her right shoulder. Unfortunately, he knew the countermove and managed to stay on his feet. But now he was beside her and not directly behind her.

Still bent over awkwardly, she punched the guy's groin with her fist. As hard as she could. He grunted and his arm loosened, but he didn't let go. She punched his go-nads again, this time using an uppercut with all of her strength behind it. He let go that time and stumbled back from her, also bent over now, swearing luridly in some language she didn't know.

Coughing, she sucked in air desperately, and the stars in front of her eyes cleared. She straightened, and just in time, for her attacker charged her headfirst, grasping her around the waist and driving her down to the ground.

She didn't mind being on the ground; she had a ton of jujitsu training that was all about grappling on the ground. To that end, she used her legs in a fast power move to flip both of them over and landed across the guy with all her weight.

His arm around her waist loosened, probably more in surprise than from the impact, but she took advantage of the momentary loss of focus by her attacker to grab his arm and wrench it practically out of the socket.

He cried out, and she pushed harder until she felt the joint dislocate. He screamed, then.

A few men bolted out of nearby tents with the intent

to help her probably, but she'd already pushed to her feet and was now kneeling on the guy's neck.

His face rapidly turned beet red and started to go purple before she eased up and let him take a few deep breaths.

Without warning, she saw a shadow from behind rush toward her. Fast. She ducked but didn't manage to avoid the blow entirely as something hard and heavy slammed into the back of her head.

Pain exploded inside her skull. Blinding, white-hot pain.

She fell forward onto her first attacker as it vaguely dawned on her that someone else had just jumped her from behind.

An accomplice? Or maybe a well-meaning bystander who thought she was killing the first attacker?

She rolled off the first guy, more by reflex than ability to form conscious thought, and jerked her feet up in the air just as a second man jumped her. Her feet caught him squarely in the solar plexus, and he made an oomphing noise as she drove the air out of his lungs.

Kicking her legs upward with all the strength she could summon in her dazed state, she flung the second man away from her with her legs and rolled to the side as the first man swung his good arm down at her, hammer-like.

His fist slammed the ground beside her head where her face had just been. Fumbling fast in her coat pocket for her folded field knife, she gripped it in her fist and swing it at the guy beside her, letting the weight of the metal in her hand add speed and momentum to the blow.

The end of the knife handle smashed into the guy's nose, and she felt the hot spray of blood on her wrist. He screamed again as she rolled away from him and groggily pushed to her hands and knees. Laboriously, she climbed to her feet as the second man also gained his feet in front of her.

She pushed the button on her switchblade, snapping open the wicked sharp knife and wielding it menacingly in front of her. The second man met her gaze, apparently saw the grim promise of death in her eyes, and thought better of attacking her again. He stumbled backward, turned and fled into the gathering crowd.

Darn it. She didn't have enough air in her lungs or useful consciousness to give chase. Besides. She would rather question her first attacker about who in the hell he was.

She turned to do just that and was in time to see him staggering away into the crowd, as well.

Panting, she keyed her throat mike. "Two men…just jumped me… Secure the lovebirds."

Gunnar bit out a series of fast orders involving the team closing in around Piper and Zane, hustling them into a vehicle and getting them out of here.

Rebel gathered herself to head toward the rendezvous point, but suddenly, the piercing pain in her skull came roaring back full force, and she only managed a shambling jog.

A familiar voice swore colorfully in front of her. "What the hell happened to you, Rebel?"

Avi. "I told you. I was jumped. By two men."

"I thought you meant they pushed you around a little, not that they tried to kill you. The back of your head is bleeding. You need medical attention, you brave idiot."

She felt the back of her head in surprise and felt a knot rising at the back of her skull. Her palm came away sticky with blood.

Avi started to bend down and she said quickly, "Don't

even think about picking me up. I can make it back to the SUV under my own power."

"Stubborn female," he muttered under his breath.

"And don't you ever forget it," she retorted.

"I see a couple of police officers headed this way," Avi said low. "Do you want to stay and make a report to them?"

"Not particularly."

"Then we need to rock and roll," he told her.

"Roger. Let's boogie," she said more briskly than she felt. Except when she tried to jog after him, every step felt like a sledgehammer to her skull.

Avi turned around, frowning, took one look at her wincing in pain and bit out, "Why didn't you tell me you're in so much pain?"

"Because I'm stubborn?" she muttered.

Ignoring her mumbled protests, he scooped her up in his arms and strode through the tents, using his long legs to full advantage to cover a lot of ground fast.

Honestly, it felt nice to let someone else do the work for a change.

"Don't you fall asleep on me," Avi warned her. "You've probably got a concussion, and I want you to get checked out before you risk passing out."

As much as she might want to argue with him, her first aid training declared him to be correct. She sighed. "Fine."

Avi set her down gently in the passenger seat of the SUV he'd driven to the soccer stadium. He paused in the act of straightening to stare into her eyes and murmur, "I can't tell you how relieved I am that you're okay."

She smiled wanly. "Me, too."

He dropped a featherlight kiss on her forehead and

then assumed a more businesslike tone of voice. "Let's get you to a doctor."

One of the American team doctors declared her concussion to be minor and suggested rest and over-the-counter pain medication for a few days. Which was good news. She couldn't exactly afford to stop cold in the middle of chasing down a dangerous team of terrorists.

Avi tried to take her directly back to her room to rest, but she insisted on going with him to the Israeli headquarters to debrief with the rest of the Medusas.

By the time the two of them arrived, Torsten and the others were perusing security film from the soccer stadium, trying to assess if the guy who'd followed Piper and Zane out of the stadium had accomplices in the stadium.

One of Avi's men, a guy named Zebediah, was already running facial recognition on an image of the guy in the stadium, in fact.

Rebel spoke quietly, in deference to her splitting headache, "Is there any footage of the two men who jumped me?"

Major Torsten glanced up at her. "We're just starting to work on pulling that footage, now."

On cue, Gia called out from her laptop, "I've got it. I found the fight."

"Put it on the big screen," Torsten ordered.

Rebel grimaced as she watched herself get jumped, toss her attacker over her shoulder and then pummel the dude's groin. It was weird watching the second man sneak up on her, clearly visible in the video from this bird's-eye angle. She wanted to shout at her past self to look out. To at least duck the blow she knew was coming.

The guy swung some sort of small truncheon at the back of her head, and she watched herself in slow motion, sensing the blow at the last second and ducking, deflecting the brunt of the impact upward from the back of her neck to her skull.

As much as it had hurt, she'd been lucky not to take that hit on the unprotected back of her head. The bastard could have killed her if he'd connected solidly with that blow.

Avi winced beside her as video showed her dropping to the ground and rolling, now fighting off two men at once.

Gunnar commented, "Nice work getting your feet up into that guy's gut."

Beneath the conference table, Avi's hand gripped her knee tightly for a moment. Without moving his lips, he muttered for her ears only, "I'll kill him for hurting you."

She glanced sidelong at Avi. "I broke one guy's nose and threatened to slice open the second one. I think I made the point for myself."

Avi's head turned and he stared openly at her. After a long moment, he began to nod slowly, almost as if to himself. "I think I finally get it. You really are a full-fledged Special Forces operative."

"Praise the Lord and pass the potatoes," she responded. "It's about time you took me seriously. I may not be your equal, but I can hold my own."

His gaze flashed over her shoulder to the screen on the wall. "I'd say you come pretty damned close to being my equal."

"I'm no better than any of my Medusa teammates. We're *all* the real deal."

Abruptly, she realized everyone else had gone silent and was listening to her exchange with Avi.

He shook his head in what looked like amazement. "What the hell have you created, Gun?"

Gunnar interjected soberly, "I told you. An all-female

Special Forces team. No more, no less." He paused, then added sympathetically, "Don't be too hard on yourself, Avi. Most male operators underestimate my ladies."

Avi laughed ruefully. "Color me a little slow on the uptake. I finally get it. The Medusas are the real deal."

Rebel exhaled in profound relief. Finally. Now, he understood who and what she was. But then, an alarming thought exploded painfully in her brain. What if he wasn't attracted to her anymore? What if being able to defend herself against multiple attackers and behave just like him in a fight turned him off? Had part of his attraction to her been his need to protect her from harm? Did he want a weak, needy little woman like all the other men she'd ever dated?

Oh no. Had she just ruined everything between them?

Chapter 13

Avi insisted on bringing Rebel back to his hotel room to rest after the briefing, and he called Gun to make sure she was removed from her next couple of regular Olympic security shifts. That taken care of, he made her lie down in bed, closed the blinds for her and ordered up a super-sized chocolate milkshake for her from room service.

"Really, Avi, you don't have to spoil me like this."

He smiled down at her. "Ahh, but I like spoiling you. And you deserve it after fighting off two aggressors like that."

"You act as if that's not part of my regular job."

He snorted. "It's not. Even I don't get jumped on a regular basis, and I live in a country chock-full of wanna-be terrorists."

"I am a little tired," she sighed.

He sat down beside her and smoothed her hair off her forehead. "Close your eyes. Take a little nap. I'll wake you up when your milkshake gets here."

He watched as her eyelids drifted closed, relishing the delicate beauty of her face, the clean symmetry of her facial bones, the curve of her cheek, the flawless satin of her skin. How had he ever missed how beautiful she was?

He eased off the bed and moved over to the desk so she could sleep in peace. He pulled up the CCTV feeds of the Olympic Village and venues, cruising them for any sign of Mahmoud Akhtar or any of his men. They had four faces of his probable teammates, now—the one from the park yesterday, the guy who'd followed Piper and Zane out of the stadium, and the two men who'd jumped Rebel.

Gia hadn't seen the face of the guy who'd jumped her at the soccer game, and the closed circuit TV footage of the venue hadn't captured a usable shot of Gia's attacker. He'd fled when Gunnar had arrived to help Gia, and Gun hadn't seen his face, either.

Slowly, but surely, the Medusas were getting a handle on who they were chasing. But the investigation was still moving too slowly. Mahmoud and his team were, without question, planning something big. But what?

If he were a terrorist, he would go for a big crowd. A venue where everyone was packed in like fish in a barrel. But which one? Every day, dozens of crowds gathered to watch various competitive events, not to mention attending festivals, concerts, medal ceremonies and a dozen other public parties. The summer Olympics were such a target-rich environment he didn't even know where to begin narrowing down possible points of attack.

He hated having to wait and react to Mahmoud's next move. Ideally, he and the Medusas would get out in front of whatever the bastard had planned and stop it before anything bad happened. *Ideally.* Which was not where he and Rebel and her teammates were operating at the moment.

Urgently, he scanned video footage until a quiet knock on the door announced the arrival of Rebel's treat. He opened the door, took the tall glass full of chocolate goodness and turned toward the bed.

Rebel was awake, watching him sleepily. At the moment, she looked like a kitten, curled comfortably on the pillows, warm and sleepy. Of course, he knew now that she was a kitten with sharp claws that she definitely knew how to use. And damned if he didn't find her sexier than ever.

He carried the milkshake over to the bed and sat down on the edge of it, loving how she snuggled up to him, wrapped around his back and smiled up at him.

"Can I interest you in something sweet, cold and chocolate?" he asked.

"That sounds like manna from heaven."

"It may not be *that* tasty, but it should make your head feel a little better."

She smiled and sat up, propping herself up with pillows at her back. She took the milkshake from him and took and long, appreciative sip. "Oh, that's yummy."

"Would I serve you anything that doesn't taste fantastic?" he responded.

She smiled over the drink at him. "Not likely. You really do spoil me too much."

"There's no such thing as spoiling a person too much."

She groaned. "Remind me never to put you in charge of disciplining your children."

His children? Maybe more like their children?

The idea stopped him in his mental tracks. He'd never seriously thought about starting a family. He had plenty of time to get around to that. Except he was sliding down the back side of his thirties, and at some point, women of childbearing age would start to look like children to him and not appealing to marry and spend the remainder of his life with.

Was he getting *old*?

The thought horrified him.

"You okay, there? You got a funny look on your face," Rebel murmured.

"Umm, yeah. Fine." *So not fine.* Where had the time gone? One year had stacked upon the previous one until he was nearly twenty years into his career, no closer to having a place to call home, let alone anyone to call family.

He had all his Spec Ops brothers, of course. But they wouldn't warm his bed or eat breakfast with him in the morning—or make him laugh, or love him with open arms...

Since when was he worried about all that stuff?

He swore under his breath. Since when did men have biological clocks? Apparently, he had one, and furthermore, it was ticking. Loudly.

He swore again. What was he supposed to do about that? It wasn't like he was ready to drop to one knee and propose to Rebel here and now. She was just getting started on her career, and she lived thousands of miles away from him, for crying out loud.

Well, color him hosed. He'd finally found a woman he might one day consider settling down with, and she was completely unattainable. Didn't that just figure?

"What's wrong?" Rebel asked quietly.

He stared down at her wordlessly. He had no idea how to answer that question.

Rebel held out the tall tulip glass to him. "Here. Take

a swig of my milkshake. Chocolate fixes everything…
at least temporarily."

He sucked on the straw, and rich, creamy chocolate
filled his mouth. He swallowed, and then leaned down
to kiss Rebel. "I'd rather taste that on your lips than from
a plastic straw."

"It's a paper straw," she corrected. "Plastic straws
harm marine life."

"Oh, so you're a conservation activist, too, are you?"
he murmured, smiling as his mouth descended toward
hers.

"I'm a lot of things you don't know about, yet," she
mumbled as his lips closed the remaining gap and captured hers for a long, deliciously chocolate kiss.

He kissed his way down the smooth, soft column of
her neck. "Do tell," he murmured against her skin. "What
don't I know about you?"

"Uhh," she exhaled, "I don't know."

He lifted his head to stare down at her, into those big
blue eyes of hers that never failed to captivate him. "Tell
me something about you that I don't know."

"I secretly wish I could dress up and put on makeup
and wear pretty clothes, sometimes. Not all the time,
mind you. But sometimes."

"So why don't you?"

"Because it seems silly to get all dressed up and then
sit at home by myself."

"Ahh. So you want to dress up and have somebody see
you and appreciate you for the beautiful woman you are."

She frowned up at him.

"Don't overthink it, Rebel. It's fine if you want to express your feminine side from time to time and be appreciated for it. You are, in fact, a woman in addition to
being a soldier."

"But soldiers shouldn't want to play dress up," she responded doubtfully.

"Why ever not?" he exclaimed. "You didn't sign up to be G.I. Joe. You signed up to be a soldier and still be you."

She shrugged. "The good news is that it doesn't really matter. I pretty much live in combat boots—or in serviceable tailored suits that will conceal my sidearm."

"I don't care what you wear or don't wear, Rebel." He leaned in close again and paused millimeters from her lips with his mouth. "I see you, regardless. And you're a beautiful woman, inside and out."

A gust of laughter caressed his face. Rebel responded wryly, "You do know that saying a woman is beautiful on the inside is code for telling her she's ugly, right?"

"It is not!" he exclaimed indignantly. "I know any number of stunningly attractive women who are complete bitches, or worse, stupid bitches. I'm not so shallow that I only judge women by their appearance. Yes, you're physically an attractive woman. But you're also smart and funny and kind and honorable. Why can't I respect all of those qualities, too?"

She stared up at him, her eyes wide, and maybe a little disbelieving.

"How giant a jerk was your father? Or all of your past boyfriends, for that matter?"

"I'm starting to think they might have been bigger jerks than I realized," she said thoughtfully.

He took the empty glass from her fingers and set it on the nightstand before gathering her in his arms and carrying her very gently down to the mattress. "I can see I have my work cut out for me to convince you that they were idiots. All of them. You're a rare and precious woman, and none of them treated you the way you deserve to be treated."

She smiled up at him, her arms looped lightly around his neck. "Do tell, Mr. Bronson."

"I'd rather show you." He added, "Carefully. So we don't make your headache come back."

The corners of her mouth turned up. "I'm willing to risk a headache if you'll make love to me. Admittedly, we probably ought to take it easy."

"I'm going to take it so slow and easy you're going to scream," he threatened.

"Scream, huh? That sounds interesting. Challenge accepted, sir."

And scream she did before he was done making love to her with his hands and mouth and finally his whole body. It was sweet torture holding himself back, waiting for her pleasure to build and then to break over him, and then restraining his own release until he thought he would explode.

Finally, she cried out for the fourth or fifth time—he'd lost count—wrapping her arms and legs around him so tight it hurt. He was going to die of needing her if this went on much longer—

She whispered in his ear, "Let go for me, Avi. Come now. I want all of you. Now."

"Thank goodness," he sighed. He let go of his tenuous control and immediately orgasmed so hard he thought his entire body had turned into one giant cramp that unfurled all at once in a glorious expenditure of his soul into her body and heart.

He was careful not to crush her, even in the aftermath of mind-blowing sex. He supported his weight on his elbows and then cautiously rolled to one side, being careful not to jostle the mattress.

"I'm not made of glass," Rebel sighed blissfully. "I won't break."

"I didn't want to test that theory today, not when you're not at 100 percent."

"I feel pretty darned good right now," she replied lazily. She turned onto her side and reached out to lay her palm on his chest. Her fingers drew circles in his chest hair, and delight unfolded inside him at the casual intimacy of it.

"Sleep, Rebel. It's late, and a good night's rest is just what the doctor called for."

"Mmm. Sweet dreams," she mumbled, already drifting off.

He followed suit, and his dreams—of her—were sweet, indeed.

Rebel woke slowly. Morning light came in around the heavy curtains, and the first thing she registered was the spicy clean scent of Avi nearby. She flung her arm wide and encountered only cool bedsheets. Her eyes popped open, and he was sitting across the room at the desk, shirtless and barefoot, wearing only a pair of jeans slung low on his hips. His bronze back was a sculptor's dream of muscles on top of muscles as he hunched over his laptop computer.

"Find anything interesting?" she asked. *Whoa.* Her voice was husky from sleep this morning. "What time is it?" she blurted.

"Almost noon. You slept for upward of fourteen hours," Avi answered mildly in that deep, sexy voice of his. "How does your head feel?"

She checked in cautiously. "Good, actually. Those painkillers the doctor gave me are awesome."

He stood up and sauntered over to the bed while she took in the sight of his bare chest with fully as much relish as she had his back. Her gaze lifted to his, and his

eyes glinted with amusement and masculine appreciation of her. She realized abruptly that she was naked and
the sheets had pooled around her waist when she sat up.

She started to reach for her chest to cover it with her
hands, but Avi got there first, capturing her hands and
holding them away from her body. "Don't be shy. You're
beautiful, and I love looking at you."

"Just looking?" she asked a little peevishly.

He laughed, a rich sound that reminded her of last
night's milkshake. "That, and other things. Like this."
He leaned forward and captured one rosy nipple in his
mouth and sucked on it just hard enough to make her
back arch in pleasure.

"And this." His mouth latched onto her other breast,
and this time his tongue swirled deliciously around the
hard bud of her nipple.

"Oh my. What else do you like to do?" she asked
breathlessly.

"Sweet Rebel. You can't begin to imagine the things
I'd like to do to you."

"Show me one of them," she challenged him.

His eyes darkened abruptly and intensity poured off
him. "Are you sure?"

"I dare you."

His eyes went positively black.

He threw off the sheets all at once, baring her entire
body to him. Without warning, he tipped her over on
her side, grabbed her hips, and pulled her up onto her
hands and knees, open and vulnerable to his stare. And
his hands.

He stood up, unzipped his fly, and his erection sprang
free, hard and ready. He pulled her back to the edge of the
bed, and standing up, entered her from behind.

The position allowed him to penetrate so deep inside

her she thought she might burst. Furthermore, his shaft rubbed against parts of her she'd had no idea before were so sensitive.

He started to move and she gasped at the sensation of him moving slowly, powerfully, in and out of her. When her entire body was trembling with pleasure, her arms threatening to collapse from it, he reached around in front of her and found the swollen, slick flesh between her legs and rubbed his finger across it once, twice.

She cried out, shoving her hips back against his, begging silently for more.

He obliged, picking up the pace and gripping her hip bones to hold her in place for him while he drove into her faster and harder.

Higher and higher the tide of pleasure clawed within her, wringing moans and groans from her throat, making her whole body shudder with it. Her entire being coiled, and then as Avi shouted and slammed home one last time, her body, mind and soul exploded together in an orgasm too incredible for her to contain it. Her arms collapsed and she buried her face in the mattress, shouting her pleasure in a wordless cry.

And then Avi's body was heavy and hot on top of hers for a moment as he gathered her in his arms and rolled to one side. She spooned back against him, loving how they fit together like this, loving how his breath rasped roughly in her ear, loving how hard he was breathing against her back.

"Are you okay?" he asked anxiously. "That was probably too rough for you with your concussion—"

"My head is fine, and so is the rest of me. More than fine. Fantastic."

His mouth moved in her hair and she felt him kiss

the top of her head. "I can't tell you how glad I am to hear that."

She plucked up her courage and muttered, "I do have a request."

"Name it."

"Could we do that again sometime?"

Silent laughter shook Avi's chest against her body. "I think that could be arranged."

"And I'd like to try it in the shower. I've never made love in a shower before."

"Done."

"And maybe…" she trailed off, embarrassed all of a sudden.

"I'll make love to you every single way you can possibly imagine, and a few ways you haven't thought about," he said quietly into her ear. "I'm game for anything and everything that gives you pleasure."

Hmm. That opened up some interesting possibilities she'd never really allowed herself to fantasize about before.

Avi chuckled again. "I can practically hear your mental wheels turning, Rebel. What are you thinking about?"

"I'm just pondering what it would be like to have that big, gorgeous body of yours all to myself to play with."

He lifted himself up on an elbow and she shifted onto her back to stare up at him. He said quietly, "Consider my body your personal playground. You may do anything to me or with me that you'd like."

"As long as you'll do the same with me," she answered, startled at how out of breath she was at the idea of no holds barred between them.

"That's a deal."

"Seal it with a kiss?" she murmured.

"A kiss…and more." He came up for air from their

openmouthed, wet-tongued, tonsil exploration only long enough to mutter, "You're following doctor's orders today and not getting out of bed. At all."

Oh my. That sounded amazing.

Chapter 14

Avi rolled over lazily and stretched, sore and well-rested all at once. Sore from the athletic—and imaginative—lovemaking he and Rebel had indulged in over and over during the past twenty-four hours, and well-rested from falling asleep beside her last night long before midnight. He rarely slept more than four or five hours a night, and last night he'd slept nine.

He felt like a new man. And not just because he'd gotten such a great night's sleep. That woman, the things she did to his head, the way she made him feel—like he could conquer the world with her at his side.

He eased out from under the covers and lifted aside the curtain to watch sunrise turn the thin, high layer of clouds lavender, then pink, then brilliant orange. He relished the quiet of the moment. How long had it been since he'd stopped to notice a sunrise? Five years? Ten? More?

Hands touched his sides and slid around to hug his

waist. He lifted his right arm and Rebel stepped up beside him to watch the new dawn. He draped his arm
over her shoulders, and her body was warm and relaxed
against his.

"Do you have to be anywhere today?" he asked her.

"No. The doctor made me take today off. How about
you? What's your schedule?"

"I have to babysit an Israeli archer at 4:00 p.m., and
then I have to work a boxing event. Israel actually has
a gold medal hopeful in the men's welterweight class."

"What ever will we do with the whole morning to ourselves?" she murmured.

He smiled down at her. "I have an idea, if you think
your doctor wouldn't mind you getting some exercise."

She snorted. "What he doesn't know won't hurt him.
Not to mention we exercised pretty athletically last night,
and I'm still standing."

Avi grinned. "True. You'll need sunblock, then."

Are you taking me surfing?" she asked eagerly.

"Do you want to give it a try?"

"Love to!"

He grinned at her infectious enthusiasm. They dressed,
collected towels, sunblock and sunglasses, and headed
for the beach. Before he let her get anywhere near the
water, he bought both of them surf shirts and knee-length
surf leggings. They slathered the rest of their exposed
skin with sunblock, rented surfboards and headed out
into the water.

Still on shore, he showed her how to lie on her board,
how to paddle and how to pop up to her feet. Rebel's balance was excellent, and with her core strength, she was
able to do pretty much everything he showed her.

"Time to head out in the water," he announced.

They waded and swam out about chest high in the

water, and he held her board for her while she laid on it. "I'll give you a push when a good wave comes along. Ride it in toward shore, and try popping up onto your feet," he instructed.

She wiped out the first half-dozen tries, but then she managed to get to her feet and wobble her way almost back to the beach.

She swam back out to him, grinning from ear to ear. "Again!" she cried.

He called a break after about an hour to go ashore and down big bottles of water and reapply sunblock. In the next hour, he let Rebel learn to catch her own waves, paddling furiously toward shore until the wave face caught her board and pushed her ahead of it.

Her shout of triumph when she caught her first wave carried to him above the roar of the swells pounding the beach.

She swam back out to him and flung herself into his arms for a salty kiss. "That was awesome!" she exclaimed.

He replied, "A few more waves, and then I'm going to make you quit. Otherwise, you'll be so sore tomorrow you won't be able to walk."

"Aww, c'mon."

"Trust me, darling. You'll feel it in places you didn't know you could hurt."

She shrugged, looking over his shoulder out to sea. "Fine. In the meantime, here comes a nice set of waves, and there's no lineup waiting to catch them."

He laughed. "Look at you, flinging around surfing slang."

She stuck her tongue out at him and paddled out to where the waves were starting to break. He followed on his own board, enjoying the view of her perky tush as she paddled ahead of him.

Indeed, only a few other surfers were lined up, belly down on their boards, watching the set roll in. One after another they caught the big waves and raced past him and Rebel.

"Here comes a good one!" he shouted at her.

She nodded and turned to face shoreward. The wave rushed up behind her and she paddled like mad, catching the face. As the wave lifted her and flung her forward, she jumped to her feet, angling her board just right to run along in front of the curl.

She flashed past, her face wreathed in pure joy.

He knew the feeling. He loved the power of the ocean surging beneath his feet. It made him feel like a conquering god taming nature's power.

He caught the last, largest swell of the set and ripped toward shore, cutting back and forth across the face of the wave in perfect trim with the curl on his right and the swell on his left.

The swell carried him all the way to shore and he finally jumped off his board in knee-deep water. He scooped up his board, tucking it under his arm and jogging down the beach to where Rebel was just wading out of the water.

"Hungry?" he asked her.

"Ravenous."

They returned their boards and retrieved their personal possessions out of the locker they'd rented. He led her to the grungiest, busiest grub joint he could find along the beach. The surfers would know best where the food was tasty, plentiful and cheap.

He ordered them two surf plates and carried them over to a table overlooking the beach. Rebel stared at the mounded plate he set down in front of her.

"Are you kidding?" she muttered.

He grinned at her as he slid into his seat across from her. Their plates each held a huge mound of mashed potatoes topped with a steak and fried eggs, the whole slathered in brown gravy.

"There's enough to feed three people on this plate!" she exclaimed.

"Start eating," he suggested. "Let's see how much is left when you stop feeling hungry."

As he expected, Rebel demolished most of her meal, and he did demolish all of his. Surfers routinely burned four thousand calories in a day out on the ocean.

As they pushed back their plates, a glance at his watch showed it was time for them to return to the real world. Or at least the world the two of them worked in. He wasn't sure how real it was compared to what most other people would consider normal.

Rebel was quiet as they drove back to the Olympic complex.

"Penny for your thoughts," he said to her as downtown Sydney rose around them.

"I can't remember the last time I've had that much fun," she commented.

"I'm wounded. Last night wasn't fun?"

She rolled her eyes at him. "That was different. That was…magic."

Mollified, he replied, "I can live with being magical."

She laughed under her breath. "Men and their egos."

"So here's a question for you, Rebel. Are you happy?"

"What?"

"Don't think about your answer. Just yes or no. Are you happy?"

"Yes."

He exhaled a long breath of satisfaction. "Excellent. My work is done."

"I beg your pardon?" she challenged.

"You said when we first met that happiness doesn't exist. That only pleasure exists. I set out to prove to you that happiness is real, and I have accomplished my goal."

She was quiet as they left the restaurant and drove back to the Olympic Village. Good. Hopefully, she was reevaluating her philosophy of all work and no play.

He pulled to a stop in front of the American security headquarters and glanced over at her. Alarmingly, she was frowning at him. And she looked anything but happy.

She asked with ominous calm, "Is that was all of this was? An elaborate plan to prove that you're always right?"

It was his turn for his brows to twitch into a frown. "All of what?"

"All the time you've spent with me? The meals? The dancing? The seduction? The sex?"

"No! Not at all. I've loved every minute of being with you. I simply hoped you would feel the same way about spending time with me."

"So, it wasn't your primary goal to prove anything to me?"

"Well, it was at first. But then I got to know you—"

She cut him off. "Right. Got it. I was a challenge to you. A conquest to be proved wrong."

"No! That's not it at all—"

"You win, Avi. You made me feel happy. Congratulations."

Without giving him a chance to say another word, she burst out of the SUV and ran up the steps into the lobby of the American security building.

Sonofa—

He really, *really* needed to go after her and sort out this stupid misunderstanding, but he was due at the Israeli team building in ten minutes to escort the archery team to the event venue.

Swearing, he stomped on the gas pedal, spewing gravel from his tires, an act that perfectly expressed his frustration at the moment.

Rebel stood in the shadows just inside the lobby of the American security headquarters and watched Avi drive away. Angrily.

Had she overreacted to him pointing out that she was happy? Her gut told her she had. Except she really did believe happiness was a myth. Avi didn't understand. Her entire worldview was built on that one principle. Work mattered. Duty mattered. Responsibility, morality, discipline. All of those were important. But not happiness. Not joy. And certainly not love.

Not only did such fleeting emotions not matter, they were definitely not the stuff of a substantial life. A life of importance. Of making a difference.

Oh, she knew Avi would argue that being happy was all that really mattered in life. After all, he was a complete hedonist, devoted to experiences and sensations, physical and emotional. He was a man of feeling.

She was a woman of thought. Of facts. Of logic. Reason.

As much as she'd enjoyed the past day and night with him, it was merely an interlude out of her real life. An anomaly. Nothing more.

Then why, as she turned to head for the operations center, was her heart so strangely heavy?

This is what she got for letting Avi draw her into his ridiculous notions of living life solely for pleasure and—fine, she would call it what it was—happiness.

She stepped into the ops center and Gia looked up

from a computer monitor, calling, "Oh good. You're here, Rebel. I need you to look at something."

Pushing aside her misery and her anger at Avi, Rebel hurried to join her teammate. She leaned down over Gia's shoulder to study the screen.

Three tall towers, built of lumber scaffolding and of differing heights, stood around a broad, dusty space, empty of anything but a few target dummies like the military would use in a live fire exercise. Partially covering one corner of the whole setup was a wadded pile of what looked like beige camo netting.

"Where is this picture from?" Rebel asked.

"American surveillance satellite captured the image in Iran a few hours ago. It's from the same training facility the Israelis say Mahmoud Akhtar used to train his latest team."

Whoa. "What's the weather like in Iran today?"

Gia glanced up at her. "Big windstorm. Are you thinking what I'm thinking? The storm blew that camo netting off of this training mock-up?"

Rebel nodded. "That's what I'm thinking. But what is it a mock-up of?"

"Looks to me like sniper perches," Gia commented.

"I concur. We should show this to Major Torsten."

"And to your hot Israeli," Gia added slyly.

"He's not *my* anything."

"*Suuure*, he's not. I've seen the way he looks at you. I'm not an intelligence analyst for nothing, Rebel. I know what that look in his eyes means. He's totally into you. Like totally."

"Yeah, well, being into someone is one thing. Possession of a human being is another thing entirely. He's not mine and I'm not his."

Rebel hated the idea of seeing Avi right now. As in

hated it. Aloud, she mumbled, "I don't think we should go to the Israelis until we have more information. They're tense enough as it is. We don't need to encourage them anymore."

Gia frowned a little. "The way I was taught my history, they have cause to be tense."

"Yes, but this thing with Mahmoud is a personal grudge for the Israelis." She intentionally didn't say Avi's name aloud. She was not going to think about him!

"You say that as if it's not a personal grudge for us. Mahmoud and his boys kidnapped our teammate. Our sister. Aren't the Medusas all for one and one for all?"

"Well, yes. Of course." Thinking fast, she added, "Exactly my point. Mahmoud and Yousef and the other Iranians should be our kill. Not the Israelis'."

"I don't care who takes them out, as long as they get taken out," Gia declared.

"Fair enough," Rebel conceded. "But I still think we should figure out what we're looking at and how it correlates to the Olympics—if it correlates to the Olympics—before we brief anyone else."

Gia shrugged. "Fine by me. But I still think Avi—"

"Could we *please* stop talking about him?" Rebel asked under her breath.

"Touchy, touchy. But I get the message. I'll back off," Gia responded.

"I'm sorry. Just because Avi's being a jerk doesn't mean I should take it out on you."

"How's he being a jerk?" Gia asked quickly.

Rebel spotted their boss winding through the desk toward them, and merely muttered back, "Long story."

"Later," Gia mouthed.

Not likely.

"What have you got, ladies?" Torsten asked briskly.

Rebel stood back and let Gia explain what they'd identified. After all, the find was Gia's, anyway. Avi was going to be fascinated by this discovery. He was as convinced as she was that Mahmoud had a big attack planned. And, he was also frustrated at not being able to get out in front of Mahmoud's plan. This image might be just the break Avi and the Medusas needed.

Torsten straightened a moment later. "So we're thinking Mahmoud's team is going to set up a sniper attack? Are we looking at multiple shooters, or are those three towers set up so a single sniper can practice a shot from differing angles at a target?"

"Unknown," Rebel answered.

"Can we get a height on those towers and then develop a list of possible shooter's perches of similar height around the Olympics?" Torsten asked.

"Of course," both women answered simultaneously.

"I'll leave you to it, then," Torsten said tersely. He didn't need to add aloud that they had to work fast. The Olympics were already underway, and Mahmoud could strike at any moment.

The shortest tower was around fifty feet tall, and the tallest one was nearly ninety feet in height. The open space between the towers stretched for approximately a hundred yards.

Rebel sat down at her own workstation and commenced examining maps of the Olympic Village, venues and surrounding city, looking for any wide-open spaces flanked by structures from fifty to ninety feet in height. Over the next few hours, she came up with a list of nearly a hundred locations.

Not helpful.

There had to be a way to narrow down the possible sites of a sniper attack.

She looked for easy egresses from the various buildings, towers and other tall structures, and was able to narrow her list down to about thirty possible targets. Still too many to cover and protect effectively.

She sat back, thinking hard. Would the Iranians go for an individual, high-value target, like a famous athlete, celebrity, or maybe a high-profile government official? Or would they instead go for a mass shooting of random targets to maximize the number of dead and wounded? She could see the logic in either type of target.

She stared at the satellite image Gia had forwarded to her screen. Those half-dozen target dummies scattered around the space between the towers stared back, faceless and featureless except for the bullet holes riddling their straw-stuffed bodies.

To the credit of whatever Iranian sniper or snipers had shot at the targets, all six dummies' heads were shredded.

Head shots were the most precise form of kill shot. The intent of the attack, then, would be to kill, and not cause random fear and panic. Which led her to conclude a specific target or set of targets was the goal.

But where? And who?

If only she wasn't mad at Avi. She would love to call him and ask his opinion of all this. But he was working an Olympic event right now, and the fact remained that she was furious at him for treating her as a casual challenge—to seduce her and prove her wrong about pleasure and happiness.

What she wouldn't give right now to be able to read Avi's mind.

Heck, what she wouldn't give right now to be able to read Mahmoud Akhtar's mind.

She picked up her cell phone and called her teammate, Piper.

"Hey, Rebel," Piper said in surprise. "I thought you weren't supposed to go back to work today."

"You know me. The eternal workaholic."

"No kidding," Piper laughed.

Rebel blinked. Really? Her teammates truly thought she was a workaholic? That was saying something, given that all of the Medusas worked insanely hard at being the best they could be.

"I tried surfing this morning, thank you very much."

"You? Surfing? Will wonders never cease!" Piper exclaimed.

Rebel rolled her eyes. She wasn't that hopeless at balancing work and play. Was she? Sure, she wasn't Avi, who seemed to live to play. But she wasn't always on the job like, say, Gunnar Torsten.

Rebel jerked her attention back to the phone call and her teammate, asking, "Hey, Piper, is there any chance you could grab Zane and come down to the ops center? Gia and I have something to show you, and I'm hoping you two can shed a little light on how our friend Mahmoud thinks."

"Yeah, sure. We'll be right down."

Rebel sat back in her chair, staring at the training mock-up the errant windstorm had revealed, more certain than ever that something bad was about to happen. Something very bad.

Chapter 15

In the afternoon, Avi glared his way through the archery elimination round—the Israeli woman won her match and would be back tomorrow in the round of sixteen. After an early, entirely tasteless supper, he scowled his way through the boxing match, which the Israeli gold medal hopeful lost to a Cuban boxer no one had ever heard of.

The match was a lopsided rout, at any rate. The Israeli boxer wouldn't have to live with any regrets over having almost won. And the kid was young. He would be back for the next Olympics all the wiser, and four years stronger, fitter and more mature.

Avi loaded the Israeli boxing contingent into the athlete bus for the return trip to the Olympic Village. The big, cumbersome vehicle pulled away from the bus stop with him glowering out the window at nothing in particular.

Why couldn't Rebel understand he only wanted the

best for her? It hadn't been some stupid challenge in his mind to prove her wrong about happiness. He'd genuinely enjoyed being with her, watching her discover some of life's finer pleasures, and making her happy. She was an amazing woman and he was fascinated by her!

He could see where she got the two-week-fling vibe from him. Initially, that had been what he expected to share with her. But then he'd gotten to know her and quickly realized she was so much more than fling material. So much so that he had no idea what to do about her now.

Should he let this misunderstanding separate them now so the parting wouldn't be so hard in two weeks? Should he track her down and try to convince her that he had real feelings for her—

Whoa, whoa, whoa. Real feelings?

Well, hell.

Sure, he had real feelings for other women he'd had relationships with. But they were friendly feelings. Companionable feelings. Comfortable feelings. Not these desperate, all-consuming, passionate feelings roiling around in his gut—

His cell phone rang in his hip pocket, and his pulse leaped. Was it Rebel? Calling to apologize, maybe, for overreacting? Inviting him to dinner, perhaps?

Nope. Israeli security headquarters.

Simple security check-in? Change of schedule? Maybe a reroute around a traffic jam for the bus? Unfortunately, his gut shouted that something more serious was up.

One of the security shift supervisors said tersely in his ear, "Avi, there has been a shooting at an open-air concert. We need you to get over there right away."

A lump of lead dropped into his stomach. *No. Nono-nononono.* The lead heated up, a ball of failure and fury burning through his stomach wall. What had they missed? Had there been a signal, a hint that could've stopped this?

"How bad is it?" he managed to choke out.

"Bad. Just get over there."

Swearing under his breath, he jumped out of his seat and headed for the bus driver. "I need you to stop the bus. I have to get off. Now."

"But—" the driver started.

Avi flashed his security credentials. "Now."

"Yes, sir."

Over his shoulder, he told the Israeli athletes and coaches, "Don't get off this bus until it stops in front of your dormitory." To the driver he said, "Do not let anyone on this bus once you close the door behind me. Anyone. Is that understood?"

"What about police—"

"*No one.* No matter what credentials they show you," Avi snapped. "Got it?"

"Umm. Yes. No one comes aboard."

"It's for your security as much as the security of the athletes on board," Avi said more kindly. "Trust me. There's been an incident, and you need to trust nobody."

"You want me to take your orders and trust you—"

Avi didn't have time for this civilian. He cut the guy off. "Don't let me back aboard once I get off the bus, either. I said no one, and I mean *no one.*"

"All right, already. I get it."

Avi spun and stepped off the bus. He turned and watched the door close and nodded tersely as the driver got out of his seat to lock the door behind him. As the bus pulled away from the curb once more, he looked around, getting his bearings.

The concert venue, about a dozen blocks from here, was a broad plaza bordered on one side by dormitories beyond a tall fence, just inside the Olympic Village, bordered on two more sides by office buildings, and on the fourth side by an expansive park. Not an ideal location for catching an active shooter.

He sprinted a half-dozen blocks and started to meet the crowd of panicked civilians fleeing the scene of the shooting. He dodged from side to side, pressing forward grimly against the human flow of fear.

Avi burst out at the edge of the square and ran smack into a line of policemen. After flashing his security credentials to the cops, they let him through the barricade without hassle.

He looked around in dismay. A half-dozen bodies sprawled on the ground in pools of blood. Most of their torsos and heads were already covered by jackets, shirts, or other makeshift shrouds.

Avi spied an American wearing a navy jacket with big white letters on the back, FBI. He sprinted over to the agent and asked, "Any idea where the shots came from? Witnesses, maybe? People who spotted the muzzle flashes or heard the direction of fire?"

The FBI guy shook his head without looking at him. Instead, the guy was studying the tall buildings around the square. "Superloud rock concert was playing, complete with special effects and pyrotechnics. No one saw anything, let alone heard any shots."

Avi swore under his breath. The shooter had picked his target wisely. Which was a problem. Smart, organized criminals were often extremely hard to catch.

The FBI agent continued, "People just started dropping in the crowd. Took a minute or so for anyone around them to realize that anyone had been shot. It took a while more for the crowd as a whole to realize there was an active shooter. The panic and stampede was delayed for up to three minutes after the first victim fell."

"One shooter took all of these shots?" Avi followed up. "How long was the shooter active?"

"It appears that all the shots were taken in the course of a minute or two."

"How many shots confirmed?"

"We count a total of nine known shots. Six kills."

Damn. Six for nine? That was a ridiculously high kill rate, even for a professional sniper. Only a few very small spots on the human body were known kill zones. Either that, or the shooter had used highly destructive rounds to increase the chance of making kills.

Aloud, the FBI man said, "Preliminary assessment is that multiple shooters did this. But that's purely a guess at this point."

Avi looked around grimly. "One highly trained sniper could aim and fire nine times in two minutes. But to make all these successful kill shots in that short a period of time? You're talking a world-class sniper."

"Either that, or more than one shooter did this," the FBI agent allowed. A couple of shooters would mean each shot could've been set up more slowly and carefully."

"I concur with you. This looks like the work of multiple shooters," Avi declared grimly. "How many wounded?"

The agent shrugged. "Not many. Three."

"Any information on the ammunition used?"

The FBI agent nodded as if Avi was thinking along the exact same lines he was, and said, "Four of the shots were to people's heads. Two shots were center of the chest kills. From one of those bodies, a crime scene investigator has recovered a high-velocity, copper-jacketed, hollow point round here at the scene. It was fragmented all through the victim's upper torso."

Avi swore. That type of round was designed to inflict maximum damage on human flesh. A round like that would shatter on impact and tear the crap out of the person it hit. Even if a round didn't strike a lethal area, the sheer damage and blood loss could turn a normally survivable shot into a deadly one.

"Faces were torn right off a number of the victims. Positive identification's going to be a bitch," the FBI man volunteered.

"Any pattern to the victims?" Avi asked without much hope of that angle panning out.

"None. They seemed randomly selected through the crowd."

Avi shoved a hand through his hair. "Do you have any information at all on the shooters?"

"Nada," the FBI man replied sourly. "The Aussies have men searching every building in the area, and Olympic security is searching those dormitories." He pointed at the three high-rises looming beyond the tall fence ringing the Olympic Village.

"I can't even give you a rough location of where the sniper's nest—or nests—were located," the guy continued. "In the chaos, victims got turned around and moved. Some were carried out of the crowd. The scene's completely contaminated."

"Is there film footage of it?" Avi asked.

"Probably. But we haven't had time to round up video from CCTV or from cell phones of bystanders, let alone bring in any experts to analyze it."

"I know a couple photo analysts who are in town for the games. Here's my card and phone number." Avi shoved his business card at the FBI man. "Where can I contact you to share what my people find out?"

The FBI man reached into his coat for a card. "Any

help you can give us would be appreciated. This is a freaking mess."

No kidding.

Avi headed for the nearest entrance to the Olympic Village, but a mob of athletes and coaches clogged the approach to the gate. The village was on hardcore lockdown and nobody was being let in or out.

Everyone in the crowd was panicky, and those close to the gate were arguing and trying to talk the guards into letting them through. Avi understood their urgency to get off the street and get within the tight security perimeter of the village. Not that he was convinced they would be any safer inside the village than they were outside of it.

Given the location of the Olympic dormitories overlooking the plaza, it was just as plausible that the gunman had been shooting from inside the village. And given the presence of a possible terror team inside the Iranian delegation, that made the possibility just that much more plausible.

Even if this wasn't the work of Mahmoud Akhtar and his cronies, it was entirely possible one or more of the actual shooters had found a way to infiltrate the Olympic Village and take up a perch in one of the dormitories towering over the plaza.

He yanked out his cell phone and called his Israeli boss in the security center. "Any chance I can get cleared into the village in spite of the ongoing lockout? There's a huge mob out here, and none of us are being allowed in."

"Sure. I'll make the call. Which gate are you at?"

"North 2."

"Done. Get back here ASAP, Bronson."

"Mind if I swing by the American operations center first and see what they've got on the shooting?"

"That's fine. Just update me when you learn anything."

"Will do, sir. But it could be a while to learn much."

It took him nearly ten minutes to cajole and finally push his way through the huge, tense crowd of athletes and coaches to reach the actual gate. As Avi emerged from the crowd, the guard started into a spiel about no one entering or exiting, and he cut across the guy's rote recital.

"I'm Avi Bronson. Security specialist for the games. I believe my boss called you guys a few minutes ago?"

"Yes, of course. Bronson. We're expecting you. If I could see your badge, sir?"

"Of course."

The guard thoroughly inspected his credentials and waved him through, accompanied by a chorus of shouts and protests. He threw an apologetic glance over his shoulder at the frustrated athletes and coaches. Little did they know they might actually be safer where they were.

He took off running for the US security headquarters, which was much closer than the Israeli building. Truth be told, the American facility was better equipped and had more staff than his own country's operations center.

Thankfully, the American guard on duty at the front door was an ex-Special Forces type who knew Avi personally. They'd worked together in Africa a few years back on a joint task force to take out pirates in the Gulf of Aden. As soon as Avi dropped Gunnar Torsten's name, the guard let him inside the building right away.

He burst into the chaotic American operations center, not surprised to see all hands on deck to figure out what the heck had just happened in that plaza.

He spotted Rebel and her teammate, Gia Rykoff—also a photo intelligence analyst—huddled together in front of a large computer monitor.

"Have you got anything?" he asked them tersely as he approached.

"We just spotted what we think might be a muzzle flash from the top of this building overlooking the plaza," Gia answered. "On top of this building." She poked at the screen.

While she backed up a clip of video from what looked like Sydney CCTV, he glanced down at Rebel. Her gaze slid away immediately, and her brow knitted into a frown. What was that expression in her eyes? Guilt? Grief? Simple discomfort?

Gia jabbed a finger at the image she'd just frozen. "Watch right here."

The video started rolling forward again, and he spied a tiny flash of light from the top of an office building. That was 100 percent a muzzle flash. He hadn't been a special operator for almost twenty years for nothing. He knew a freaking weapon firing when he saw one.

Immediately, he yanked out his phone and called the FBI agent on scene. "We've got video of a muzzle flash on the bank building at the northwest corner of the plaza. It might be one of the shooters' nests."

"Got it. Thanks. I'll let you know what we find." Before the agent fully disconnected the call, Avi heard him shouting for agents to get up to the roof of the bank building.

He stood silent behind Rebel and Gia as the women went back through footage from various surveillance cameras of the concert, using the time stamp of that possible muzzle flash as their guidepost. They didn't spot any more muzzle flashes.

But he wasn't surprised. The video imagery attenuated to full white screen over and over as pyrotechnic explosions from the rock concert's stage overloaded the video cameras. And the noise—it was a mishmash of instrumentals, singing, screaming crowd members, and those damned stage explosions. No way would they pick out the sound of the shots firing.

And then Rebel and Gia started the grisly task of watching the video to spot victims starting to drop in the crowd. The women worked at guessing the direction shots had come from based on how bodies initially spun and fell, and where the red mist leftover from the lethal headshots lingered in the air.

It took about a half hour all told, but at the end of that time, their best guess was that three shooters had ringed the plaza, shooting down into the space from above. He swore luridly. It would have been like shooting fish in a barrel.

Had there not been so many headshot kills, he would've guessed the shooters hadn't even bothered to aim their weapons. A standing room only crowd had been *packed* into the square to see a world-famous rock band perform. Every shot was bound to hit someone.

"How many shots total are we looking at?" Avi finally asked.

"We've counted one more shot than the initial FBI report. That makes a total of ten hits," Rebel answered, her voice haggard. "The forensics guys on the scene will have to hunt down that last stray round that embedded itself in a walls or the pavement to verify our count. It is possible that one bullet did a through-and-through and caught two victims, of course. But we definitely have ten victims."

"And how long did the shooting go on?"

"About ninety seconds as best we can tell," she replied.

He relayed the information to the FBI agent, who relayed back that absolutely nothing had been found on top of the bank roof. If a shooter had been up there, he'd left no tracks, no fingerprints, no brass casings, nothing to indicate he'd ever been there.

Avi said to Rebel and Gia, "Can you start looking at video footage from closed-circuit TV of the streets around the plaza immediately after the shooting?"

"What are we looking for?" Rebel asked. Her voice was emotionless. Too emotionless. She was suppressing her emotional reaction to the incident way hard. He got it, of course. Right now, they all had a job to do, and hers was to find any information that might help law enforcement catch the bastard or bastards who'd done this. Thank goodness she had the mental discipline to do her awful job so well.

He replied as evenly as he could muster, "I need you to look for anyone carrying a bag or case large enough to conceal a sniper weapon."

"You think the shooters ran away from the scene along with their victims?" she asked.

"How else did they egress the area without anyone seeing a thing?" he responded tightly. "No weapons have been found in the surrounding buildings. No tracks, no brass shell casings. Nothing to indicate that a shooter set up a nest of any kind. Whoever did this cleaned up after themselves carefully and took all their gear with them when they left the scene."

She nodded, and for an instant, made eye contact with him. A world of pain swam in her gaze. Grief for the victims of the shooting, chagrin at not having been able to stop it and something else. Something personal and painful that he was afraid to put a name to.

She hesitated as if she wanted to say something to him, but then remained silent.

"What?" he bit out. "If you have something to say, say it. Six people are lying dead in that plaza. I'll listen to any ideas you've got that might help catch the shooter or shooters, no matter how far-fetched they might be."

She sighed heavily and squeezed her eyes shut tightly for a moment. Pain. That was definite pain etched on her face.

"I've got something to show you," she said heavily.

"What's that?"

"I should have shown it to you before. But…" A pause, then she spoke all in a rush. "But I didn't want to talk with you. I let my own selfish desires get in the way of doing my job. It's my fault those people are dead. All my fault—"

He cut her off, alarmed. "What the hell are you talking about?"

"Come with me."

He followed her to a workstation across the room. She sat down, typed at the keyboard and pulled up on her large, high-definition monitor a still photograph. He leaned down to study it more closely.

The image looked like a training facility for snipers. It was set in arid, beige dirt, featureless except for three shooting towers and a bunch of shredded target dummies on the ground. That, and a pile of camo netting tangled to one side of the shooting range.

"We got this image this afternoon from an American surveillance satellite," she said grimly. "Look familiar? Tall shooting positions around a large, open area, with targets below?"

He swore luridly. Was she suggesting that tonight's shooters had trained in that mock-up on her screen?

"Where is this training facility?" he asked harshly. Although, he suspected he already knew the answer.

"Iran. Same place Mahmoud Akhtar trained his new team."

Avi swore even more violently.

She spoke quickly. "Gia and I worked up a list of possible locations around Sydney that this mock-up duplicated. We couldn't get the list below about thirty venues and we—I—didn't want to tell you about it until I could narrow down what this mock-up was meant to be of."

He glanced down at the screen and back at her. "It is a pretty general mock-up. All you can really tell from it is that a shooter expected to shoot at a downward angle at targets from a high perch."

"Yes. But if I'd told you earlier. Maybe the IOC would have put out more security at all the big open areas with crowds."

"You couldn't have known the target would be a crowd. From that mock-up, the target could just as easily be a single individual that the Iranians planned to assassinate."

"Don't let me off the hook," she ground out. "I should've told you and I didn't."

"Fine," he replied harshly. "Next time, don't hold out on me. But I'm telling you, tonight's attack would not have been prevented even if every security delegation at the games knew about it. That's too general a mock-up to have given us a hard target to defend."

Her gaze lifted to his reluctantly. "For real?"

"For real," he said gently. Then he straightened, assumed a military commander's tone and said briskly, "Get your head out of your ass, McQueen, and get back in the game. I need you combing footage of the crowd fleeing the scene for some glimpse of the shooters. It's all we've got."

"Yes, sir," she blurted reflexively.

She spun and headed over to Gia's side smartly.

He hated using that tone of voice with her, but she'd

needed a figurative slap to snap her out of the self-recriminations and get her back to work. There would be time later to apologize to her for being a jerk.

And maybe, just maybe, she would understand. Unlike any other woman he'd ever had a real relationship with, she was the first and only actual military member. He muttered a silent prayer to whatever deity might be listening that she would understand.

He followed her back to the workstation.

Without sitting down, she looked up at him reluctantly. The expression lurking at the back of her gaze was wounded. Dammit. He'd been too tough on her. Too late to go back on it, now, though. He would have to find a way to make it up to her later.

In the meantime, he asked more pleasantly, "Can you work up a briefing on the image you showed me, in particular, highlighting its similarities to tonight's shooting?"

"I could, but then I wouldn't be able to look for anyone carrying a rifle away from the plaza."

She made a good point. He replied, "You're right. Hold off on the briefing for now. It's more critical to ID shooters and figure out where they went after they shot all those people."

"I will. But when we're done reviewing the footage, I'll get on that briefing for you." A pause. Then she asked in a small voice, "Are you okay?"

His gaze snapped to hers. "Hell, no, I'm not okay."

"I meant personally."

"So did I," he snapped.

She blinked and looked startled for just an instant, and then the professional facade was back. "I have to get back to reviewing the footage of the crowd."

He stepped back, out of her way. But as she brushed

past him, he couldn't help sucking in a sharp breath. Her gaze lifted to his ruefully. Yeah. She felt it, too. No matter what misunderstandings lay between them, there was still crackling chemistry, as well.

"Later," he murmured.

She made a noncommittal noise and continued on past him.

He wandered over to where Israeli analysts were watching video footage from inside the Olympic Village, doing much the same as Rebel and Gia were doing on the footage from the city. They were looking for athletes or coaches moving suspiciously in the crowd. People carrying bags or cases large enough to conceal a rifle.

And it went without saying that everybody was searching for the black tracksuits with green, white and red trim of the Iranian delegation.

Truth be told, he desperately hoped the Iranians were not behind this attack. The diplomatic incident and scandal would be horrendous if a nation known for harboring, aiding and supplying terrorists was linked to a terror attack.

As the night aged, he brought cups of coffee to Rebel and Gia, and as the women began to rub their eyes and squint at the computer screens, he brought them bottles of eye drops to moisten their fatigued eyes. Beyond that, there wasn't much he could do but stay out of their way.

As morning finally broke, he called the IOC security chief and asked for five minutes of the guy's time. He was granted three minutes before the morning security briefing, which started in twenty minutes.

Avi hurried over to Rebel's workstation. "I'm going to need those briefing slides as quickly as you can build them. I'm due at IOC headquarters in about fifteen minutes."

Dark circles under her eyes announced her exhaustion, but she nodded resolutely. "I'm on it. Give me five minutes."

"Come with me and give the briefing," he muttered to her.

"Why?"

"Because it's your work. You should get credit for it."

"Oh."

Not used to men letting her have the spotlight, was she? He snorted. When was she going to figure out he wasn't *anything* like the jerks she'd grown up around?

Chapter 16

Rebel had only gotten a single tour of the IOC security center upon her arrival in Australia several weeks ago, well before the games had begun. The communications center had been quiet then, mostly deserted. Not so, now. Every station was manned, and the tension in the room was electric after last night's shooting.

"This way," Avi murmured. His hand came to rest in the small of her back, as he guided her through the maze of workstations to a closed door. He knocked on the panel.

"Enter!" a voice called.

Avi introduced her to a silver-haired man, who looked unusually fit for his age. "This is Otto Schweimburg. Chief of Olympic Security. Otto, this is Rebel McQueen. Photo intel analyst from the American security team."

Schweimburg nodded tersely. "As you can imagine after last night, I'm in a hurry. What've you got?"

"Rebel?" Avi said.

"Shall we sit?" she suggested, setting her laptop on Schwiemburg's desk and opening it up. Quickly she showed him the satellite photo of the Iranian training mock-up, and her comparison slide showing how the dimensions of last night's plaza and the estimated size of the mock-up were very similar.

Schweimburg looked up at her and Avi sharply. "So, you're suggesting the Iranian government launched last night's attack? Why would they attack a target out in the city and not one attached to the Olympics officially?"

Rebel replied, "It's not my job to speculate, sir. It's merely my job to point out the similarities between a piece of recent intelligence and a more recent attack."

"Duly noted," the German replied. "What do you suggest I do by way of response to this information?"

She blinked, not accustomed to being asked for her opinion. She took a deep breath and answered, "I would recommend relocating the games to the emergency backup facilities immediately."

"You do understand the upheaval that would cause, don't you?" Schweimburg snapped.

She shrugged. "You asked for my recommendation. I didn't say it was convenient. We've had two credible attacks on the games, and both attacks have at least circumstantial links to the Iranian government."

"We've had one attack on a rock concert not officially affiliated with the games," the German snapped.

"I have to respectfully disagree, sir. I was at the swimming pool the night of the chlorine incident, and I saw two Iranian men by the pool at the exact spot I believe the chlorine was released into the water."

"Bronson briefed me on your theory. But it's only a theory."

The German's tone was dismissive at best, and insultingly condescending at worst. Nonetheless, she stood her ground. She was sick and tired of no one listening to her when her gut shouted that she was exactly right. Even Avi treated her like a cute little kitten to be petted and amused by, but not taken seriously.

"You're not paying attention to me," she ground out. "I don't make any analysis lightly or without reasonable certainty that I'm correct. And I'm telling you, something stinks about these two incidents."

"Like what?" Schweimburg demanded, openly hostile, now.

"Like why weren't more people killed last night?" she challenged baldly. "I've identified three probable directions of sniper fire in the plaza. Three snipers with ninety seconds to shoot, and they only took ten shots, total? Why not spray three hundred rounds in that time and take out dozens, or hundreds of targets? It's what I would have done if I were a terrorist looking to make a statement."

Schweimburg and Avi both stared at her, looking shocked.

"And why a stupid little chlorine attack? Why not release something really caustic that would have peeled the skin off everyone in that pool?"

"Follow the logic," Avi said tersely, interrupting what appeared to be Schweimburg opening his mouth to kick her out of his office. "Keep talking, Rebel."

She frowned. "Speaking as an intelligence analyst, the worst-case scenario is to assume that both attacks were perpetrated by the same person or persons. Starting with that, the next step is to put myself in the head of the attackers. One attack in the Olympic Village, that resulted in greatly increased security in and around athlete housing. A second attack in the city, near the games but separate from the games. It, too, has resulted in significant police resources being diverted to protecting tourists. I can only conclude that both of these small attacks were either test attacks to gauge reaction, or more likely, attempts to draw off security assets from the attacker's ultimate target."

"What's the ultimate target?" Schweimburg blurted.

"Unknown," she answered. "I would need more data to form a hypothesis. But it'll be much larger than either of these warm-up attacks."

"Warm-ups?" Schweimburg echoed. He shuddered visibly.

"Like I said," Rebel pounded home, "I'd move the Olympics now, and pray the terrorists are not attached to a delegation and don't end up moving with the athletes and officials."

"You want me to load up twenty thousand athletes, nearly as many officials and coaches, and all of their gear on a fleet of passenger jets. Then I'm supposed to fly them to Los Angeles to the facilities under construction for the next Olympic Games. And I'm supposed to resume the games—leaving behind all the spectators and media here to watch and cover the games?"

She shrugged. "That would be my understanding of how an emergency evacuation would happen. Why else do you have forty 747s sitting on the ramp at Sydney International Airport? Aren't they here for exactly that purpose?"

"That's supposed to be classified information."

She retorted dryly, "It's hard to hide forty jumbo jets. And it doesn't take a rocket scientist to figure out why they're hanging around the Olympic Games, doing nothing."

Schweimburg scowled and notably did not dispute her claim.

He did, however, counter, "What if these attacks are unrelated, and furthermore, they're all that the attackers could manage to do in the face of the overwhelming security around the games?"

"Then that's the best-case scenario, and you're darned lucky the attacks weren't worse. Believe me, sir, I would love to be wrong. But you asked for my professional opinion. I gave it."

"The IOC and *all* the Australian tourist councils would argue stridently against moving the games," Schweimburg said heavily. "I would be shouted down immediately if I even broached the subject of moving the games."

Rebel shrugged. "Your responsibility is the safety of the athletes and spectators, not the profitability of the games."

"Easier said than done," he snapped. "I'm late for another meeting. I'll take your analysis under advisement."

Which meant he was going to round file her briefing in his trash can and ignore her. Frustration roiled in her gut as she silently filed out of the office behind Avi. Even worse was her sense of being ignored. Again.

When they were completely outside the building, Avi finally broke the thick silence between them. "Are you okay?"

She whirled to glare at him. "No. I'm not okay. I'm sick and tired of not being taken seriously. Is it because I'm not experienced enough? Or because I'm under the age of forty? Or because I'm short? Or is it just because I don't—" she emphasized her next words with a jab of her finger to Avi's chest with each word "—Have. A. Penis?"

He threw up his hands in mock surrender. "I don't

have any problem with you being a woman! Personally, I'm thrilled that you're a woman!"

"And yet you didn't think I could take care of myself in that park. You keep protecting me like I'm some hand-wringing, delicate flower? When are you going to look at me and see a soldier? When are you going to look at me and see your *equal*?"

He sputtered as if he had no idea how to respond to that concept.

"I may not have twenty years of Spec Ops under my belt, Avi Bronson, but the United States Armed Forces are pretty damned good at training special operators. And I'm one of them. Stop patting me on the head and treating me like I'm a weak, helpless kitten!"

"Uhh, got it," he said as he took a cautious step backward, away from her. "No kittens."

"I happen to be one of the top-rated real-time, photographic intelligence analysts in the United States government. I know my job, and I stand by every word I said in there. You tell me why last night's shooters only took ten lousy shots!"

"I'm sure I have no idea," Avi said carefully.

"My analysis is spot-on," she snarled.

"I believe you."

She snorted. "Right now, you're scared of me because I'm pissed off. You'll say anything to appease me."

That brought him up short. He stopped backing away from her and his spine straightened. "Actually, no. I won't lie to appease anyone. I do believe you. I think your analysis is exactly right. I also think Otto Schweimburg is a political hack who needs to grow a pair of *cojones*."

Rebel stared at Avi, surprised. "Seriously?" she asked with slightly less heat.

"Swear to God. He's an ass and you're right."

Some of the wind went out of her tirade. She asked more calmly, "What do you suggest we do next?"

"You and the Medusas and I have to go back to the drawing board. I'm inclined to believe you and trust your analysis of the situation. It hadn't occurred to me to wonder why more people weren't killed in the plaza, but as soon as you mentioned it, it made total sense that something is off about that attack."

"Do you think I'm correct that security resources are being drawn away from the real target?" she asked.

"It's as good an explanation as any. And it's worth following up on. What places have had their security contingents reduced because of the two attacks?"

"Easy," she answered. "The event venues. Particularly the big ones with large security teams. Otto and his people deemed them well enough protected to be able to spare some of the warm bodies patrolling them for other duties."

"Great. There are ten venues that seat more than a thousand spectators—some of them in the tens of thousands. How are we supposed to cover all of those with our little working group?" Avi groused.

"No idea. We'll just have to keep an eye out and hope to catch a break. If we could get decent surveillance on Mahmoud and his crew, we might stand a chance of thwarting whatever they're planning."

Avi shook his head. "The bastard's gone to ground and no one's seen even a glimpse of him since you saw him at that swimming pool."

At least Avi believed her when she said she was sure it had been Mahmoud Akhtar she'd seen.

"I need to get back to my desk," she announced. "There's still video to comb through."

"You worked all night," Avi responded. "You need a

bite to eat and to take a nap. Once you've rested, you'll be much more effective."

She snorted. "I wasn't effective at all in that meeting with Schweimburg."

"Hey, you called it correctly. He's just stuck between doing the cautious thing for security and pressure from the business interests around the games. It's a hard balancing act, and he made his best call. You and I just happen to disagree with him. Regardless, we still have to do our jobs and actually protect the event."

Avi steered her toward the dining hall, and she let him order her an omelet and stack her plate with toast, bacon, fruit, potatoes and stewed tomatoes.

"I couldn't eat half of this if I tried!" she exclaimed.

"Fine. I'll eat the rest. And then you sleep. After that, you and I need to have a talk."

She looked up at him sharply, then her gaze skittered away from his. That was a whole lot more intensity in his eyes than she was prepared to deal with right now. Not when she was exhausted and frustrated by Schweimburg's failure to take her seriously, and she felt terrible about those six innocent people killed in the plaza last night.

To say that he was frustrated was an understatement. Avi went to the head of the Israeli security team with Rebel's pictures, and he put forward her theory that many more people should have been killed in the plaza.

As a result, the Israelis doubled up the security on their athletes and posted more armed guards around the athlete's quarters, but that was about all they could do without the cooperation of the International and Australian Olympic Committees.

It also meant Avi spent every waking minute pulling

security details for the next several days. Rebel moved back to her own room and answered his text with one-word replies that were completely uninformative. Dammit. She'd retreated all the way into her emotional shell and wasn't planning to come out anytime soon.

She'd slipped away from him.

Or maybe he'd never really had her in the first place. But he'd really thought they'd forged a connection. Something that went deeper than just dynamite sex. He'd really thought he'd broken through her ridiculous notions of happiness being a myth.

He sent her ridiculously expensive handmade chocolates, and he even had the best pizza in Sydney—a deep-dish concoction a full two inches tall—delivered to her room.

He got back single word texts. "Thanks."

That was it. Just thanks.

What the hell was wrong with her? He was clearly indicating to her that he still wanted to be with her. That he missed her. That time was slipping away from them. They only had three weeks together, here, and nearly two of them were gone. He felt the end of the games approaching far too quickly; each day that slipped past was one less day he had to win her back.

But how was he supposed to win her back if she wouldn't even speak with him, let alone be in the same room with him?

And it wasn't as if his schedule was completely free, either. Every time he tried to arrange some time off to correspond to Rebel's downtimes, something always went wrong or fell through, and he never got off work at the same time she did. It was almost as if the Fates were conspiring against him to keep them apart.

He was growing desperate enough that he actually

considered approaching Gunnar Torsten and confessing how he felt about Rebel and asking Gun to arrange their schedules so Avi could spend some time with her.

But the Americans had quietly stepped up their security measures, too, and nobody on the American security team had any more time off than he did. Everyone was scrambling to anticipate and prevent the next attack before it happened. For the one thing both nations' security teams were in agreement on was that another attack *was* coming.

He felt an external clock ticking down to disaster as inevitably as his internal clock was ticking down the impending loss of Rebel for good.

And nothing he said or did seemed to slow down either clock, let alone stop them.

Chapter 17

Rebel sat listlessly through the morning American security briefing as the speaker went through the day's assignments and special details. The main events were drawing toward their conclusions, and the finals of numerous competitions were drawing the largest crowds of the already-record-breaking attendance at these games.

Great. Just what Mahmoud and his team needed. The largest crowds in history, all crammed together like sheep for the slaughter. It was good of the IOC to line up such juicy targets for the Iranians.

Not a soul would listen to her warnings that something terrible was about to happen. Otto Schweimburg had not even brought up the idea of moving the games to the emergency backup site. She was convinced the only reason the head of the American security contingent had taken any action at all was as a personal favor to Gunnar Torsten and not because the guy seriously believed anything bad was in the offing.

People in the operations center looked at her like she was a nut ball and avoided even speaking to her as she sat at her desk, combing through the video feeds of the games and its surroundings hour after hour, day after day.

The briefing ended and she trudged back to her desk to resume the mind-numbing and hopeless task of trying to spot Mahmoud or one of his known associates in the hundreds of thousands of faces passing across her monitor every day.

She'd been at it for maybe an hour when her computer beeped an incoming email message. Please let it not be another passionate entreaty from Avi to give him a chance to explain himself to her, to express his feelings for her, to make things right between them.

Nothing could be right between them again. He'd made a science experiment out of her, and she could never trust him again when he said he cared for her.

She opened the email, startled to see that it came from CIA Headquarters in Langley, Virginia. She read the note quickly—it was from the Middle East Desk. They'd received her request for any further information available on a classified training facility in the heart of Iran.

A satellite had been rerouted to pass over the region in question as part of another, higher-priority mission, and the photo intel folks had taken the opportunity to take more pictures.

She scanned down through the attached images quickly. The only new thing she saw was that the camouflage nettings had been replaced over the mock-up of the plaza, and the shooter training range was no longer visible from the sky.

She almost didn't bother scanning all the way to the end of the lengthy series of still images captured from the surveillance satellite.

But she did scroll to the end, and she did read the final paragraph the analyst attached to the end of the email.

We do have an asset inside the facility in question. If you would like me to forward you a redacted version of the asset's reports from inside the training building, that could be arranged.

She lurched in her seat. The CIA had somebody who could tell her what was inside that giant warehouse?

She hurried across the ops center to a properly secured computer and fired off a response email requesting the *unredacted* reports from inside the training facility at the Middle East Desk's earliest convenience, in particular, any images obtained from inside the training building, to be sent to this secured computer. She didn't have the authority to call it a national security matter, but she invoked Major Torsten's authority and called it a national security matter, anyway.

She hit Send and went back to her desk to wait.

It took about a half hour, but a communications specialist called out across the operations center, "McQueen! You've got a classified email!"

Yes.

Impatiently, she signed the receipt log, waited for the email to be decrypted, and then sat down at the classified message station to open the email.

The written note was brief.

Here are the images you requested. Quality is dubious, but these are all we have. No detailed analysis has been performed on these images as they were determined to be of no immediate intelligence value.

She peered at the poorly lit images of a cavernous space, struggling to make out features. Slowly lights and doors and large structures came into focus. She grabbed a pad of legal paper and began to sketch a rough layout of the interior of the facility as she deciphered the various images and figured out at what angles the photographs had been taken.

It appeared that the photographer had frequently shot pictures from down by his or her hip, maybe concealing the camera, most likely a cell phone, in his or her hand.

Getting a feel for the layout of the building was a laborious process, but slowly, she began to understand what she was looking at in the pictures. And as she did so, her blood ran colder and colder.

This was it. The missing piece of the puzzle they'd all been looking for ever since she spotted Mahmoud Akhtar here in Sydney.

"McQueen, other people need to use that workstation," a communications specialist snapped behind her.

"Sorry," she replied absently. "These images are classified and I can't take them over to my workstation. Feel free to use my computer if you need it—"

"What I need is for you to get out of my chair."

She laid down her pencil and swiveled in her chair, not bothering to stand. "You'll have to take it up with my boss. I guarantee what I'm working on right now will be more important than anything you can even imagine doing today."

"Who in the hell do you think you are?" the comm guy exclaimed. "You're just some low-level grunt—"

She did stand up then. She was a full six inches shorter than the communications man, but she stared at him so coldly, and with such a promise of violence against him if he didn't get out of her face, that he actually took a step back from her.

She was *sick* and *tired* of these self-important yahoos not taking her seriously. The next one who crossed her was going to get broken into a whole bunch of tiny, painful pieces.

Apparently, this particular yahoo had at least a minimal self-preservation instinct, for he stomped off toward Gunnar Torsten's office, muttering obscenities under his breath.

It took about sixty seconds for Gunnar Torsten to come out of his office and stride over to the computer station. The comm guy looked smug behind her boss.

"What have you got, Rebel?" Torsten asked her.

"The CIA obtained photographic images of the interior of the training facility Mahmoud used to prep his team for the Olympics."

"Are you kidding me?" Torsten exclaimed under his breath. "What have you found?"

"The images are terrible and it's taking me a while to figure out what I'm looking at. And then that guy came over and tried to kick me off this computer."

Torsten whirled around and snarled, "Lieutenant McQueen will have full and undisturbed access to this computer for as long as she needs it, today. If anyone has a problem with that, they can take it up with me. Is that understood?"

"But—" the communications guy started.

"She's working on a matter of national security. Rebel, let me know if this guy gives you any more hassles. I'll be happy to take him out back to the woodshed."

The comm guy spluttered a bit more but moved away from her.

Torsten ground out low, "Anything you need, Rebel.

Anything at all. Just get me the layout those bastards used to train for their mission over here."

"I could use Gia's help. I'm trying to build a 3-D representation of the training area, but it's hard with a pad of paper and a pencil. I could use her expertise with designing a computerized model."

"Done. I'll get her over here if I have to take her security detail myself," Torsten replied.

He was as good as his word. In about fifteen minutes, Gia hustled into the operations center and rushed over to Rebel. "What's up?"

"I need your eyeballs to help decipher these images. And I need you to build a 3-D images of what we see."

With Rebel working on the actual images and Gia working on her laptop computer, the two of them slowly constructed a recreation of the contents of the warehouse. It took most of the afternoon, but they finally sat back, nodding grimly at each other.

"I think that's got it," Rebel declared.

"I concur. Want me to call the Medusas together?"

"I think we'd better."

"Are you gonna call Avi?" Gia asked slyly.

Rebel huffed. "Fine. I'll call him. But I'm telling you, nothing's going on between us. As in *nothing*."

"Methinks she doth protest too much," Gia sang.

She told her teammate succinctly what she could do with that sentiment.

Laughing, Gia headed for Torsten's office to start calling in the team. Reluctantly, Rebel pulled out her cell phone and dialed a familiar, painful number.

"Rebel? Is that you? Thank God. I was beginning to despair of you ever speaking to me again. You have to let me explain—"

She cut him off. "This is a work phone call, Major Bronson."

He fell silent.

The silence stretched out for an uncomfortably long time.

His voice rough, strained, infinitely pained, he finally said, "What's going on, Lieutenant McQueen?"

"I need you over here as soon as possible."

"That's going to be difficult. I'm scheduled to work until 2:00 a.m. tonight."

She winced. If she continued refusing to let him explain himself, then he obviously didn't want to see her. Matching his formality, she said, "We've had a breakthrough that may help us determine what target Mahmoud and his team are planning to hit."

"I'll be there in ten minutes."

The line went dead in her ear.

That was it, then. She'd officially killed any chance at a reconciliation between them.

It was over. She should be relieved. *Right?* Why then, did it feel like she'd just extracted her heart from her own chest with a spoon?

Avi paused outside the conference room door and took a deep breath. He could do this. He could look at Rebel, sit beside her, have a professional conversation with her, without giving away how wrecked he was by her rejection.

Initially, he'd thought it was just a simple misunderstanding between them. The sort of thing they could talk out in an adult conversation. But as the days had dragged on with her refusing to even speak with him, let alone see him in person, it had dawned on him that something larger was afoot.

Not only was she mad at him for setting a personal goal of making her happy and achieving it, but she was soul-deep angry that he'd challenged her worldview and, ultimately, proven it false. Maybe that was what she couldn't forgive him for.

Thing was, he couldn't be sorry for showing her that there was more to life than work. That happiness was an essential and wonderful part of being alive. She might never forgive him for it, but at least he had the bitter satisfaction of knowing he'd made her life immeasurably better.

Too bad that knowledge wouldn't keep him warm at night, or laugh with him, or grow old with him.

"In or out?" someone said behind Avi, startling him into realizing he'd been standing there with his hand on the doorknob for a stupidly long time.

Swearing, he opened the door and walked into the conference room. The impact of seeing Rebel again was a punch in the gut. Delicate violet circles under her eyes suggested she wasn't sleeping any better than he was, and she appeared to have lost some weight. There was a hollowness to her cheeks he didn't remember from before.

What kind of a monster did it make him that he'd given her happiness, and now she had to live with awareness of its absence. God. Had he actually ruined her life? He needed to make it right. There had to be a way to fix the damage he'd done.

"Thanks for coming, Avi," Gunnar Torsten said grimly.

"What's up? Rebel said there's been a breakthrough."

"She found it, so I'll let her tell you about it."

He gathered the rest of the Medusas had already been filled in, for they all looked expectantly at him and not at Rebel.

Clenching his jaw, he reluctantly lifted his gaze to her at the end of the conference table beside Torsten. For just an instant, she met his gaze. Her expression was quietly ravaged as she stared back at him.

Then she turned away from him and flashed a very dark, fuzzy photograph up on the wall-mounted large screen behind her. She said emotionlessly, "I'm going to flash through the actual images very quickly, because it took me and Gia hours to decipher what we were actually looking at. But I wanted to give you an idea of where our diagrams came from."

He nodded and watched as several dozen equally dark and meaningless photographs of the interior of some building flashed past.

She spoke again. "I was notified by my government that a series of photographic images had come in from the interior of the training facility Mahmoud Akhtar and his team have been using for the past eight months or so."

Avi lurched in his chair. That was huge! His gaze flashed back to the screen and the blurry image on it. That was Mahmoud's training setup? He asked urgently, "What did the two of you figure out from analyzing those images?"

Rebel pressed a button on a remote control and a computer-generated, 3-D image of a series of boxes placed around a large space popped up on the screen. "This is a crude rendering, of course, but we're fairly certain the dimensions are accurate. Inside the warehouse-style facility is a large, open training area similar to what we—or you Israelis—would use to mock up a mission and practice it before actually executing it."

He nodded impatiently. Every Special Forces unit on Earth routinely ran mock-ups for training and for mission planning purposes.

She continued, "As far as we can tell, the Iranians placed a series of large, wooden crates around the open space. The placement is not random—most of the boxes line up with one another one way or another. Our guess is the crates were built to specific dimensions, because they are all of differing heights and widths."

"Maybe they just slapped some obstacles together without worrying about the dimensions?" he suggested. He didn't particularly believe that, but they needed to consider all the possibilities.

Rebel shrugged. "It would be hard to stack and store boxes of so many different shapes, and it would waste lumber—which is neither plentiful nor cheap in Iran— not to reuse these simulated obstacles."

He nodded, satisfied that the dimensions of the crates were intentional. "Continue," he murmured.

Rebel said, "As you can imagine, we've been trying ever since we called this meeting to match any places at the Olympics or in the surrounding areas of Sydney to this topographical layout."

"And?" he prompted.

"No success, yet."

"Can you run some sort of comparison against satellite imagery of the whole area?" he asked.

"Easier said than done," Rebel replied. "The first problem is that it would take sophisticated software and mainframe computer access, neither of which we have readily at our disposal, to run the kind of comparison you're suggesting. We can ask a couple of different agencies in the US government to set up that sort of matching comparison, but it would take too long. The games will be over in less than a week."

His gaze snapped to hers, and hers to him as she uttered the words.

Less than a week to sort out whatever had gone wrong between them and get their relationship back on track—or from her point of view, he supposed, less than a week left to dodge and avoid him until she could return to her regularly scheduled miserable existence.

"The second problem with identifying what this is a mock-up of is that this could as easily be indoor as outside. We can't rule out lobbies of large buildings, shopping malls, or Olympic venues as the targets."

"So we'll physically have to walk through each building and look at the interior setups for a match," he declared.

Gunnar interjected, "If I were them, I'd be planning a hit where the most people will be crowded together."

Avi responded, "So, you're thinking the interior of an event venue, or a nightclub. Maybe a party of some kind." He thought about it for a few seconds. "I concur. It's what I would do if I were them, too." He glanced up at the diagram on the screen. "I'd go for maximum death in minimum time."

Rebel shook her head. "I don't understand why they didn't just spray that crowd at the concert with automatic weapon fire. They could have killed hundreds of people and wounded hundreds more. There were nearly three thousand people in that plaza, packed shoulder to shoulder. The carnage would have been spectacular."

Avi responded, "We can only assume that they have an even-larger death toll in mind for their ultimate attack."

A moment of grim silence around the table greeted that observation.

"Third problem," Rebel continued, "The heights of the crates in the warehouse may not correspond exactly to the heights of the obstacles in the actual target location.

Roughly half of the boxes in the warehouse are about two meters tall—tall enough that the attack plan may include using them for cover or moving around them, but won't include climbing over them."

"So they could be pillars or other vertical structures instead of just crate-shaped obstructions," he verified.

"Correct," Rebel responded. "And some of the crates could be simulations of corners with hallways extending at ninety-degree angles from them."

Damn. That would complicate identifying the target. "Still," he said, "we have the basic layout of some sort of structural obstacles. That should be enough to figure out what they're planning to hit. It's a hell of a lot more information than we had a few hours ago."

"One last conclusion we can draw," Rebel added. "They most likely are planning some sort of quickly executed tactical strike, and they plan to get away alive, or else they wouldn't bother running the mission through a detailed mock-up like this. The intel report that came with the photographs of the training facility said this setup was in place for several weeks and only dismantled about two months ago."

Avi breathed, "A few days before the *IRAN Jahan* sailed."

Rebel's startled gaze met his. She hadn't made that connection, huh? She nodded slowly. "The timing is perfect."

Gunnar asked, "Do you want to take this to Otto Schweimburg?"

Avi pulled a disgusted face. "He has steadfastly refused to listen to any of my suggestions that the Iranians are up to something. I have no reason to think he'll believe me—or you—now."

Gunnar grunted in agreement.

"I think we should go out and find a matching location to the diagram and then show it to Schweimburg. If nothing else, maybe we can convince him to put extra security on the target we identify."

That got nods all around the table.

Avi looked around at the Medusas. "What are we waiting for? Let's get out there and start searching for the target."

Gunnar replied, "We may not have much time before the attack. We'll have to work smart and not just randomly run around looking at floor plans. I propose that we build a list of gathering places in descending order of crowd size. We'll start at the top and work our way down the list."

"You're assuming the Iranians will go for the biggest, most visible target," Avi retorted. "It's just as possible they'll pick a smaller target with less security in a bid to ensure a successful attack."

"Fair point," Gun answered. "Why don't you work up a list of targets based on the amount of security at each one? Half of us will work on the size-based list, and half of us will work on the security-presence-based list. Any locations that duplicate, we'll cross off the other list as soon as one team inspects it. Piper, Zane, Rebel, Lynx, you're with me. Tessa, Beau, Gia, you're with Avi."

Avi didn't know whether to be relieved or dismayed that he didn't get to work with Rebel. Inspecting facilities with her might have given them a chance to talk. But they both needed to focus 100 percent on this search. Thousands of lives might depend on not missing something important.

They all spent about a half hour with their heads together in the conference room, sorting out possible target locations into the two lists. When they'd categorized every building and gathering place in or around the Olympic venues and village, they adjourned to start the search.

He headed out with his team, a print copy of the 3-D diagram in hand. It was harder than it looked to match an image on paper to actual places, full of people, signs, posters, kiosks, vendors and other distractions to obscure the actual structures behind them.

They drove from one location to another, painstakingly searching each one for a possible match to the diagram. After a while, he had the diagram memorized cold and could pace off the distance between pillars or walls or stairwells in buildings without even having to refer to the sheet of paper in his hand.

The two teams worked all afternoon, but nobody came up with a match. Avi's team grabbed sandwiches from a vendor at the big basketball field house and continued working as they gulped down the food.

At about 7:00 p.m. his cell phone vibrated, and he noticed that his companions also reached for their phones at the same time. He read the message scrolling across his screen.

Bomb threat at boxing venue. Evacuation in progress. All Group B security personnel report to Sydney Convention Centre, south entrance, for bomb sweep.

Group B personnel constituted about half of all the people assigned to any given event at any given time. Group A personnel wouldn't leave an assigned venue under any circumstances, but Group B'ers could be moved to help out in an emergency.

He immediately called Gunnar. "What's up at the Convention Centre?"

"Bomb threat. Deemed credible, and the venue is being evacuated as we speak. Then they'll sweep the building, and if it's all clear, they'll rescreen the spectators and let everyone back inside."

"What event's running in there, tonight?"

"Men's semifinal in basketball. USA vs. Russia."

"Packed house, then," Avi commented.

"Packed to the rafters. Standing room only. I'm guessing it'll take a half hour to clear the place out, another half hour to run the bomb dogs through, and another hour to get everyone back in their seats. The IOC says it wants the event to go on tonight, though. It'll throw off the overall event schedule too much if the game doesn't happen."

"You already checked out the Convention Centre for matches to our mock-up, right?" Avi asked.

"Affirmative. No match."

Dammit. Avi's team was nearly done with its search list. Only small targets with crowds measuring in the hundreds or a few thousand at most remained. His gut said Mahmoud would go for a significantly more spectacular target than anything that small. He asked, "Hey, Gun. How are you guys coming on your list?"

"Most of the way through it. You?"

"Same. We're scraping the bottom of the target barrel. I think we missed something. Regroup at Ops and form a new plan?" Avi suggested.

"Maybe we check out the Convention Centre again—" Gun started.

Avi interrupted. "You guys were thorough and didn't miss anything there. Don't second-guess yourself, brother. You and I both know we're on the right track. We have to keep going with this line of investigation."

They had missed *something*. He just couldn't figure out *what*.

"My conference room in ten?" Gun responded.

"Make it five," Avi replied grimly.

Chapter 18

Rebel didn't relish seeing Avi twice in the same day. It had been hard enough briefing him in before. It had been all she could do to maintain a professional demeanor when her heart was shattering into a million pieces.

She waited nervously in the conference room for him and his team to arrive. *Cripes.* Her palms were damp, and she was breathing too fast. She knew better than to let him have this kind of an effect on her. But as it turned out, she had no control over her reactions to him, like it or not.

Which was both frustrating and informative. No matter how hard she wanted to deny it, she had fallen for him hard. And walking away from him was turning out to be much harder than she'd anticipated.

It *was* the right thing to do. They had no future together living and working halfway around the world from each other, let alone the fact that their worldviews were diametrically opposed, or that he had never taken her seriously as a Special Forces operative.

No. There were just too many obstacles for them to overcome.

Maybe if one of them wasn't in the military, if they could find a way to be in the same place at the same time, maybe then she might have been willing to give the whole notion of life as a happy experience more serious consideration. But if the past couple of weeks with Avi were any indication, the pursuit of happiness directly interfered with her ability to do her job.

The conference room door burst open and Avi, Gia, Tessa and Beau stepped inside.

Torsten said briskly, "Where are we, Rebel? Give us a quick summation."

She appreciated him trusting her intelligence analysis skills enough to ask her to lead this critical meeting.

"We've pretty much exhausted the interiors of any venues as the target, assuming the mock-up we're working off of is actually a representation of the final target. Are we still in agreement that this is a rational working assumption?"

Nods all around the table.

Gunnar's cell phone beeped and everyone looked at him as he read the message. He announced, "A device was found in the Convention Centre. Crude, not powerful, and a dud to boot. The IOC is still having a bomb unit remove it from the building, but it's been made safe."

"Where was it planted?" Rebel asked quickly.

Gunnar typed into his cell phone, and a moment later answered, "Main concourse, tucked in a Food Services supply closet. It would not have caused any structural damage to the building. Just a lot of noise and concrete dust."

"What kind of bomb was it?" Avi asked.

"Less than a kilogram of C-4. Blasting cap. Simple detonator. Cell phone activated. No backup detonator in case someone tried to disarm the device."

Wow. That was crude. Even the most rudimentary training in bomb-making would produce a more sophisticated device than that.

She commented, "I'm confused by this whole bomb threat at the Convention Centre."

"Why's that?" Avi asked quickly.

One thing she had to give him credit for. He'd never questioned her intelligence or thought process. She answered, "Why put a tiny device in such a huge building? It would cause chaos, but no damage. If we're also working on the assumption that Mahmoud Akhtar is planning something spectacular, that bomb was anything but. Easily found. Easily disarmed. And why call in the bomb threat in the first place? Who made that call?"

Gia jumped in. "Maybe someone on Mahoud's team got cold feet and made the call."

Zane shook his head. "When I was undercover with him, Mahmoud didn't let any of us have cell phones of any kind, and he continuously monitored us to make sure we didn't sneak away and call anyone or even use the internet. Given the degree of preparations he's gone to for whatever he has planned here, I have to believe he hand-picked fanatics like himself. They'll have intense military discipline, and nobody will deviate from his plan."

Rebel nodded. "Fair enough. That means if Mahmoud's guys are behind this little bomb at the Convention Centre, it was part of their plan to call it in." She continued, "The timing of the call is suspect, too. Why call it in before the basketball game starts? Why not wait till everyone is settled in their seats, maybe late in the game when many people have been drinking and are half-sloshed? Olympic security would have a much harder time evacuating the place, and if chaos was the goal, you'd get much more of it by waiting."

Torsten said, "Good point. We have to assume Mahmoud is more interested in pulling off security from another venue at a specific time than he is worrying about the effect that calling in the bomb threat will have."

Avi lurched in his chair and blurted, "Which means it's a diversion. Whatever Mahmoud has planned is going down tonight. Maybe right now!"

Rebel nodded grimly. "I have to concur."

Gunnar said, "Our next guess has to be right, then. We'll only get one shot at this. Mahmoud has pulled off half the security personnel from whatever venue he plans to hit. What did we miss, Rebel?"

She gulped. This was what she'd signed up for. To be the pointy end of the sword, to live on the firing line, handling the toughest crises imaginable.

"I thought about that this afternoon as our search of venues kept coming up negative. I think we have to go back to the drawing board in our assumption about the kind of attack Mahmoud is planning. If he's not planning to do something up close and personal like wade into a crowd with a bunch of guys wielding automatic rifles, he's probably planning something more hands-off, but that will affect more people."

"Go on," Torsten murmured.

"Given that Olympic security were pulled off of event venues by the bomb feint, I think we can rule out civilian targets. He's planning to hit something in the village or at a venue."

Everyone nodded in agreement, and she pressed on. "The only kind of attack that's guaranteed to result in mass casualties that doesn't involve bombs or guns is some sort of chemical, biological, or nerve agent style attack."

That elicited a low groan around the table.

"What if the mock-up is of the roof of an event venue? Those could be air conditioning units and ventilation fans. What if, instead of looking inside the buildings, we should be looking on top of them?"

Torsten leaned forward to speak, but Gia was already typing on the laptop in front of her. She said, "I'm pulling up satellite imagery of the Olympic village and venues, now."

An image of Australia from space came into view, and she zoomed in quickly on the east coast of the continent, then on Sydney, and then on the Olympic cluster of facilities. Rebel and Gia stared at the images in silence, and everyone else said nothing, letting the photo analysts do what they were best trained to do.

Gia muttered, "I'll start on the right. You start on the left."

Rebel nodded, never taking her eyes off the large screen.

"There!" she exclaimed. "What's that building?"

Avi was first to reply. "That's the new Addison Field House. The gymnastics venue. Women's individual event finals are running there, tonight. They get underway in about ten minutes and will run till after midnight."

"Capacity?" Torsten asked.

Avi's answer sent a chill down Rebel's spine. "In excess of thirty thousand. And the women's gymnastics finals will fill every seat in the place."

Gia zoomed in on the big arched-roof building with futuristic ribs stretching across it, clamshell fashion. Puffy sections rose between the ribs.

"Right here." Rebel pointed at the screen. "Gia, can you superimpose our diagram of the mock-up on top of the roof and slide it around to see if we get a match?"

"It'll take me a minute," the analyst muttered.

While she did that, Avi spoke up. "The Addison's roof is held up by air pressure. To get in or out of the building, spectators have to pass through revolving doors that hold in the air. It has a giant ventilation system that cools and pumps air through the facility. It would be a perfect target for some kind of gas attack. Dispersion rates would be lightning fast because of the building's need for constant airflow." He continued, "There've been complaints among various security teams that it's too slow a building to evacuate. Not enough exits to move out a large crowd quickly."

Gia started moving around her image, revolving it and trying it over different segments of the building's extensive power and air units standing around the edges of the roof.

It took several minutes, but everyone yelled, "Stop!" at the same time as, suddenly, the drawn image matched up almost perfectly with a collection of air conditioners and ventilation fans.

Torsten said quickly, "Before we barge over there and climb up on the roof, I want everyone to gear up in full tactical kits. These guys will be violent, armed and prepared to die. I'll put in a quick call to our superiors to get an emergency green light, but barring that, I'm willing to operate under the Israeli green light. Are you willing to take responsibility for the operation, Avi?"

"Hell, yes."

"Rules of engagement?" Rebel asked.

Torsten responded, "This is going to be a political hot-cake no matter how it goes down, particularly if Mahmoud and an Iranian sponsored hit team show up on that roof, tonight. We're going to have to make an effort to stop them with nonlethal force."

Avi retorted quickly, "And when that fails, *then* we'll operate with extreme prejudice." Which translated to, shoot first, ask questions later.

Torsten responded, "I know you want these bastards, Avi. We do, too. But we have to cover our asses in this operation or all of our careers will be dead in the water after tonight. We need to record everything we do for evidence after the fact because we will be called out on the carpet for whatever we do."

His implication was clear. Without ironclad evidence that Mahmoud and his team were doing something illegal, any attack on them would cost the Medusas their careers.

Torsten looked around the table grimly. "If any of you prefer not to participate in the mission, I release you now. It's entirely possible that the bureaucratic fallout from this will be toxic to anyone who participates."

There was no question in Rebel's mind what was the right thing to do. If they could stop an attack that might kill thousands of people, and once and for all take out an international terrorist, her career was a small price to pay. "I'm in," she declared.

One by one, everyone else at the table echoed her sentiment.

Torsten took one last, hard look around and nodded. "I'll do everything in my power to protect all of you, and if necessary to take the fall for you. Don't let concern about what might happen after tonight affect your performance on that roof. I've got your backs."

And that was why the Medusas loved him. He was a hard teacher, a hard taskmaster, a hard man. But he was a good leader and his honor and loyalty to his team were ironclad.

"We're clear on the battle plan, then?" Torsten summarized. "We will collect photographic evidence of wrongdoing. Rebel, I'm going to put you in charge of that because you know what needs to be in the images to justify our mission."

She nodded and Torsten continued, "When Rebel has the imagery she needs, we'll attempt to arrest Mahmoud and his team. If they fail to surrender, we shift to a strictly take down–take out operation. Kill everyone up on that roof who isn't a good guy."

Everyone around the table verbally acknowledged their understanding of how this engagement would go down.

Avi asked, "Do you have a kit for me, or do I need to head over to my ops center to gear up?"

Torsten eyed Avi. "You're about my size. I've got what you need."

Rebel moved over to a printer where Gia had sent images of the actual roof for everyone to study in the next few minutes. Normally, they liked to spend hours or days planning a mission, but they didn't have that luxury, tonight.

Torsten said, "We'll access the roof from the nearest stairwell and make our way across the roof in a standard clearing operation. Form a line, walk forward, challenge anyone we find. Improvise as needed. Rebel, get me the nearest roof access point and a building schematic. I'll have one of the Medusas bring your gear to you while you do that." He looked around the table. "Questions or comments?"

Verbal negatives sounded around the table.

As everyone stood up to go get ready, Torsten said,

"Avi, I know you've operated with Americans plenty of times, but buddy up with Rebel just to be safe. She may need some extra cover while she records the situation as we encounter it."

Avi glanced over at her and asked quietly, "Are you okay with that? No harm, no foul, now's the time to speak up if you don't want to work with me."

Rebel winced as Torsten looked sharply back and forth between them. "We'll talk about this later," Torsten bit out. "What say, you, Rebel? Good or not, with Avi?"

"I'm good."

"All right. Get me that stairwell location." With that, Torsten and Avi left the room, leaving her in silence to pull up a quick building schematic, print out the relevant portions of it and spot a roof access point about two hundred feet away from the air-conditioning units in question.

She gathered the paperwork just as Lynx, the team's junior member, arrived in the room carrying a large duffel bag of Rebel's tactical gear.

"Thanks, Lynx. How are you feeling? Calm? Tense?" It was Lynx's first actual field operation.

"A little of both," Lynx confessed.

"Just do it like we do in training. The reflexes you've spent all these months building won't let you down. Don't overthink. Just do what you know how to do. And remember, we've all got your back."

The younger Medusa nodded and smiled at her. "And I've got your back."

They bumped fists, and Rebel shrugged into her flak vest, strapped on her utility belt, loaded spare magazines of ammunition in her thigh pockets and did a quick inventory of her video recording equipment designed for low- or no-light conditions and with image stabilization technology so she could film while running and still get a usable image.

She strapped on her helmet, parked her NODs—night optical devices—on top of her helmet, and pulled the thin microphone boom attached to her helmet into place at the corner of her mouth.

"Radio check," she transmitted.

Over the built-in earphones in her helmet, Torsten responded, "Five by five. Meet us out back. You'll both be in the front SUV. We're waiting on you and Lynx."

"On our way." She picked up her urban assault rifle, highly customized for the Medusas to be light, maneuverable, and deliver a crap-ton of lead on target in no time at all. She felt herself settling into the focused calm she took into any mission.

With a nod at Lynx, she led the way out the door.

"What the hell's going on?" a desk jockey across the room squawked when he saw the two women emerge from the conference room in full tactical gear.

"Talk to Torsten," Rebel bit out as she passed by the guy without stopping.

"We're not authorized to use deadly force!" the guy yelled after her.

"Speak for yourself," she called back as the operations center door shut behind her.

She took off running down the hallway with Lynx on her heels. They burst outside and jumped into the first vehicle, which Avi was driving. The SUV pulled out even before her door was fully shut.

They all felt the urgency of the moment. Time was against them. That bomb diversion at the Convention Centre meant Mahmoud had a limited window to do whatever he was planning to do, and that window was already in effect.

The interior of the SUV was silent as everyone studied the images of the roof, the building schematics and the diagram of the mock-up the Iranians had trained in. Rebel was lucky. Because of her job training, she could memorize a visual image with barely more than a glance. Still, she studied the images carefully to make sure she hadn't missed any crucial details.

Torsten made a phone call from the backseat of the SUV to brief someone in the US military command structure. He'd undoubtedly been passed up the chain of command with his request to launch a full tactical assault on an Olympic venue and was now having to repeat himself.

Rebel knew her boss well enough to hear that his request wasn't going well. His voice remained even and reasonable, but she sensed an undertone of frustration.

He ended the call with, "I'm not asking for permission. I'm telling you this is going to happen. We have credible intel that one of the world's most wanted terrorists is, as we speak, launching a major attack on the single largest Olympic sporting venue. We're operating under the umbrella of the Israeli government, which has requested our assistance in this operation."

Even Rebel heard the shouting from the other end of Torsten's phone. He weathered the storm admirably, though, ending with, "By all means. Call your counterparts in the Israeli Defense Forces."

He hung up and, from the driver's seat, Avi glanced in the rearview mirror to grin at Torsten. "This is a Mossad operation. By the time your people run up through the IDF chain of command, cross over to Mossad, and run down that chain of command, this op will be long over."

"That's the idea," Torsten replied, grinning back.

Rebel had to love operators who knew how to work the political apparatuses of their countries effectively. Special

Forces soldiers had to be careful when and where they sidestepped the system, but now and then, they could get away with an end around like this.

The drive to the Addison Field House took under ten minutes. The interior of the vehicle was silent as they approached the building, everyone mentally preparing in whatever way they did for a mission. Rebel heard several of her teammates practicing four-count breathing to calm themselves and clear their minds. She followed suit.

The SUVs pulled up behind the Addison Field House. Rebel climbed out of the SUV and fell in behind her teammates. Here went nothing.

Chapter 19

They'd elected to enter the venue via a loading dock, well away from the crowds who would undoubtedly panic at the sight of a full tactical team racing past them.

Rebel ran with her teammates along a service corridor underneath the facility to the stairwell they'd chosen for their approach to the roof.

Once they entered the building, they all went silent, relying purely on hand signals to communicate as needed. They'd run so many scenarios together over the past year plus of training together that there was little need even for hand signals. They all knew who would do what and when.

They jogged up a dozen long flights of stairs to reach the roof. Torsten paused and signaled for them to go hot. The safeties came off their weapons, and Rebel reached forward to place her hand on Tessa's shoulder. When everyone had a hand on the person in front of them, Torsten crouched low and eased open the exit. It was entirely possible a sentry had been placed to watch this stairwell.

Silence.

Torsten eased outside, sliding left, scanning back and forth for hostiles. Gia went next, sliding right and checking that quadrant for movement. One by one, they slid outside until they stood in an arc about thirty feet across.

Torsten eased forward and everyone else followed suit.

There was a reasonable amount of ambient light up here, but Rebel still pulled down her NODs. They would automatically adjust to the current light level. The roof jumped out in lime light and black shadows. Human heat signatures would show up as bright white blobs.

They took their time, creeping forward slowly and stealthily. Various maintenance structures, steel support beams crossing in front of them at an angle, sloping toward their right, and the first air conditioning unit were approached, moved around cautiously, cleared and put behind them.

From the right end of the line, Gia held up a fist.

Everyone froze.

She indicated by hand signal that she had movement in her one o'clock position. The team pivoted slightly to the right to center up on the target and moved forward even more slowly now.

Contrary to the gunslinging, shoot-out reputation of teams like theirs, the object in any mission was to slide in completely undetected, accomplish the objective and slide out completely undetected. Tonight had potential to be the exception to that rule, but the Medusas would still move in as if they planned for no one to know they'd ever been here.

A large white blob suddenly lifted away from the roof

and resolved into some sort of bird. A vulture maybe. Its wingspan was easily six feet.

The team continued forward.

It was a painstaking process, but they entered the area of the roof that matched the mock-up. It was eerie moving in and among the cluster of ventilation and air conditioning units for real. The crates from the warehouse, their diagrams, and the satellite imagery all came together in Rebel's head and came to life around here.

They made it all the way across the area covered by the mock-up without spotting anything out of the ordinary.

Crap. Was she wrong? Had the mock-up itself been a giant misdirect? Was Mahmoud out there right now, attacking some other crowd of innocent civilians while the Medusas sat up here, in the wrong place, doing nothing?

Torsten signaled the team together and they crouched in the shadow of a huge air conditioner some twelve feet tall and twice that wide and long.

"Thoughts?" Torsten breathed.

"Maybe we were wrong," Rebel went ahead and said aloud, since she knew they were all thinking it.

Surprisingly it was Avi who came up immediately after her and said, "No. I think you got it right, Rebel. I vote that we sit tight for a little while. Let's spread out and get angles on this whole area and see if our tangos join us. They've got a three-hour or more window left to attack in before that basketball game finishes and the Group B security people move back to their original positions."

Torsten glanced around. "Devil's advocates?"

Zane, who knew Mahmoud better than any of them, weighed in. "Even if we're wrong, we've got nothing else to go on. Where else would we go if we weren't sitting here? This is the only spot we found in an exhaustive search that matches Mahmoud's training mock-up. The guy is thorough and obsessive. He would plan a large-scale attack down to the tiniest detail and not deviate from it. I think we've correctly identified his target. If not tonight, he'll come up here tomorrow night or the next night. But this is the place."

"We sit tight then?" Torsten asked.

Everyone nodded. In truth, this wasn't a democracy. The team would do whatever Torsten decided to do. But a good leader gave everyone a chance to be heard and to add their thoughts if there was time to do so before making a final decision.

Torsten ordered, "Beau, Tessa, set up watch here for now."

The pair turned and faced opposite directions, looking outward from the group, and commenced scanning the roof for any movement. While they did that, Torsten laid his copy of the drawn diagram on the ground. The others clustered over it.

"Since we've got the time to set up an ambush, let's do it. We'll surround this entire area." He started pointing at positions on the drawing and assigning pairs of Medusas to each. "Rebel, Avi, you'll go here. It should give you the best overall view of the area so you can film whatever you need to."

Torsten quickly reviewed fields of fire with everyone and even called in Tessa and Beau to take a look at the setup before they returned to scanning the roof.

In any situation where a fire team was surrounding a target and shooting inward, it become vital not to shoot one's own team members by accident. It was a maneuver they practiced exhaustively because of the inherent risks, but Rebel still appreciated the reminder to everyone of how this would go down.

Torsten pocketed the diagram and murmured, "Move out."

Tessa and Beau were a trained sniper team, spotting for each other and tag team shooting, and they moved off to climb on top of the tallest structure in the area, an enormous metal box with fan blades behind a grill that was at least eighteen feet tall. From there, Tessa and Beau would have the best vantage point to perform a true overwatch function and knock out threats invisible to the Medusas moving around at roof level.

Rebel and Avi moved to their designated hiding spot, behind a small maintenance shed.

Avi murmured, "You know, we could move inside this shed and take out the ventilation grill in the bottom of the door. We'd have better cover and could move around more to observe the area and record video."

She nodded and pulled her lock picks. Avi smiled briefly and stepped out of her way. They'd already established she was the better lock picker. The door sported a well-made double-action dead bolt, and it actually took her a full minute to get through it.

They slipped inside. While she quickly shifted and stacked equipment out of the way in the back corner, clearing a space in front of the door, Avi unscrewed the two-foot-wide and about one-foot-tall metal grill from the door and set it aside.

He lay down in front of the door, rifle cradled in his elbows, and she joined him in the same pose. Her entire side plastered against his, and her focus and calm derailed in an instant. *Well, hell.*

Avi, of course, immediately sensed her disquiet. He whispered off-mike, "Breathe."

"I know what to do," she whispered back.

"Look. I know this is uncomfortable for you. It's not

easy for me, either. I'm sorry for everything. I would like to talk later and work it out. If you never want to see me again, or you just want to be friends, or you want to give a long-term relationship a go, we can both be adults about this and arrive at an amicable resolution."

God. Did he have to be so reasonable all the time? Continuing to scan the area, and continuing to whisper off-mike, she replied, "Fine. We'll talk later. But there isn't much to talk out."

"I shouldn't have treated you as a challenge. I was wrong," Avi whispered.

"I probably should thank you for showing me happiness, truth be told," she admitted.

He actually glanced over at her for a moment before yanking his gaze back to the roof. "Then why are you mad at me? Is it because I blew up your worldview? Do you resent me suggesting that there's more to life than work?"

She hadn't articulated her anger in exactly those terms, and she took a moment to consider it. "That's part of it," she responded. "But the other part of it is that you've never taken me seriously as an operator. You keep treating me like a little lady who can't take care of herself."

He exhaled on a silent gust of laughter. "Oh, I've not mistaken you for that ever since I saw you totally prepared to take out that guy in the grove at the park, single-handedly. And I certainly had no illusions about your skills after you took on the two guys who jumped you outside the soccer stadium."

"Then why do you insist on treating me like I can't take care of myself?" she asked in frustration.

"Because part of how I show esteem and affection for someone is to take care of them. I feed them and entertain them and make sure they're safe and happy. It's just who

I am. I treated my mother that way, and I treat my friends that way. You're no different. You're…family…to me."

She'd been in the Special Forces world long enough to understand the significance of that. Operators classed everyone as not-family or family. Those who made it into the inner sanctum of trust were few and far between, but once a person was dubbed family, an operator would do pretty much anything for that person. Up to and including dying for them.

Had she been misinterpreting Avi's behavior all along? Had it been nothing more than him giving her his unreserved trust? She felt her walls of anger and distrust start to crumble around the edges, and the sensation scared the hell out of her.

She'd lived her entire life in a hard, protective shell she'd carefully constructed around herself. No one got in. No one made her feel deeply. No one hurt her.

In retrospect, it had been how she defended herself from her father's rage and her mother's apathy. It had been how she'd walked away from previous relationships without ever looking back. And it had been how she'd become the Special Forces operator she was today. She had a rare ability to compartmentalize her feelings, fears and doubts, not letting anything emotional distract her from the mission.

But then, along came Avi.

She blurted, "How is it you can feel things and still go out in the field and maintain complete focus?"

"It's not easy sometimes. Like now. Not only am I worried about your safety—" He added hastily as she started to make a noise of protest, "And that of your teammates. But I'm also jonesing to nail Mahmoud Akhtar once and for all. The bastard has been a thorn in Israel's side for longer than I care to think about."

"Same for the United States," she agreed.

"It's not that I feel much when I'm on a mission. I shut most of my emotions down. That's what all those exercises you've learned for calming and focusing self are for."

She smiled wryly. "I always thought those techniques, tricks and exercises were overkill. I naturally compartmentalized and never felt much need for external ways to do it."

It was Avi's turn to pull a wry expression. "Welcome to the world the rest of us live in. We all had to do it the hard way and learn to forcibly contain our emotions."

"Oh."

He replied dryly, "Yeah. Oh."

Clearly, when she got back to Louisiana, she had some work to do. She was going to have to go back through all those training exercises and relearn them. And this time, she would have actual emotions in need of suppression. She wasn't sure whether to be grateful to Avi for that or furious with him.

"I don't know if I can do it," she confessed.

"Of course you can. You're one of the smartest, bravest, strongest women I know. You can master anything you set your mind to. Including your feelings."

The vote of confidence from him meant the world to her. But now was probably not the time to express that to him.

"There's still the issue of you living in Israel and me living in Louisiana," she threw out in desperation.

"That *is* a problem," he allowed. "I've been thinking about—"

She interrupted him tersely. "Movement. Six o'clock."

Avi went perfectly still beside her, breathing so lightly and quietly she couldn't hear him, and she was only inches away from him. She was massively relieved when her own breathing settled, calming and slowing into utter readiness for violence.

Thank goodness for all those months and thousands of hours of training Torsten had put the Medusas through. She took her own advice to Lynx and reminded herself to trust the training and not to overthink anything.

Tessa murmured into Rebel's earphones, "Four tangos have emerged from the same stairwell we used, more coming. They're moving fast. Not exercising stealth tactics. Each one carrying a bulky duffel bag. Faces obscured. No positive ID available."

That might be the last verbal Rebel's teams used tonight, for as their targets approached the Medusas all fell into the frozen stance of predators waiting to pounce.

"Rebel, call out when you have the video you need," Torsten breathed.

She clicked once in the back of her throat in acknowledgment of the order. She started recording as the first hostile came into view. It was a man based on general height and build beneath a baggy hooded sweatshirt. The man wore a baseball cap pulled low on his forehead and the hood of his jacket was pulled up over it.

In a few moments, a total of eight people moved into view in her viewfinder. Two were smaller and slighter in build than the others—probably female. The rest were male. Each one of them had a very large bag slung over a shoulder, perhaps five feet long and two feet or more tall and wide. The group moved as if the bags were very heavy.

She couldn't make out any facial features at all. It was impossible to tell if this was Mahmoud and his people, but then, how could it not be? Only Mahmoud's team had spent months training in a mock-up of this very location.

She tried to pick out the team leader based on how the hostiles moved around one another, but to no avail. They, too, were highly practiced in what they were doing up here. They didn't speak. They barely looked at one another. Each person seemed highly focused on doing what they'd specifically come up here to do.

As tempting as it was to call for the attack now, in point of fact, the intruders on the roof hadn't done anything yet to indicate that they were about to stage a terrorist attack. She continued filming, waiting for them to do something damning that would condemn them without question. She had to wait to call for the takedown until the people in front of her actually took hostile action with the intent to harm civilians.

Then, and only then, would the Medusas, Avi and the Israeli government have legal cover to justify slaughtering eight people up here on this roof. As it was, it was going to be a huge stink—

She set the thought aside. Avi knew what he'd gotten his government into in green-lighting this operation, and Torsten knew what he'd gotten himself into by participating in this mission. They would deal with the fallout later.

Inhale. Count to four. Breathe out. Count to four.

Her thoughts stilled.

She watched dispassionately as the hooded team spread out among the air-conditioning units and opened their bags. She was mildly startled when they all pulled out what looked like plastic hazmat suits—full-body jumpsuits that they stepped into, pulled up and zipped shut over their clothing. Then, they pulled out full-face respirators and donned them. So. Her guess about a gas attack of some kind had been correct.

Next out of the bags were thin latex gloves followed

by thicker rubber gloves. The team members took turns duct taping the tops of the gloves to the plastic suits.

Wow. These guys were taking no chances with whatever material they were handling. Her alarm climbed as she pondered just how lethal an attack they were planning to launch up here. Thank God the Medusas had finally gotten ahead of Mahmoud and were here to stop the unfolding disaster.

She could probably call the attack now. But Torsten had been sharply concerned about getting solid evidence of a crime before they attacked. She let her camera roll a bit longer.

The hostiles moved in pairs to two of the air-conditioning units and to two huge ventilation intake fans. They pulled out long rolls of flexible plastic tubing about the diameter of her wrist. Each tube had a round plastic attachment on it that looked like an oversize shower cap. This elastic-banded cap was placed over a small fan the hostiles pulled out of the duffel bags. The fans were like one she might use in her house to cool a stuffy room.

There was a noticeable pause in the action then. Whether they were waiting for a timed mark to all continue together, or they were just taking a pause to breathe deeply and prepare for the next step, she couldn't tell.

But, as one, the hostiles reached into their bags one last time and pulled out large metal tanks like scuba divers would use. Rebel flashed back to the pile of identical tanks in the storage room in Iranian security headquarters over a week ago. She felt Avi's miniscule jolt against her side. He remembered seeing those tanks, too.

As soon as the tanks came out, the people in front of her started to move very slowly, with extreme caution. They were obviously terrified of whatever those tanks held. She continued filming, making sure to capture the tanks and the blower/tubing setup clearly designed to deliver the gas in the tanks into the field house's ventilation system.

She hoped it went without saying that, when the shooting started, no way would any of the Medusas hit one of those tanks and release whatever poison was inside. Not only would a potential poison cloud be released that might drift over civilians in the vicinity, but none of the Medusas wore or had on them any protection against an airborne agent. A pressurized gas tank, when hit by a hot flying lead slug at high velocity, also stood an excellent chance of exploding, which could release a large, lethal gas cloud up here on the roof. It would likely kill everyone not wearing the proper protective gear. Which was to say, she and all of her teammates would die.

The attackers pulled out rolls of duct tape and commenced taping plastic tubing to the tanks' outlet valves and running the tubing into the the ends of the long tubes down into the intake shafts of the massive air units.

She'd seen enough.

"I've got what I need," she muttered into her mouthpiece.

She barely had time to pocket the video camera and pull her weapon into place against her right shoulder before Torsten shouted from his hiding place in Farsi, "Freeze. Put your hands up where I can see them!"

The reaction by Mahmoud's team was swift. They dropped to their knees, reached into their bags, whipped out short-barreled automatic rifles and jumped, some diving for cover and others dropping flat on their bellies in firing positions that minimized their target areas.

As one, they opened fire on Torsten's position, no doubt targeting the sound of his voice. The barrage was deafening.

The Medusas wasted no time and unleashed its own return fire of lead at the hostiles. Their body cams would record that the hostiles fired first and that they merely returned fire in a defensive manner.

Several of the terrorists' bodies flew backward, but other shooters rolled to the side, taking up new positions that gave them a better angle to target the now-revealed positions of the Medusas.

One of the hostiles who'd been sent flying by the initial fusillade staggered to his feet again, and commenced walking forward, firing his weapon in a continuous barrage of lead, sweeping back and forth in front of him.

"He's wearing body armor!" she shouted into her mouthpiece.

"They all are," Zane shouted back.

Tessa bit out, "Neck shots. Back of the head. Leg shots. Those facial respirators are metal and ricocheting rounds off of them."

Not good. The Medusas were limited to difficult to hit or nonlethal targets, all while having to tightly control their fields of fire not to hit their own people, and having to be exceedingly cautious not to hit the gas tanks. Meanwhile, Mahmoud's team could shoot its high-caliber weaponry back and if not kill with its shots, incapacitate Medusas with the sheer firepower impacting the Medusas' flak vests.

And then one of Mahmoud's guys picked up a gas tank and held it across his body, using it as a shield while he advanced toward Rebel and Avi's firing position.

Swearing, she lifted her finger away from her weapon's trigger. She dared not chance hitting that tank.

Avi bit out beside her, "We won't win this in a firefight. We've got to close in to hand-to-hand range." He jumped up, pulled a K-Bar knife out of an ankle sheath inside his boot and opened the door.

Rebel was close on his heels. He was right, of course. But it was also suicide for Avi to rush out there into the middle of an active firefight with Mahmoud's other men shooting away like crazy. No way was Avi going out there without her help!

It was undoubtedly suicidal of her to join him. But they *had* to stop these terrorists at all costs. Up to and including her life and Avi's.

By God, if he was going to die, she planned to die beside him.

Chapter 20

The only thought that passed fleetingly through Avi's mind as he raced out to engage Mahmoud's men up close and personal was that it was going to suck to die, having just found the love of his life. He'd finally found a woman he could share his whole life with, grow old with. And now neither of them was going to get any of that. The irony was rich.

He focused on the bastard charging toward him with that damned gas tank cradled across his torso. Deeply wary of the hostile possibly opening the outflow valve and trying to shoot a puff of whatever poison was inside the tank at him, Avi took a deep breath and held it as he charged forward, coming in low.

He closed on the terrorist and swung up hard and fast with his right hand, arcing up and under the gas tank, aiming for the lower end of the guy's flak vest under that plastic hazard suit.

The bad guy slammed the tank down on Avi's wrist. Hard.

Which was the plan. Avi let his right arm fall to his side, giving way before the blow, momentarily stung into uselessness, as he flashed in high with his left hand. He dropped the wrist blade he kept strapped under his left sleeve into his hand and stabbed hard into the hostile's neck with the short, double-edged blade.

The Iranian stared at him in frozen shock for just a second as his carotid artery, jugular vein and trachea were severed in one violent blow. Then his legs buckled, and Avi dropped to his knees fast to catch the tank as it fell out of the mortally wounded terrorist's hands.

A series of massive blows hit Avi in the middle of the back, pitching him forward violently. Gunshots against his body armor. He smashed forward onto his face, but thankfully, the downed terrorist was directly in front of him and cushioned the gas tank between their bodies.

Avi tried to draw a breath, but his chest muscles were temporarily paralyzed by the violent blows against his back. With his last remaining useful consciousness, he dragged his right hand up and forward, reaching for the gas tank valve. He gave it a twist to make sure it was tightly secured.

He registered a female voice behind him, uttering a scream of primal rage. Lying prone across the cold, hard cylinder of the tank and the warmer, softer body of the terrorist, he tucked his chin and glanced back over his shoulder.

He was in time to see Rebel come flying out of the maintenance shed and jump on the back of the terrorist who'd been peppering his back with bullets. She wrapped her legs around the guy's hips and her arms around the guy's throat.

The terrorist dropped his weapon with a clatter and

turned, clawing at her arms, but was too late. Rebel made a vicious slash across his neck with a dark, hungry blade.

The hostile dropped to the ground with her atop him. She grabbed at his forehead, yanked his head up and made a second slash, half severing the man's head from his body.

That's my girl.

She wasn't messing around. She'd made darned sure the terrorist was never standing up again.

She rolled off the tango and pushed to her feet, racing forward and diving to the ground beside Avi. "You okay?" she demanded.

He tried to speak but had no air. Instead he flashed her a thumbs-up and hand signaled her to keep moving forward.

She nodded and jumped up, spinning around the edge of the air-conditioning unit in front of her in search of more prey. Her knife was held low and ready, exactly the way a trained knife fighter should wield one. God, he loved that woman.

He lay there for several more seconds, waiting for his diaphragm to engage once more. In the meantime, he went limp, playing possum in case any more of Mahmoud's men got the bright idea to finish off anyone alive but wounded on the ground.

All of a sudden, he gasped hard, sucking in a desperate lungful of air.

It hurt like hell to breathe, but he drew in several more deep breaths. Oxygen flooded his brain and full awareness of the situation around him came back all at once.

He pushed to a crouch and looked around. Everywhere around him, Medusas and terrorists were grappling in hand-to-hand combat. Mahmoud's men must also be deeply wary of an ongoing gunfight with those tanks of poison gas now rolling around underfoot.

Where was Rebel?

He followed her around the air-conditioning unit and was horrified to see her bowed backward in the grip of a much-larger hostile who was pushing a knife toward her throat with all his strength. She had her forearms up between the blade and her throat, but she was running out of space and flexibility to avoid that blade.

He reached for his right hip as he charged forward, shouting at the top of his lungs.

The terrorist looked up reflexively for just an instant.

It was all Avi needed. He whipped out the pistol at his hip and fired twice, double-tapping two shots millimeters above Rebel's face and directly into the bastard's throat.

The terrorist dropped and Rebel went down beneath him. Blood, black in Avi's NODs, sprayed everywhere.

Please God let none of that be Rebel's. Please let that guy's blade not have fallen on her throat or cut her somewhere else!

Frantically, he darted forward. Adrenaline roared through his veins and he tossed the two-hundred-pound-plus corpse off her as if it weighed nothing.

"Are you hurt?" he demanded. "Did he cut you?"

"I don't think so."

He ran his hands over her face, her neck, down her arms. In the heat of battle, warriors often felt no pain and had no idea they were shot or otherwise grievously wounded for minutes or even hours.

Thank God. He felt no torn flesh, no welling blood.

He nodded tersely at her, and she whirled, placing her back to his.

"Move to your right," he muttered.

Back to back, the two of them moved beyond the air conditioner in search of more hostiles.

"Your nine o'clock," Rebel muttered.

"Tally ho," he replied. One of the women had fled the fight and was now hesitating some forty feet away from them, staring back at the carnage as the Medusas inexorably wiped out her teammates.

"Gun!" Rebel called as the woman reached for a hip holster similar to Avi's.

He raised his pistol and took aim as the woman whipped out her pistol—

And lightning fast, raised it to her own temple.

The ring of that single gunshot echoed across the roof, and the woman dropped to the ground.

"Spin to your right," Avi ordered. "Two hundred seventy degrees."

Rebel completed the move, pivoting across his back without ever losing shoulder-to-shoulder contact with him—although truth be told, her shoulder blades hit him closer to the middle of his back.

They crab-walked quickly around the next ventilation unit over and both yanked their weapons up to shoulder height as they encountered Piper and Zane also back-to-back, clearing their zone.

As a foursome, they circled back to the middle of the hot zone, searching for any remaining terrorists. They ran into Gia and Lynx also coming in from their zone.

"Overwatch, are we clear?" Avi radioed tersely.

"No hostile movement up here. Move in to confirm kills," Beau answered.

"Check in," Avi radioed next.

"Rebel, good," Rebel reported.

"Tessa, good."

"Beau, good."

"Piper, good."

"Zane, good."

"Gia, good."

"Lynx, good."

Silence fell over the channel.

"Gunnar?" Avi asked.

Nothing.

"Gun? Check in."

Still nothing.

They took off running as a group toward Torsten's last known position, where he'd shouted out the initial order to Mahmoud's men to freeze.

He lay prone in a pool of blood so big that Avi feared the worst. Quickly, he rolled Torsten onto his back and reached for his neck.

"I have a pulse. Thready. Weak. Who's the medic?"

Lynx pushed forward and dropped to her knees. "He's strangling on his own blood. I'm going to open a tracheotomy. He needs blood now. I didn't bring a full crash kit with us. Torsten's O positive. Who's a match?"

"I am," Gia said quickly.

Tessa and Beau worked over Gia's arm to find a vein and set up a needle while Lynx did the same to Torsten's arm.

When lifesaving blood was flowing through a latex tube into his brother, Avi said, "We've still got work to do. Piper, Zane, confirm kills in the left field. Rebel and I will take the right."

He moved off with Rebel at his side. They approached each downed body with caution, weapons at the ready. He pulled back the hoods of the hazmat suits and yanked off the face masks. One by one, they confirmed that the terrorists were dead. Rebel took a picture of each person with her cell phone camera.

They met Piper and Zane at the far end of the fight area. "All dead," Piper reported.

"Same," Avi replied.

Rebel said, "We need to collect those tanks and make them safe. I suggest we put tape over the outflow valves and then bag up each tank, maybe in a hazmat suit we take off the bodies?"

Zane commented, "The suits will be shot full of holes, but they'll be better than nothing until we can get a proper hazmat team up here."

Lynx's voice came over the channel. "We need to call for air evac to the nearest hospital. I've got Torsten stabilized, but he's going to need more blood and immediate surgery. He's taken at least four rounds in the torso."

Avi made the call to the Israeli operations center. He asked for the medevac and reported that Mahmoud Akhtar and an Iranian terrorist strike team were neutralized. Additionally, he asked for a hazardous materials team to come up to the roof of the field house and to be prepared to make safe at least a dozen tanks of poison gas.

That got a squawk of surprise out of his supervisor. "What the hell's going on up there?"

"Later," Avi bit out. "We've got a man down and a scene to secure."

The paperwork on this op was going to be epic. But thankfully, Torsten had had the good sense to insist on getting plentiful evidence on the attack before turning his Medusas loose.

It took about ten minutes for a helicopter to show up and do a tricky hovering maneuver, holding the skids mere inches off the roof. The inflatable main portion of the roof was not built to take the weight of a chopper, and the hardened area with the ventilation equipment was too crowded for the helicopter's blades. The Medusas made a makeshift litter by linking their arms underneath Torsten's body, picked him up, and ran him over to the chopper. Lynx climbed in first, protecting Torsten's tracheotomy.

Avi was not surprised to see the IV tube in Torsten's arm now hooked up to Lynx's own forearm. Special operators took care of their own.

The chopper lifted away in a violent downwash, and they all ducked and ran back to the hot zone to finish securing the tanks of gas. He hesitated to imagine what lethal poison Mahmoud had gotten his hands on. The bastard had the money and backing of the Iranian government, which surely had access to the worst chemicals on earth from some of its less savory allies.

It took nearly an hour for the scene to be cordoned off, handed over to the hazmat guys, and for him to make an initial report to Otto Schweimburg, who showed up in person with a huge contingent of IOC security people to take over the scene.

The German announced, "I'm placing all of you under arrest pending a full report on what the hell just happened up here. You had no authority—"

Avi cut him off. "I had authority from my government to neutralize an international terrorist who was number one on our watch list. We will be happy to turn over photographic evidence to you of the attack that was attempted up here tonight. Just keep in mind, we not only did your job for you, but we also saved the lives of thirty-thousand people in the building beneath our feet."

That seemed to take a bit of the starch out of Otto's spine.

Avi continued grimly, "And as for your arrest, we've got a man down. We'll be at the hospital until we know he's going to be all right. After that, you may feel free to arrest and question us to your heart's content. But until then, get out of our way. We have somewhere to be."

Otto actually stepped back, or maybe fell back in the face of Avi's verbal onslaught. But either way, Avi barged past him and felt the Medusas following close on his heels.

They retraced their steps down the long stairwell, under the stadium, and out to the loading dock, where their vehicles were now hemmed in by a traffic jam of emergency response vehicles.

"We'll never get our cars out of this mess," Rebel said in dismay.

He nodded and wove through the worst of the press of ambulances, fire trucks, and Olympic security vehicles to a SWAT van at the edge of the crowd. He knocked on the back door, and a fully armored SWAT officer opened up.

"Any chance we can make our weapons safe in your vehicle and beg a ride to the hospital? One of our guys was shot and has been airlifted out."

"Yeah, mate. Get in," the SWAT guy replied.

It was a tight squeeze with a SWAT team on the benches lining the sides of the vehicle and the Medusas sitting on the steel floor. As the vehicle sped away from the scene, the Medusas unloaded and cleared their weapons.

At last, the adrenaline charge of the op began to drain out of his blood, leaving Avi both exhilarated and exhausted. "Everyone okay?" he asked over his microphone.

The Medusas had performed brilliantly tonight, but they were a young team and relatively inexperienced as Spec Ops went. They all checked in, sounding calm and unrattled by the bloody encounter.

Torsten had trained them well. It was one thing to

stand off and shoot at distant targets that were more moving objects than actual human beings. But hand-to-hand
combat was up close and personal. You had to look a guy
in the eye as you gutted him. The act of killing another
human being in a situation like that took some real steel
in a person's psyche. But these Medusas had it.

Not that he'd doubted it for a second. Rebel had proven
her mettle to him time and again over the past several
weeks.

He had to find a way to hang on to her. He would
never, ever find another woman like her.

Rebel took the SWAT guy behind her up on his offer
to lean back against his shins. As her jacked-up combat
senses came back down to normal, utter exhaustion of
mind and body set in. She would never forget seeing Avi
charge out of their hiding spot, attacking that hostile by
hand, and then seeing another shooter come up behind
him. Her whole future life had flashed before her eyes
as that shooter laid into Avi, firing a barrage of lead at
the man she loved.

And then, seeing Avi go down—she'd died right there,
with him.

She'd never experienced anything to compare to the
rage and despair of that moment, and she hoped never
to experience it again. Even that horrible moment of silence when Torsten had failed to check in on the radios
hadn't been as bad.

She closed her eyes and let her head fall onto her
knees, which she hugged close to her chest. The anony-
mous man at her back reached forward and massaged
her shoulders, and she let his hands work some of the
tension from her neck.

They arrived at the hospital and she stood up wearily,

sparing a nod of thanks to the guy, who nodded back. People in their line of work understood each other without words in situations like this.

The Medusas piled out of the van and stripped out of the rest of their tactical gear, handing over flak vests, utility belts, knives, pistols and their assault rifles. It took a few minutes for the SWAT team leader to write out a receipt for all the equipment and hand it to Avi with a reassurance that it would all be cleaned and locked up for them at Sydney police headquarters. They could come by and pick it up whenever they were ready.

Rebel fell in beside Avi as he led the way into the emergency room. Nurses, patients and family members in the waiting room reacted with visible alarm as they strode in.

Even without their gear, she supposed they made for an intimidating sight. Most of them were spattered with blood, and they all had to look fully as grim as she felt.

"How is Gunnar Torsten doing?" Avi asked the nurse who stepped forward hesitantly to ask if she could help them. "He was medevaced in by helicopter about an hour ago."

With a glance over their shoulders at the frightened faces in the lobby, the nurse wisely said, "Why don't you all come with me?"

She put them in a large examining room with three beds in it. "I'll call up to surgery and see if I can get you a report. Meanwhile, are any of you injured? That's a lot of blood on your clothing."

Avi snorted. "You ought to see the other guys."

The Medusas chuckled as a group, and Rebel felt more of the night's strain draining away. Man, Avi was good. He knew exactly how to handle a team coming off an extremely violent mission.

The nurse came back into the room and Rebel stared apprehensively at the woman along with the rest of her teammates.

"Your colleague has extensive internal bleeding and is going to be in surgery for some hours to come, but the surgical team has every reason to believe he'll live."

Rebel's whole body felt like it crumpled, her relief was so great.

Strong arms went around her, and Avi pulled her tight against his big body. Unashamedly, she put her arms around his waist and hugged him back.

"Walk with me," Avi murmured.

They slipped out of the examining room, leaving the others to get looked over by a nurse for any minor cuts and wounds. They walked down a long hall until they found a bench seat in front of a large window. Avi guided her down to it and took both of her hands in his.

"Rebel, I don't care what it takes. I have to find a way to be with you. Up there on that roof tonight, when I thought I was going to die, my only regret was that I wasn't going to be able to spend the rest of my life with you."

He took a deep breath and continued, "Look. I know this is fast. But as it turns out, I've been waiting my whole life for you. I'm sure you're the one woman for me. And I'll do whatever you need me to do, be whomever you need me to be. But I can't lose you. I love you."

Rebel's heart did a weird flip-flop and then felt like it grew about three times larger in her chest.

"Rebel, I know you're cautious emotionally. And I know I'm asking you to take a giant leap of faith and trust me. To trust in us. To believe in us. But I'm willing to wait for you, and to fight for you. As long as it takes for you to have me."

She stared down at their intertwined hands, his big and tanned and callused, hers smaller, but also callused and capable. They were so alike, the two of them. They fit each other.

Perfectly.

She knew in her heart of hearts that he was right. That they would be great together. But still. It was a giant leap of faith for her to open up to him all the way. He was asking for forever.

Could she do it—

Oh, who was she kidding?

She looked up, gazing into his dark, soulful eyes. Eyes she could joyfully lose herself in. "Of course I'll have you. You're perfect, Avi Bronson."

He stood up in a rush and swept her into his arms. He kissed her so passionately, so thoroughly, she lost all ability to think. Heck, to breathe. All she could do was feel—his love, his care, his happiness.

And it was wonderful. And it was all hers.

Epilogue

Avi pushed Gunnar in his wheelchair outside into the humidity and heat. If this was winter in Louisiana, he hated to think about what summer was going to be like. The good news: he would be here, with Rebel, to find out.

"You're clear on the exercise today?" Gunnar asked him.

"Yup. I've got it. We'll split into tracker teams and hunt each other down. It'll be fun," Avi commented as the Medusas piled out of the training building behind him.

"Man, I can't wait to get out of this thing and get back in the field with you guys," Gunnar groused.

"Patience, brother. Your doctors said you'll make a full recovery if and only if you give the inflammation around your spine time to heal."

The bullet that had lodged perilously close to Gunnar's spine had been successfully removed, but the soft tissue damage was taking a while to recover. In the meantime,

Gun had asked him to take a temporary assignment to the United States to work as a foreign-liaison-training officer with the Medusas.

Which was just as well. There had, indeed, been protests lodged by the Iranian government and a fair bit of political flap after eight of its operatives were killed in Sydney. Rebel's videos had quickly quieted their outcry, however.

As for the gas in the tanks, it had been deadly Agent VX, one of the most toxic nerve gases ever created. One lungful would kill anyone. The amount in the tanks would have taken out everyone in the field house without question. Even if some of the athletes and spectators had made it out alive, they all would have been dead in a few hours.

Avi's superiors felt it would be prudent for him to lie low for a while, get out of the Middle East and off the Iranians' radar. So, this mission to help train the Medusas and share Israeli commando techniques at a supersecret training facility completely off the grid of any foreign government had been the perfect solution.

Not to mention, he got to spend a full year here with Rebel, which also carried him through his last year of service before becoming eligible to retire from the Israeli Army. His plan was to leave active duty with the IDF and accept the permanent training position Gunnar had already offered him with the Medusas.

As for Rebel, she was coming along nicely in learning to embrace happiness. They'd moved into a little house and were building a life together. He did the cooking, of course, but she made it a cozy, loving home.

In fact, tonight, he was going to present her with the engagement ring currently tucked in his pocket and make it official. And then he would have his very own Medusa to love, honor and cherish.

Forever.

He couldn't wait.

* * * * *

COMING NEXT MONTH FROM

H HARLEQUIN®

ROMANTIC suspense

Available August 6, 2019

#2051 THE COLTON SHERIFF
The Coltons of Roaring Springs • by Addison Fox
In the midst of his reelection campaign, Sheriff Trey Colton
has made a startling discovery. His fake engagement to his
best friend, Aisha, has turned serious. Maybe even real...
But will the serial killer he's hunting put this new relationship
in danger?

#2052 COLTON 911: BABY'S BODYGUARD
Colton 911 • by Lisa Childs
Rae Lemmon isn't happy when Forrest Colton finds a body
in her backyard, and she's absolutely terrified when someone
threatens the life of her baby if she doesn't get rid of her
new bodyguard—Forrest. But as they get closer to finding
the threat, Rae may be in danger of losing her heart along
the way.

#2053 CAVANAUGH'S MISSING PERSON
Cavanaugh Justice • by Marie Ferrarella
Kenzie Cavanaugh is searching for a missing person, but
when fellow detective Hunter Brannigan realizes it ties into
one of his cold cases, they're pulled into a much deeper
conspiracy than they ever believed possible.

#2054 FIRST RESPONDER ON CALL
by Melinda Di Lorenzo
Paramedic Remo DeLuca finds Celia Poller on the side of the
road after a car accident. Severely injured, Celia has short-
term memory loss and the only thing she's sure of is that she
has a son—and that someone is threatening both their lives!

HRSCNM0719

Get 4 FREE REWARDS!

We'll send you 2 FREE Books
<u>plus</u> 2 FREE Mystery Gifts.

Harlequin® Romantic Suspense books feature heart-racing sensuality and the promise of a sweeping romance set against the backdrop of suspense.

FREE
Value Over
$20

YES! Please send me 2 FREE Harlequin® Romantic Suspense novels and my 2 FREE gifts (gifts are worth about $10 retail). After receiving them, if I don't wish to receive any more books, I can return the shipping statement marked "cancel." If I don't cancel, I will receive 4 brand-new novels every month and be billed just $4.99 per book in the U.S. or $5.74 per book in Canada. That's a savings of at least 12% off the cover price! It's quite a bargain! Shipping and handling is just 50¢ per book in the U.S. and $1.25 per book in Canada.* I understand that accepting the 2 free books and gifts places me under no obligation to buy anything. I can always return a shipment and cancel at any time. The free books and gifts are mine to keep no matter what I decide.

240/340 HDN GNMZ

Name (please print)

Address   Apt. #

City   State/Province   Zip/Postal Code

Mail to the **Reader Service:**
IN U.S.A.: P.O. Box 1341, Buffalo, NY 14240-8531
IN CANADA: P.O. Box 603, Fort Erie, Ontario L2A 5X3

Want to try 2 free books from another series? Call 1-800-873-8635 or visit www.ReaderService.com.

Remo took a very slow, very careful look up and down
the alley. The side closest to them was clear. But the
other? Not so much. Just outside Remo's mom's place,
the man Celia had so cleverly distracted was engaged in
a visibly heated discussion with another guy, presumably
the one from the car his mother had noted.

Remo drew his head back into the yard and hazarded
a whisper. "Company's still out there. We can wait and
see what happens, or we can slip out and make a run for
it. Move low and quick along the outside of the fence."

Celia met his eyes, and he expected her to pick the
former. Instead, she said, "On the count of three?"

He couldn't keep the surprise from his voice. "Really?"

She answered in a quick, sure voice. "I know it's
risky, but it's not like staying here is totally safe, either. A
neighbor will eventually notice us and give us away. Or
call the police and give Teller a legitimate reason to chase
us. And at least this way, those guys out there don't know

BOUND TOGETHER BY DUTY, THEY ARE THE FIRST LINE OF DEFENSE.

THE MISSION MEDUSA SERIES CONTINUES

Intense training has prepared Special Forces member Rebel McQueen for anything...that is, except sexy security specialist Avi Bronson. They are complete opposites, and yet only Rebel and Avi believe in an imminent terrorist attack. Together, they must protect thousands of innocent lives. But who will save Rebel from certain heartache if she dares to succumb to Avi—and her most dangerous attraction?

$5.75 U.S./$6.75 CAN.

ISBN-13: 978-1-335-66207-1

50575

9 781335 662071

EAN

S

CATEGORY
SUSPENSE

HHARLEQUIN®
ROMANTIC
SUSPENSE

harlequin.com

Happily-ever-after.
It's our promise,
whatever kind of love story you're seeking—
passionate, dramatic, suspenseful,
historical, inspirational…

With different lines to choose from
and new books in each one every month,
Harlequin has stories to satisfy even the most
voracious romance readers.

Find them in-store, online or subscribe to
the Reader Service!

HARLEQUIN®

ROMANCE WHEN
YOU NEED IT

SeriesIBC2018

ISBN-13:978-1-335-66207-1

that we know they're here. Right now, they're trying to flush us out quietly."

"As long as you're sure."

"I'm sure."

He put a hand on Xavier's back. "You want to ride with me, buddy?"

The kid turned and stretched out his arms, and Remo took him from his mom and settled him against his hip, then reached for Celia's hand.

"One," he said softly.

"Two," she replied.

"Three," piped up Xavier in his own little whisper.

And they went for it.

Don't miss
First Responder on Call *by Melinda Di Lorenzo,*
available August 2019 wherever
Harlequin® Romantic Suspense books
and ebooks are sold.

www.Harlequin.com

HRSEXP0719